GR

laike

THE **EINSENBERG EFFECT** BOOK THREE

TRIGGER WARNING

PLEASE READ THIS SECTION!

Seeing this note means the book that you are about to read could contain triggering situations or actions. This book is subject to one or more of the triggers listed below. **Please note that this a universal trigger warning page that is included in Grey Huffington books and is not specified for any paticular set of characters, book, couple, etc. This book does not contain all the warnings listed. It is simply a way to warn you that this particular book contains things/a thing that may be triggering for some.** This is simply my way of recognizing the reality and life experiences of my tribe and making

sure that I properly prepare you for what is to unfold
within the pages of this book.

violence
sexual assualt
drug addiction
suicide
homicide
miscarriage/child loss
child abuse
emotional abuse

PAPERBACKS
HARDCOVERS
SHORT STORIES
AUDIOBOOKS
MERCH
AND MORE...

STAY IN CONTACT

want live updates?
text **greyhuffington** to 1 (833) 315 2372

instagram.com/greyhuffington

GREYHUFFINGTON

laike

THE **EINSENBERG EFFECT** BOOK THREE

PROLOGUE

laike

"I'M COMING BACK for good so let them niggas know it's mine," I belted the lyrics of one of my favorite joints. That nigga, Bryson Tiller, was either in his bag like a motherfucker or he, too, had that one girl holding down the number one spot of the roster that he planned to snatch up one day. Shit, maybe even in another lifetime, but the point was still valid.

Ping.

The sound of my phone caused the music to stop briefly before picking back up. In an effort to be strategic with my time, I ignored the message. I was well aware of my procrastination easily becoming a hindrance in some cases. I knew that if I entertained whoever it was blowing up my line then it would easily add thirty to forty minutes to my prep time, and I only had twenty minutes to be out of the door and at dinner.

"That shit ain't up for grabs. Where you at on the map? I come to where you at. Fuck around and end up your last," I spat word for word.

It was one of the few songs that I knew from beginning to end, not a single lyric tripping me up when in rotation. It was also one of the few songs that put me deep in my feelings and even deeper in my bag. I couldn't take feelings to the fucking bank or the utility company. They only accepted cash, so that's what I pursued – not feelings. That shit was fleeting.

Ping.

The reminder text hadn't come yet. Two minutes hadn't passed. Hearing the sound again let me know that I'd been texted a second time. Before I could wrap my head around anyone finding the need to text me twice in a row without any type of discipline or self-respect for themselves, it sounded off, again.

Three times in a fucking row? I questioned with flared nostrils and forehead lines that pushed my eyebrows closer together. Not only was the line in question one that prohibited such behavior, but it was

2

fucking up my sound. I could hardly hear what Bryson was singing about because the pinging continued.

By the fourth time, I secured the knot of my high-top Dunks and fought my way through the madness of my closet before re-entering my bedroom. The texts were still rolling in as I scooped the phone from my bed. Frustration and aggravation were among the things I was experiencing when I unlocked my phone to see that Ashlyn had texted me five times.

"Your pussy not even good enough to be blowing down this line like that, baby girl."

The words flowed from my mouth as I scanned the five paragraphs she'd sent. It would be a cold day in hell before I read any of that shit. Instead of pretending that I was, I tapped the contact at the top of the screen and followed up by pressing the call button when the screen changed. I wasn't sure if it had even rung fully before I heard her voice on the other side of the line.

"Laikie," she cried, "why are you doing this to me?"

The outpouring of emotions was baffling. I assumed I was missing pieces of whatever puzzle she'd put together in my absence, but there was no earthly reason for any contact in my burner phone to be on any of our calls with tears running down their faces. Shit with us was never that deep – not with her or anyone else.

"Don't call me that shit, Ashlyn. My name is Laike and you're fucking with my music by sending all of these texts."

3

"Why didn't you reply?" She huffed, struggling to contain the big feelings she was experiencing for no apparent reason.

"Because I'm not reading that shit. Don't ever fix your fingers to send me long ass messages back-to-back again. What's up? What's so urgent?" I cradled the phone between my shoulder and ear as I spritzed my skin with the Chanel cologne that my sister had gifted me recently.

"Why don't you come see me anymore? I've been calling you for weeks. What is the problem? What did I do to deserve this type of treatment?"

"Ashlyn, is that all you want? You're holding up my line with this stupid ass shit."

"You don't miss me?"

"Not even a little."

"Laikie!" she bawled.

Her voice was beginning to irritate me to the point of no return and tonight wasn't the night for that. I had plans to enjoy my night and there was no way I was going to allow a woman who already knew the stipulations of our arrangement before she entered it ruin it. Anything beyond what I'd agreed to offer was beyond my control. Dick, that's what I'd promised her and that's what I'd given her. Plenty of it, too, so I didn't understand why she was crying on my line.

Feelings. That's why she was tripping. They'd wreck you every single time. She was caught up in hers, and I didn't have the equipment to reel her back in. My hands and my heart were tied.

I ended the call at the sound of her whimpers. My parents had named me Laike Eisenberg. That's what I was to be addressed by. When she decided to give me a pet name, I should've stepped away from our situation then.

As soon as the call ended, the music began again. But, before the nigga could release two words, my phone began ringing. Ashlyn was calling me back.

"Listen," I began to explain through gritted teeth, "let me explain something to you, Ashlyn. Check your feelings. I never promised you anything but dick and you got plenty of that. If you're beating yourself up wondering why I don't miss you and aren't calling you, then chill. If you were assuming you could change the terms of our situation then that's on you, baby girl. I made it clear to you that my heart is not up for grabs. Never will be. As far as this dick, you could spin on it any day, but you've fucked that up for yourself. I appreciate a woman who is on her shit, one who prioritizes her hygiene. That's not you."

"What do you mean? I do prioritize my hygiene, Laike. What does any of this have to do with you and me?" she yelled.

"Everything. I went into your bathroom three times in the last month, Ashlyn. The same empty toothpaste tube has been on the counter since the first time."

"I've been meaning to get new toothpaste! You're breaking up with me over some toothpaste?"

"We were never together, Ashlyn. And, na. If bad breath, plaque buildup, and bumpy gums are your thing, then who am I to interfere with that? It's the simple fact that you expect me to risk my health because of it. A dick covered in germy saliva doesn't appeal to me. If you're not brushing your teeth at the house, then I know you're not visiting your dentist regularly. As a man who loves his dick sucked, that's an issue. It makes me wonder if you're keeping your pussy clean. That's an issue. Handle your shit, baby girl."

I didn't wait for a response. Ending the call would free up my shoulder and help me get out of the house in a few minutes. That was the goal before the call and still was after. A new song began once my line was clear, but it didn't last long. Ashlyn had dialed me back. I quickly ignored the call and unlocked my cell again. When I entered our message thread, the gray bubble popped up immediately.

Before the message she was typing could come through, I tapped the contact icon at the top of the screen and then scrolled to the bottom of hers. The red Block This Contact button was the next thing I pressed before shutting my phone down again and continuing to perfect my final results.

"I can love you with my eyes closed."

The new tune that was played was a very familiar one. It was just as good as the last one. As I rocked to the beat, I brushed the tapered portions of my cut. Once they were smooth, I rubbed in the cream I'd stolen from Lyric months back. As long as she had a stash of hair products, mine would never be short of amazing.

I need to get this shit cut down an inch or so next week, I noted, rubbing the cream through the brown loops the world called curls. They were stacked on top of each other and all over the top of my head. I hated when they grew longer than two or three inches. The same cream worked wonders for my beard, so it was next in line.

"Don't nobody care about your heart like I do. Girl I'm down for you just the way that you're down for me."

Nobody. The word stood out as I bobbed my head, working the cream into my unruly facial hair. Just as I smoothed them down with my hands, the alarm sounded on my personal line. It was the same alarm, every month on the final Sunday at six forty-five. Dinner was at seven, always, and it was always imperative that I was prompt and present.

How you valued one's time was a direct reflection of how much or little you valued them. My father had instilled it in us as children and it stuck with us through adulthood. If we could help it, you could always expect the Eisenbergs to be on time, no matter the occasion.

After a final once-over in the mirror, I stepped out

of my bedroom and into the hall. Black and cream furnishing, accent pieces, and decor covered every inch of my home. Because of the psychological effects of color combinations and choices, I refrained from slathering black paint on the walls. Coming in from a rough day to black walls would only anger me more or pull me deeper into the matrix I was trying to escape.

Though black was the richest color, in my opinion, I was aware that it wasn't the best option for mental stimulation and elevation. So, I stuck with accent pieces and selective decor to reflect my adoration for it. It paired well with cream. The two were astounding.

Neither of the two sets of stairs was appealing to me or appropriate for my mood. So, instead, I found myself standing in front of the elevator where I pressed the glass button. The doors slid open immediately. There wasn't anyone in the three-story, customized home but the owner – me. I wasn't expecting there to be a wait at the elevator. There never was, not since I'd moved in six months ago.

The music that I'd been enjoying in my bedroom continued inside the elevator. I wasn't familiar with the new song that was playing, but I wasn't opposed to the tune. From the second to the first floor, the elevator transported me. I stepped off and headed straight for the kitchen. The keys to my Challenger were on the counter where I'd left them. I pressed the start button twice and waited for the most beautiful sound ever.

The engine of the Hellcat roared as I closed my

eyes and allowed my lips to stretch across my face. That sound never got old. Though my car was tucked away in my garage, it made its presence known throughout my home.

Loud, barbaric, uncompromising muscle howled in anticipation of its freedom. The open road was heaven for an engine like mine. But here in The Hills, there wasn't much of that. In fact, the streets were paved with the thought of going under forty miles per hour.

At the edges of the hills that our community was perched on, the limit was thirty. If you didn't want to get yourself killed, then it was best to follow the rules around the borders of The Hills. They were dangerous and even a nigga like me knew to abide.

I grabbed my wallet from off the counter and stuffed it in my jeans. The Patek watch on my wrist glistened as I reached for my .40 briefly after. The bracelet beside it beckoned for my attention as it slid slightly down my wrist and collided with the diamond-encrusted timepiece.

I patted my pockets to make sure that I'd stuffed them with cash. Between Essence, Emorey, Elle, and Lucas, I wasn't sure that I'd have much left when I returned. They'd even taught the tiniest one of them all to stick his hand out. But it was all good. That bunch was the closest I'd ever get to having children of my own, so it was only right that I spoiled them as if they were mine.

Sometimes, I felt like they were – especially that

badass Lucas. He reminded me so much of the child that my parents described me as. He was a hothead and always into something. They'd visited the emergency room with him one too many times for him to not have even reached the age of two yet.

Unlike the girls, he was adventurous. Neither Luca, Keanu, nor I could get rid of him when he was in our presence. He swore he was one of the guys. The only exception was when we rolled our trees and smoked them. He wasn't allowed to hang then and for good reason. We were all against it.

I entered my garage and smiled at the sight of my baby. Black on black with a yellow stripe across the bottom of the grill. Bumble was her name. I'd put a shitload of money into creating a fucking problem on the streets. She was my partner, so it was only right that she mirrored me.

Once inside, I unlocked my personal cell and tossed the other two onto the passenger's seat. That's where they'd remain until my night ended. There were to be no interruptions during dinner. I tapped the lock on the screen. It opened the security application for my home. I double-checked the status of every door and window of my strategic design. *Secured*, they all read.

Satisfied with their status, I, then, checked the cameras around the front of my estate. There were four of them, one closest to the garage for moments just like this one. Although my home was gated and well-secured, niggas studied hard when their survival was in question, and I didn't underestimate their ability to carry out a mission for the right price.

Underestimating niggas was the exact point that most niggas went wrong. I didn't plan on being one of those niggas. Aside from the bushes and greenery blowing with the wind, there wasn't any movement.

My phone connected to the Bluetooth system automatically as I punched in the four-digit code that caused my radio screen to retract and reveal the hidden compartment behind it. Inside was a small .22 and five thousand dollars that were stashed in the event of an emergency. However, neither of those captured my attention.

It was the tin can on top of the money that caught my eye. I removed it before pressing the power button on the stereo. As the screen repositioned itself, I busied myself with the task of opening the tin. I pulled on the top and bottom then watched as it slowly slid apart to reveal six perfectly rolled blunts.

They'd been waiting for me all day. I'd rolled them while watching the sports analysts talk their shit as part of my morning routine. It wasn't until I ran out for the meeting with Luca and our team that I placed them in the tin where they belonged.

"I like your vibe and you're really the shit. We done got low to the flo in this bitch."

I matched 6lack word for word while putting fire to my blunt. Because I knew I'd be needing the tin again, I tossed it over on my passenger seat and hit the button to lift the garage. While it raised, slowly, I removed the .40 from my waist and placed it on my lap. Clutching the handle, I watched my rearview mirror. Any sign of movement, and I'd be unloading.

Confirmation of the absence of an intruder led me to shift the gear. I reversed out of the garage and lowered it once my car was completely out. Before backing out of the automatic gate, I waited until my garage door contacted the cement of my driveway. Precautions, as vexatious as they were, were obligatory.

I hadn't survived this long being stupid. Or, maybe I'd survived this long because other niggas weren't stupid enough to try their luck. Either way, I wouldn't change the way I managed my home and life if my practices were keeping me and my family safe. It didn't matter how exasperating the tasks were.

My engine bellowed in the darkness as I exited the gate and began down the street. With my music pumping, I set forward on the path that would lead me to my destination, and in four short minutes, I'd arrived.

The big B on the back of the SUV that was pulling into the gate ahead of me identified its owners before I saw either of their faces. Because they'd already opened the gate, I didn't have to. I trailed them through it and around the winding driveway. As they took their time exiting, I hit my blunt twice more before putting it out. It wasn't until I saw the passenger door pop open that I hopped out of my ride and made my way around the back of theirs.

A smile curled my lips upward on my face as I watched baby girl climb out of the truck. Her belly pierced the air, clearing the path that she was on long before the rest of her body reached it. The thought of Lyric delivering my niece in a few months was still breathtaking. She was still a baby herself. Though well over thirty, she was still my baby. And Luca's. And our father's.

There were days the idea of her bearing a child knocked the wind out of me. Her growth in the last two years was commendable, but I wasn't ready for her to exercise her independence just yet. I wasn't prepared for her not to need me anymore. Even in marriage and after birth, I desired unlimited communication and closeness. We'd been a unit all our lives and now that she had her own, it was a daily struggle not to step on anyone's toes or invade her personal space.

Our father had given her away at the extravagant wedding they'd had, but I hadn't. Neither had Luca. We were still holding on with a death grip. She was our little sister. Setting her free was easier said than done. We honored her wishes and gave her the space she needed to create a life for her husband and future family, but we didn't wander too far.

It was by the grace of God that the man she'd chosen to make a life with was my best friend. That shit was a gift and a curse. It had taken time to acclimate myself to their newly formed union, but after I'd finally come to terms with it, I realized nothing was different. Our circle was still intact and nothing had changed.

Her arms stretched as she headed toward me. Her belly reached me first and was given a bit of the overflow of love that I had for the being carrying it around. With everything in me, I loved Lyric. That would never change. I could hardly wait until Keanu Jade was born so that I could bestow the same love on her.

"I'm your favorite uncle, remember that, Keanu," I whispered to her belly while rubbing both sides. "I got candy and snacks on deck and you're always welcomed over. Well, after you start walking and get out of that diaper. I love you to the moon and back, baby girl."

"Oh my God, I feel like I haven't seen you in ages," she whined as she impatiently waited for me to stand up straight and address her.

Same, I thought.

"It's only been, what? Four days?"

"Four days too many."

As she wrapped her arms around me, I could smell her expensive ass perfume. I prayed it didn't stick to my clothes, but that was wishful thinking. It always did. When she pulled back, I watched her nostrils swell with suspicion.

"Is that my luxurious curl cream in your head?" she asked, sniffing the air.

"What?" I chuckled with a tilt of my head, acting as if I was unaware of what she was talking about.

"This nigga stole that shit like two months ago. He

threatened me 'cause he knew I would tell you," Keanu told her as he rounded the truck.

He extended a hand. I grabbed it just before he pulled me in for a hug. *My nigga*, I thought as my shoulder collided with his chest. Since his true intentions for my sister had been revealed, there had been a shift in our relationship. For the first few weeks, it had been placed on ice as I dealt with my personal feelings surrounding the union, but once the ice thawed, we'd somehow become closer. I wasn't sure how that was possible, but it had happened.

The truth was, I wouldn't want my sister with anyone else. Keanu treated her just as we did. She was his moon and his stars. It was the secrecy that had me in a chokehold and unsettled. This wasn't any nigga. This was *my* nigga, Ken.

It didn't matter what the fuck Lyric said, he was supposed to feel comfortable coming to me with that type of information. He'd said over and over that he did feel comfortable revealing that bit of information, and I wanted to believe him. However, his actions proved otherwise.

"Yet you still snitched!"

"Well, she knows now, so technically, I didn't."

"I would've figured it out eventually, anyway. I have been looking for it. Do you like it?"

"Yeah. It's cool. Shit almost gone. I'm surprised you're just noticing."

"I had braids for a month and then I went to the

salon the following few weeks. I'm too tired for all of that now. I just want to shampoo my hair and call it a week – until the shower, at least."

"About that," I started as I reached into my pocket, "here. Put that on something."

One of the wads I'd stuffed my pockets with was already gone. I'd forgotten to calculate her into the equation. She was the biggest lick of them all. She'd empty both pockets and then go do the same for Luca – although her husband was never too far. She picked his pockets daily, though, so we gave him the break we knew his wallet needed. Fucking with Lyric and his accounts would be in the negative if he wasn't making it as fast as she was spending it. That was another reason I was appreciative of his presence in her life. He could afford the lifestyle we'd created for her without an issue.

"What is this, Laike?" she questioned, looking at the stack as if it was poisonous.

"Some money."

"This is not money, brother. This is me you're talking to. I'm assuming you're joking right now," she sassed as she leaned forward and stuck her hand in the other pocket.

With a sigh and shake of my head, I allowed her to rob me of every dollar I had on my person. When she pulled out the other knot, the mug she wore quickly faded and was replaced with a sly smile.

"Now, that's more like it."

"What am I supposed to give to the kids if you've taken everything?" I probed, tossing both hands in the air. She was uncompromising when pertaining to paper, but that's exactly how the Eisenbergs preferred it.

"Fuck them kids," she joked, causing us all to cackle. We knew she didn't mean it, but that didn't make it any less hilarious.

"Y'all coming inside or y'all staying out here while we eat?"

It wasn't necessary to turn around. I could identify Luca's voice even in a crowd. The adlib that his side-kick added was the final confirmation. No one understood what the little nigga was saying, but I could almost bet that he was backing his father up.

"We're starving," Lyric admitted as she rubbed her belly, "So, we're coming in."

"Niggas don't even speak anymore. Just start asking dumb ass questions," Ken hissed.

"'Cause he knows damn well we're coming in," I added.

"Then come the fuck in, then. And, you niggas at my crib. I'm not speaking to y'all asses. Address me when I appear. That's how that shit works."

"Who this nigga think he is?"

"King of the castle it sounds like," Ken replied.

"Hey, baby girl," Luca said to Lyric as he wrapped his arm around her shoulder and neck before pulling her in. He kissed her forehead and then her cheek. "We're saying grace in fifteen minutes."

"Thanks, Luca. I'm going inside. I refuse to be a part of whatever is about to go on."

We all watched as she disappeared into the house with my money in both hands.

"I need to borrow some money," I said to the guys.

There was a brief silence before we all looked at each other and tossed our heads back in laughter.

"She done cleared me out, fam," Ken admitted with a shrug. This was nothing new for him and definitely nothing new for us.

"I'm next, nigga, but I got a few dollars right here. Can't have you walking in there empty-handed. The girls won't let you make it. Emorey going to swear you're broke."

"I am."

Belly-curling laughter erupted from us all, again, reminding me why I loved the niggas beside me so much. In the line of work that I'd committed to since a teenage boy required stillness, caution, rigidness, attentiveness, and slight paranoia. There wasn't much room for laughter and freedom. It wasn't until my circle of friends and family surrounded me that I felt both, immensely.

"Put your toy in the house while I finish my blunt," I warned Luca.

"Toy? This nigga is an Eisenberg. Don't ever refer

to him as a toy," he replied, defending our honor. However, it wouldn't win this battle.

"The seed of Chucky to be frank," I emphasized.

As we engaged in more laughter, Luca leaned down and put Lucas on the ground. He was now a thriving one-year-old with legs that ran a mile a minute. He'd been walking since he was ten months, thanks to his sister, and had been causing hell since he learned to crawl at five months.

My sister-in-law couldn't catch a break. She'd given up and handed him off to his father. Lucas was officially Luca's problem, and he was fine with that. The two were inseparable. He hardly dotted the door without Lucas at his side.

The pair almost made me consider a mini of my own, but that shit was not happening. He and Lyric would have enough to supply our parents with a bus load. There was no need for me to add to the equation. I'd settle for empty pockets and scheduled tea parties that I otherwise hated.

"Fuck you," Luca spat in my direction before taking off toward the house.

I knew it wouldn't be long before he returned. In the meantime, I jogged to the car and grabbed the blunt that I'd put out to greet Lyric. I was sitting on the top of my hood seconds later. As I watched Luca and Lucas make their way inside, I fired it up and took a puff.

"You good, nigga?"

Ken's silence was alarming. Though he hardly said

much, I could tell that something was on his mind. Because I knew he wouldn't come right out and tell me, I had to ask.

"Just tripping about how this nigga has a shitload of children, and I'm shitting bricks thinking about my first being born. I can't say I've ever been scared of anything in my life, but this shit has me spooked. As Lyric inches closer to the end of her pregnancy, I'm inching closer to the brink of my insanity."

"Not big, bad Ken shaking in his motherfucking boots," I toyed.

The fear was apparent in his eyes. Since he'd stepped out of their whip, I'd noticed it but couldn't put a finger on it. Now that I had confirmation of what it was, it made sense. I hadn't recognized it because it was foreign territory for us both.

"Feeling like a little ass boy right now. Yet, she's poised as always. I'm losing my shit on the low."

"Aye. On this one, I don't blame you dog. Not only is childbirth an experience of a lifetime, but it's the closest one to death and women do that shit every day. Since discovering she was pregnant again, I've been in my feelings. Real talk. The amount of women I see struggling through childbirth has never sat right with me. But the number of Black women struggling and suffering from complications of childbirth is alarming for me. Unsettling, to say the least. Even the thought is taxing on my mental. And, the coin toss after. Too much to consider. Ever was perfectly fine after the birth of three children. Then, she had that knucklehead, and I thought we'd lost my sister-in-law for good. That shit is so unpredictable. You just never know and that fucks with me daily. Lyric is my heart. The only girl that can ever truly say that. I'd be a mess if anything happened to her," I explained.

"The only girl that can ever truly say that?" Ken chuckled, "She's your sister, homie. Baisleigh... that's your heart."

"Any fucking way, nigga, we're on the same page. We're both scared."

"Scared of what?" Luca asked with his hand out as he rejoined us.

I handed him the blunt in my hand before revealing what we'd been talking about when he walked up.

"Up in our feelings about Lyric and the end of this fucking pregnancy."

"She'll be aight. As long as she has us, there's nothing to worry about. Her and KJ will be cool," he assured us before placing the blunt at his lips.

"Easier said," Ken added with a shake of the head.

"They're ready to eat," he informed us. "I was sent out here to deliver the message."

"Pass that shit so I can go eat," Ken insisted with his hand out.

Luca obliged before heading toward the house again. I was right behind him, leaving Ken with his thoughts as he finished off the blunt. We wouldn't start dinner without him, so I knew he wouldn't be long.

Me, on the other hand, was ready to see the little people that made Sunday dinner a little more interesting. Though they didn't stay downstairs during most of our family dinners, the small amount of time I spent with them prior to sitting down with the adults fueled the rest of my week.

When I stepped into the house, Elle was trying to make her way out of the door. I bent down and scooped her right into my arms. She'd turned three two weeks ago and, in my opinion, was going on thirty-three. We considered her the old lady of the bunch. My mother was rubbing off on her a little too much.

"Where you going, little lady?" I asked, tossing her into the air.

"Uncle Ken," she cackled, "Uncle Ken."

"Uncle Ken will be in here in a few minutes. He's not going anywhere. Neither are you," I assured her.

She'd long ago taken a liking to Ken. Aside from her parents, he was her favorite person. Whenever he was near, she wouldn't let him breathe too long without acknowledging her presence. Their relationship was as complex as it was comical. The two fought as hard as they loved each other.

"What him doing? Him come here to me," she saddened.

"He will, Elle. For now, Uncle Laike is here."

"Uncle Wake," she replied with a frown. "Emoweeeeee!"

I chuckled as I lowered her to the ground.

"Emoweeeeeee. Uncle Wake. Uncle Wake," she screamed, taking off down the hall to find her sister.

She was hardly interested in me, but she knew that my Em would be. Essence, too. She was growing like wildfire and requesting larger sums of money each time I saw her.

"They're already upstairs. The little one snuck off in search of her favorite person," Ever explained.

She appeared from around the same corner that Elle had run around with the escapee in-hand. She was definitely an Eisenberg. There was no doubt about it. We made our own rules and didn't give a fuck who didn't like it.

"Where is he, anyway?" Ever asked, knowing as well as anyone else that if she sent Elle upstairs without meeting her wishes, San would have hell the entire dinner.

Just as the question fell from her lips, Ken stepped in behind me. The loud, prominent smell of marijuana hit my nostrils and turned them upward in pleasure. It was the most beautiful smell one could ever encounter.

"Uncle Ken!" Elle cheered.

Like the little gymnast she was, she leaped from Ever's arms and into Ken's. He caught her mid-air and helped her land on his chest. With a shake of the head, I left the trio in the foyer to hash out their issues. My tribe had already gone upstairs and that was slightly disappointing.

When I made it to the kitchen, everyone was seated already. Before sitting at the elongated table that I'd customized for Luca with moments like the current one in mind, I grabbed a whiskey glass from the bar area. I scanned the wide selection of browns and clears before discovering my liquor of choice.

Hennessy White.

I poured approximately three shots into the wide-mouthed glass and topped it off with a splash of the cran-grape. It was the first option of two other juices that had been poured into large glass pitchers with long snouts.

When I finally made it back to the table, the chatter had calmed a bit and everyone was finally seated. Ken stared at the glass in my hand, regretfully. I tilted my head a few degrees as I stared back at him. The stare-off commenced but didn't last long before my mother cleared her throat to chastise us both.

"I raised you so I know you've got some manners, Laike. And, Ken, you, too! Both of you need to open your mouths and address the room that you walk into."

"Heathens," my father followed up with. He was always co-signing his wife.

"She's already yours, Pops. You don't have to be a tail kisser," I reminded him.

"Sometimes, I regret letting my soldiers march that night you were conceived," he hissed.

"I'm the best thing that has come from that saggy sack of yours, old man. Have some respect," I responded.

Before he was able to conjure something foolish to release from his lips, I continued, "Furthermore, the table should be greeting me when I step in the building. You commoners are in the presence of royalty. Has that not registered yet?"

"This nigga is so full of himself." Luca sighed.

My wit failed me due to the blunt trauma I suffered to the head. My mother had taken off her flat and tossed it across the table. Her aim was perfect.

"Don't play with me, Laike," she fussed.

I could see the steam rising from her ears. She was the cutest when she was upset, which was why I loved taking it there with her as often as I could. She considered me her dark child for a reason. It was me that brought that side out of her most.

"Wow, you got them without snagging me a pair?" Lyric gasped.

"I tried to get you to come to the store with me but you passed me up on the offer. Dena had called to let me know they'd gotten them in."

Dena. That name crossed the dinner table enough times for me to remember her though I'd never seen her face. She was their sales representative at the Chanel store. Any time she called, they came running. I was wondering why my dad hadn't found a way to block her, yet. She was the reason four and five figures would come up missing from his bank account on any given Saturday of the month.

"I just got hit across the head and instead of calling Child Protective Services, you're worried about an ugly ass flat that looks like something Grand would've worn to church on Sunday?"

Grand was my mother's mother. She and my grandfather had both died in their home eight days before my thirteenth birthday. Though long ago, I'd never forget the day. It was the first time I saw my father shed a single tear. There was a gas leak in their home that no one was aware of that ultimately killed them both in their sleep. That was the only detail that my father admired about their death. They'd died peacefully in their sleep, together. He felt, in some way, that it was how it was supposed to be.

"You're a grown ass man, though I have to be reminded of that myself sometimes," my father chastised. "Now get your mother her shoe before I throw mine at you next, and I won't be so gentle."

"Y'all always been this abusive or is it just clearer now?" I asked.

My father leaned forward, and I understood that it wasn't to give me a lecture. He was reaching for his shoe, too. I placed my hands in the air so that he could see there was no need to reinforce his wife's actions.

"Here. Give the woman her shoe before I have to carry your ass to the hospital," Ken whispered as he nudged me in the side.

I lowered my left hand and grabbed the shoe. When I passed it to my mother, she nearly took my hand off accepting it. When I retrieved my semi-numb fingers, I blew her a kiss.

"What's up, everybody? Y'all good?" Ken started.

He'd learned his lesson simply by watching me succumb to mine. The heat that I was willing to receive, he wasn't. Now that I'd been made an example, he wanted to fly the straight and narrow.

"Pussy," I whispered through a cough near his ear as the responses filled the room with chatter.

Just as it subsided, I stood from my seat and waved my glass in the air for dramatic purposes.

"I'd like to take this opportunity to greet each and every one of you individually. I'll start with my mother since her temper is shorter than a tic tac. Laura, hello. It's so very nice of you to join us. Liam, umm hmm." I tilted my head in his direction without as much as a glimpse.

"Aight," Luca interrupted as he waved his hand from side to side, "no one else cares to be addressed, my nigga."

"Very well, then."

I ended my speech with a bow. When I took my seat, I could hear Lyric release an exaggerated sigh. She and Luca were the epitome of haters. If the word was ever discovered in a dictionary, their pictures should appear underneath it.

"Can we eat, now?" Lyric blurted, obviously the hungriest of the bunch.

"Yes. We've already blessed the food," my mother replied.

Stuffed salmon, stuffed chicken, ranch-style garlic potatoes, green beans, fried cabbage, cornbread, and Kool-Aid that Ever had decided to make us at the last minute were all on the menu. Instead of using too many brain cells to decide on the perfect combination, I opted for two plates. There wasn't a dish untouched once my plate was complete and prepared for consumption.

The blunt I'd faced before getting dressed and the one I'd helped finish off left me with a hell of an appetite. The chatter around the table caused sporadic laughter and cheer, but I was locked in with the determination to finish off my plate. Everything was hitting.

"But he needs a companion," I overheard Luca express.

"The dog that you haven't had since you bought the little nigga needs a companion?" I butted in.

"Yes. He does."

"We're not getting another dog, Luca," Ever chimed in.

"And, I'm not taking another one in," my mother added.

My father stayed silent, causing a chuckle to escape my mouth.

"He wants another dog," I called him out. "Look at his face."

"Exactly!" Luca exclaimed.

"Well, if I was a dog, I'd want some pussy from time to time, too," my father explained. "So in his defense and mine, I think he needs him a woman."

"We all do," Ken agreed.

The entire table silenced as their eyes landed in my direction. Taking that as my cue to shut up and mind my business, I lowered my head and put my eyes on my plate. We weren't having this discussion, not now.

"Mom, you said there was something you guys wanted to talk to us about," Lyric proclaimed.

The silence grew eerie as my eyes left my plate and found my parents. The authenticity of my mother's smile didn't reside in the one that she'd mustered after Lyric's comment. My father cleared his throat and nodded his head. He laid his napkin on the table and scooted his chair a bit closer to my mother's.

"Uh. Yeah. There is something we wanted to share with you guys," he confirmed.

I glared intently at my parents, unsure where the uneasiness was coming from. When my vision led me to Luca, I noticed the unsettling of his spirit through his darkened eyes. He met my gaze, both of us saying everything that needed to be said without uttering a word. My stomach knotted as the silence pressed on.

"Well," Lyric chuckled nervously, "what is it?"

She, too, felt it.

With every set of eyes in the room on her, my mother smiled as she began to speak.

"I – uh. My –my cancer has returned."

The color faded from my light brown skin. I grew a bit more pale by the milliseconds as the words my mother spoke planted themselves into my brain for permanent residency. The food that I'd chewed sat in my mouth, unmoving as I was. I felt like I'd been hit with two bricks against my chest, and they'd knocked the life out of me.

The loud ringing in my ears was constant, blocking every word my family spoke in my presence. I could feel nothing but pain, uncompromising pain. Pain that was too much to be expressed with tears. Pain that was far too much to express with words. Pain that crippled you. Pain that altered you – forever.

I wasn't sure when the ringing stopped or when my feet began to move but by the time I realized what was happening, I was outside with my body leaned forward as I released everything I'd consumed at the dinner table. Over and over, I heaved until everything was emptied from my stomach. The sound of the door opening caused me to snap my neck in the direction of the house.

First there was Ken and then there was Luca. I held my hand up to stop them both. Their presence wouldn't soothe even a portion of the pain I felt. I didn't need them trying to convince me that things would be okay and that everything was under control.

It wasn't. Cancer was a deadly motherfucker and it didn't matter how much bread we had to fight it, there was a strong possibility that it would always win in the end.

I stood to my feet, barely able to hold my own weight. The potency of the pain had me wobbling toward the car as if I was intoxicated. Somehow, it felt that way, too. Sluggishly, I slid into my car and started the engine. As it idled, I lifted the glove compartment and grabbed the travel-sized bottle of Listerine. The taste that was left in my mouth was far too awful to bear.

I poured the Listerine straight into my mouth and recapped the bottle. I swirled the liquid around as my mother's words echoed in my mind. *My cancer has returned. My cancer has returned. My cancer has returned. My cancer has returned.*

I spat the liquid out into the driveway and closed my door.

"FUCK!" I bellowed from a place so deep within that I didn't recognize it.

My hands gripped the wheel as my back made contact with the seat over and over again. When that didn't feel like enough to relieve me of the pressure and pain I felt, with balled fists, I punched the steering wheel over and over again.

"Fuck! Fuck! Fuck!"

Head in hands, I surrendered to my emotions, momentarily. "What the fuck, yo?"

A knock on my window startled me. Through the tint, I could see Lyric's long frame. Against my true desires, I rolled it down. While I could ignore Luca, it was impossible to ignore Lyric for any amount of time. My heart wouldn't allow it.

"Laike, please come back inside," she pleaded.

Tears stained her face. The glossiness of her eyes confirmed that she was on the verge of even more. I couldn't stand to see her cry. It tugged at my heartstrings, whether good or bad.

"I can't do that Lyric," I admitted. "I need some time to get my head together."

"Where are you going?" she inquired.

"I don't know. Wherever the night leads me, but I'll be aight. Don't worry about me. I'm good."

"But you're not. I'm not. No one is."

"I will be."

I didn't allow her to say another word before I lifted the window, signaling the end of our conversation. Understanding that there wasn't any convincing me, she turned and headed in the house with a hand on her growing belly. I used the opportunity to pull around Luca's roundabout, carefully bypassing the family's' cars.

When I broke way, the speed limits of the suburban streets suddenly didn't matter. The smell of burning rubber permeated the air. The pavement consumed chunks of my tire's meatiness as I chased oblivion.

laike + braisleigh

HOURS PASSED me by before I released the pedal from beneath my foot and put my car in park. My engine roared as I rubbed my hands down my face. It seemed to go on forever and ever.

The stress of my mother's words were heavy on my soul. They annihilated the beauty of the night. Before walking out of my door with a joyful heart and gratitude resting on within my bones, I hadn't imagined the evening would take such a dreadful turn. *Nothing*. Nothing could've prepared me for a hammer to the chest.

Ma. The light of my life. She was forever my lady. My world easily revolved around her even when it revolved around the other woman in my world – Lyric. She was my center. Each decision I made in life was with intentions to make her a proud mother.

When the jokes subsided and I was stripped of my ability to make her laugh, I just hoped that I made her smile. *Genuinely*. She'd raised me right, and I was left with an insatiable appetite to be everything she dreamed I'd be.

With heavy thoughts and an even heavier heart, I disabled my vehicle and stepped out. The openness of the driveway made me suck the skin of my teeth while using my key fob to secure one of my most prized possessions. I hated it. The lack of privacy didn't and never would sit well with me.

Comfort wrapped around me like a fresh, warm blanket as I stepped into the dark home. I locked the door behind me and placed my keys on the hook, not loosening my fingers from around them until they'd settled. The stillness of the atmosphere was too comforting to disrupt.

Gently, I took the stairs one by one. And, with each, I felt me unraveling. Though I was still fully clothed, my gradual ascend stripped me of my layers, over and over and over. By the time I entered the dark bedroom where the most gentle, precious heart rested, I felt naked.

Silently, I released the anxiousness that swelled in my chest. Home. Physically, maybe not. My home was miles and miles away, but in every other aspect of my world, this was my home. She was my home.

"Laike," Baisleigh stirred in her sleep.

She knew. I settled in my head.

She reached up and tapped the small light above her bed. It barely illuminated the space near her side of the bed, but it helped her see who'd entered her bedroom. I heard the exaggerated exhale that left her throat at the realization that it was me.

Our eyes met shortly after. No words were shared. As I removed my shoes, pants, and shirt, we simply gazed at one another, openly and unashamed. What-ever needed to be said was, soundlessly.

It didn't matter how far I ran or how much time got between us, she was home. She held pieces of my heart that I'd never be able to get back. I didn't want them, either. She deserved them. She deserved everything.

That's why I had no problem giving her anything that was in my grasp if ever there was even an inkling that she desired it. Nothing was off limits. Not even new pieces of my heart that she conquered without even knowing. Her existence simply required the whole thing and watching her grow only made me fall deeper into the web she'd spun for me when we were just kids.

Baisleigh knew me better than anyone. She knew me better than I knew myself. That's why I wasn't surprised when her features saddened and her eyes slowly closed before reopening.

"What's the matter?" she asked me, the sadness surrounding her words.

I climbed onto her bed and pulled the covers back. Once we were skin to skin and my head rested on her chest, my walls fell to the ground. The barriers that I'd put in place to protect my heart were dismantled. I closed my eyes and allowed myself to unknot. The wetness of her chest was only the beginning of my spiral.

"Baby, talk to me," she insisted.

I couldn't. *Where are the words when you need*

them? I wondered. Keeping Baisleigh blinded wasn't my intention but speaking wasn't a privilege of mine at the time. The pain I felt was encompassing and had swallowed me whole.

"Laike, please," she begged.

The racing of her heart assured me that this wasn't a sick nightmare and that I was very much alive. She was, too, and scared to death of whatever she was waiting for to leave my lips. Desperate to level our playing field, I found my voice.

"Her cancer is back."

Baisleigh sucked in a deep breath and held it for far longer than expected. It wasn't her words that caressed me. It was her limbs. She wrapped me in her arms and leaned down to rest her lips on my forehead. The feeling of her fingers slowly gliding across my back until they reached my head was unlike anything else.

"I love you," she finally responded.

"Too much."

Much too much, B.

Comfortably we sat without another word being spoken. As many as I had to express on any given day, Baisleigh understood that I had none. Again, she just got me. I'd never had to explain myself when it came to her. It was as if she simply felt her way through our connection and was never steered in the wrong direction.

After minutes of racing hearts, labored breathing, and exaggerated sighs, she reached up and turned off the light that illuminated a very small space above our heads. She slid deeper and lower in the bed. It was nearly impossible for her to move too much because my closeness didn't allow her to. As if she could disappear at any second, I held on tight.

It wasn't until our noses touched that she settled. Immediately, I felt her lips on mine. Their softness was something that I'd always rely on as refuge from the brittleness of the world.

"I'm here, Laikie," fell from her lips just as she tucked her arm underneath mine.

I know.

laike + baisleigh

DARKNESS WAS CIRCUMAMBIENT, surrounding every inch of us. Because opening my eyes would've been pointless and still left me sightless, they remained closed. My sensitivity increased tremendously. The scent of creamy vanilla and possibly chamomile stuffed my nose. They weren't strangers in spaces that she created. I'd been in enough of them to know and remember.

Though it was silent, there was a loud ringing that rested within both of my ears. It was redundant and familiar. The taste of liquor lingered on my tongue, but it was marijuana that was most potent. I could feel everything, *especially her*.

The folds, dips, and curvatures of Baisleigh's body matched mine perfectly. Together, we fit like lost pieces to a puzzle. For every time her body pleated, mine protruded. Without guidance, they synced – even at rest.

My fingers, they strummed the surface of her skin, acclimating themselves with the fine texture all over again. The silkiness of it all made it hard to tell the difference between where the nightie she wore began and her skin ended. The two were one in the same.

Pushing through the darkness, guided by only my sense of touch, I lowered my body in the bed. My keen sense of smell kicked into overdrive and began heading the mission as Baisleigh's arousal kissed the air. It wasn't long before I met its distribution center.

Nostalgic, it was. And, beautiful. It was the most beautiful fragrance I'd ever encountered. Her sweetness combined with a divine feminine musk that left my mouth watery and my tastebuds tingling.

So many years, *too many years*, had passed me by since the last time I found my head lodged between a set of legs, but I was ready to make up for each one of them I'd missed. Baisleigh's pussy was the only one I had an appetite for, which left me starving for the better half of adulthood.

"Laike," she slurred, waking up from her sleep.

"Open up."

Without haste, she slid her legs across the thick, comforting sheets of her bed. As she slowly opened for me, I allowed the saliva that pooled in my mouth to build. I didn't want to waste a drop. It was all destined for the well that rested between her thighs.

Pantiless. It's how she'd always slept because she hated the lining of her underwear sinking into the creases of her skin through the night, and the fact that they always found their way up her round ass as if they had a choice. The damn thing would swallow a pair of jeans whole if it got the chance. Always hungry, it was.

My thumb caressed the bulge between the lips of her pussy, swelling it upon contact. Baisleigh's legs collapsed on each side of her body. A stifled moan was caught in her throat but was still noticed.

With applied pressure of my thumb, I coerced the sound from her body along with an exaggerated sigh of relief. Baby girl's build-up was infuriating. Whoever was hitting her shit wasn't hitting it right. The revelation that I could relieve her stressors and meet every desire for intimacy that she had ever mustered had me tight in the chest.

Baisleigh was a good girl. A hard-working girl. A loyal girl. A faithful girl. The least she deserved was sexual inclination – over and over and over again. She deserved to be depleted. Gutted. Left nothing to the imagination. She deserved big, uncompromising dick and that's exactly what I planned to give her. The discovery of her deficit shifted my gears and forced me to reconsider the prolonging of her climax.

With the way that she squirmed uncontrollably from my touch, I knew that her sensitivity would only increase if she wasn't unpacked of her sexual frustrations and teased instead. I didn't want that for her. Instead of hypersensitivity that didn't allow her to truly enjoy our moment, I needed Baisleigh aware of everything and down for anything that our time together required of her. So, the first order of business was to release her from the shackles of unpleasant sexual encounters, self-pleasure, and disappointing partners.

My head dropped between her thighs, again. Her scent was my favorite. I pushed her legs even further apart and found comfort in the position that I was in. Then, out of sheer habit, I inhaled her natural fragrance.

Puuuuh! The saliva that pooled in my mouth, I spat onto her pink flesh. Her pussy was so fucking pretty, and I was suddenly sick to my stomach that the dark was obstructing my view. I wanted to see it. I wanted to see her.

Baisleigh had the smoothest, dark skin and prettiest features that were perfectly proportioned and placed on her face. Whatever point God was trying to prove about dark-skinned women's superiority when sculpting B, he'd fucking done it. She was walking art. With long, black hair that didn't stop until it reached the middle of her back and a body that the gym never truly needed to experience because of her genetics, B was sickening.

Women hated to see her coming. Shit, I hated to see her coming because she reminded me of my incapacities. I'd fumbled her heart, and, because I still hadn't digested the reality she must've suffered due to that, I'd yet to face myself. Until then, I couldn't truly face her. Admittedly, she shook the ground I walked on each time she appeared. I was always unsteady, out of focus, and rattled in her presence.

Baisleigh was my heart in human form, walking and thriving outside of my chest. That always made me feel a way, especially knowing that it was no longer in my grasp. She was good without me. That helped me sleep some nights and kept me up, restless, other nights. It was a gift and it was a curse. It simply depended on the way the wind blew that day or what I'd had to drink that night.

"Laike," she whimpered.

"Turn on the light."

I wanted to see her. I had to see her. I needed to see her.

"Laike," she rushed out, breathlessly.

"Light," I reminded her.

Obliging, Baisleigh stretched her body until she reached the light. The movement brought her pussy to my face, suffocating me in the meaty pouch. If I died there, I would've died a very happy man. Not wanting to waste the opportunity, I sucked her clit into my mouth being that it was so close.

"Baby, please," she cried out, falling back onto the bed.

Darkness still blinded us.

"The light, Baisleigh," I demanded.

"I'm trying," she voiced, shakily. "Please."

I released her pussy from my mouth so that she could complete the mission. Though simple, with additional obstacles put in her path, the task was a lot more difficult. Once set free, the space above us illuminated with a soft light that allowed me to see her beautiful face, the one that I'd been enamored with since we were jits.

Our eyes met as she readjusted herself beneath me. Much more love than I deserved sat within her orbs. She'd loved me far too much and far too long, and it pained me that I'd betrayed that love to explore a world that was as bitter as it was cold. I missed her sweetness and her delicate nature, but I was too far removed from our lives together to even begin to rekindle the flame that I'd snuffed abruptly. *And for what?* I always asked myself.

She was the one I'd let get away and for the rest of my life, I'd be paying for that. While others assumed it was as easy as professing my love for her that would seal our fate, it wasn't. Pieces were broken that could never be mended – on both of our ends. I'd done that to her. I'd done that to us. While I knew that it was better for both of us, it didn't make shit any easier or more accurate.

I still felt as if I'd wronged her though I was only trying to save her. I'd killed her drive, her spirit, her peace for so long that it was hard to watch from afar. So, I found a corner of the world where my view was limited and stayed there for as long as I could because seeing her crumble due to my decision was far too much to handle. It wasn't until I knew that she was better that I emerged and the sight of her thriving swallowed me whole.

It wasn't that I wanted her to suffer without me, but it seemed as if she was so much better without me and that was a thorn in my side. That's why it wasn't as easy to pick up where we'd left off. That's why I'd promised to never interfere with her life again. I saw the damage I'd done. I saw what I was capable of. I didn't ever want her to return to the darkness I left her in. I'd never be able to live with myself. That's why I stayed away... *until now*.

My eyes faltered as I tried to force myself out of my thoughts and back into the moment. *Our moment*. I watched as the saliva I'd conjured slid down her pussy and pooled beneath her, making it glisten along with her asshole. It was all edible in my opinion, and I had every intention of indulging.

Utterly vexed by my own failures, I shoved two fingers into her canal as I watched her features expand and shrink, simultaneously. Her dimples made an appearance as her brows sagged and met in the center of her forehead. *Fucking perfect*, she was.

"Ooohh Laike." She inhaled.

"Stop letting fuck niggas in my shit if they ain't going to hit it right," I suggested as I turned my fingers upward and signaled for her G-spot.

I wanted it to come to me, so I beckoned for it. Baisleigh's eyes rolled backward, getting lost somewhere up in her head as she succumbed to my familiarity with her frame. I knew her inside out, literally and figuratively. She'd been my assignment for years. It was my job to figure her out and I had.

"Oh God. Ummmmm. Laike."

I loved to hear her call my name, no matter what mood she was in or the reason being. There was only one instance when I hated to hear it fall from her lips and that's when she was begging me to reconsider my decision to end things in order for me to explore my manhood in early adulthood. My intention to save her heart resulted in me breaking it anyway – and mine in the process.

"You hear me?" I asked as I lowered my head between her legs, again, and licked her flesh.

"Yes. Yeeeeessssss."

Baisleigh's back arched as her hands drew the sheets closer to our bodies with the tips of her fingers. I devoured her meatiness while watching her through a lens that no one else had ever been seen through. This one was curated with love, adoration, and trust. Aside from my mother, Lyric, and Ever, Baisleigh was the only woman I'd ever trust had my best interest at heart. Without a doubt, I knew that she did. Always had. Always would.

Back and forth, I swiped my tongue across her clit, focusing solely on its stimulation. I knew that without a doubt, it would unearth Baisleigh's crown after being buried beneath the mud for umpteen years. Her zenith would easily be rebirthed, and I could give her exactly what everyone after me seemed to be failing to do.

Steady and unmoving, I remained locked in place. The only movement was from my tongue as it rummaged through the pain, anger, and resentment against me that she'd built her walls with to find her center. I'd split her right down the middle and remind her of exactly who I was and why she ever fucked with me to begin with.

"Laaaaaaaaike!" she screamed.

Her legs lifted and began closing the distance between me and them. The peak that I was chasing was near. She was unraveling and could hardly wait until she mounted and bloomed. Trapped between her legs, my assault on her clit did not end. I continued to swipe it over and over until I felt her body lift my head from the bed along with it. She began bouncing as gibberish surfaced from her throat.

"Fuckkkkkkk. Oh Goddddd my. Wait. Laike. Iiiii-iiiii. Nooooo."

I continued to work my fingers, brushing against

her g-spot as I continued to tap on her clit with my tongue. Simultaneously, the moves unplugged her faucet. The pressure forced her waters to shoot into the air and drench my face – from my nose down my beard and chest.

"That's what the fuck I'm talking about, B," I cheered a splintering Baisleigh on.

I hovered over her body as she rode the wave I'd sent her on. With her legs spread wide, I could see the contractions that hit her pussy one after the other, causing it to sink before expanding again. I'd always loved seeing concrete proof of her peak and there wasn't a more rewarding sight than watching her pussy spasm.

I removed my briefs as the show went on. When the contractions subsided, I placed a knee on each side of Baisleigh and slid up until my dick touched her chin. I lifted the thick, weighty rod and massaged it. My victim was semi-conscious and still blabbering about some shit I didn't understand every few seconds. Sleep would soon find her, but not before we finished, together this time.

"Wake the fuck up, B."

I tapped the side of her face with my dick. When her eyes opened, I tapped her lips and then pushed upward until the top one reached her nose. Her perfectly aligned teeth and gums were exposed, causing me to ooze. I drizzled them both with my pre-cum.

Thick, creaminess lowered into her mouth as her lips reconnected. I massaged my dick while watching Baisleigh reacclimate herself with the taste of me. Her eyes opened slowly. She began sliding upward in bed, coming to life as if my pre-ejaculation was the magic potion she needed to be awakened from her slumber.

Her mouth slacked as she reached forward and grabbed as much of me as she could. I was nearly seven inches in length, but the circumference of my dick was the beauty of it. The thickness had ripped through pussies that promised to never partake in the challenge again.

But, B, she could handle my shit. There was never a question if she was up for the challenge. She'd mastered it. Her pussy had been altered to fit my shit, which was probably the reason niggas, who didn't meet the standard, weren't of her benefit.

She opened wide, accepting me into the second warmest, wettest hole on her body. I entered without a doubt that it wouldn't emerge until it was covered with her saliva and about ready to blow. Just watching her adjust to my girth had me ready to fill her mouth with my seeds.

"A little more," I encouraged, pushing forward to make sure that she fit as much of me inside of her mouth as possible.

Slob dripped from her bottom lip as she batted her long, enhanced lashes and fixated her gaze on me. She understood the assignment. I watched as she managed to fit more of me between her lips. Then, suddenly she pulled her head back until she was free of me. Only a second passed before she was inhaling deeply and shoving my dick into her mouth again. With an even wetter, warmer space than the last time I'd entered it, she tried sucking the brown skin off my shit.

"Damn, B," I slurred, eyes low and heavy as I watched her work her magic on me.

She was intoxicating enough alone but the sight of her lips on me and my dick slowly gliding down her throat, repeatedly, was consummately inebriating. The dark skin, oversized lips, extra-large eyes, long lashes, thick brows, and fluffy cheeks would be the death of me.

She showed no remorse as she bobbed her head, massaging my balls and urging my nut to surface. I wasn't ready. She knew I wasn't. But she found pleasure in unmanning me. However, I wouldn't give her the satisfaction of seeing me whither. Not yet, at least.

Against her wishes, I pulled back and watched as my dick fell from her mouth. Defeat covered her features. She was still insanely gorgeous, possibly even more with the scowl on her face. B was pissed, but I'd be lying if I said I gave a fuck. The bedroom was the only place she didn't always get her way. This was my territory.

I managed to maneuver on the soft sheets until our knees were beside each other. I pulled her legs upward and over her head. Missionary was my favorite with

Baisleigh. I enjoyed watching the pleasure on her face as I plowed into her relentlessly. It was her favorite, too. Well, immediately after backshots. She creamed like there was no tomorrow when she was on all fours throwing that shit back to me.

Just the thought of the waves her ass created as our skin smacked had me anxious to bend her ass over and make her cum. She wasn't little Baisleigh anymore. Baby girl had sprouted her thirty-plus hips and the grown woman's weight had her sitting really fucking pretty. That ass paired with her dripping pussy would surely create a tsunami.

With tingling buds, I lowered my head until my lips kissed her bottom set. She flinched upon contact, still sensitive from her climax. Her thighs glistened from the stretching of her legs, catching my eye as I straightened my spine.

My dick swung low, dangling to the point that it touched her pussy. We were on the same page, it seemed. It was knocking at her entrance for permission to enter, and I was waiting for her to open up.

"Spit on 'em," I requested.

Puhh! Puuuuh!

As Baisleigh spat into her hand, I held my dick in mine while spitting on her pussy. We were on one accord. Her fingers wrapped around the head of my dick to lubricate it a little more than it already was as my glob slid down and into the hole that it was meant for. And, then, I slowly penetrated her valley.

"Laaaaaaaaaaike."

I slid into her, passion dripping from each movement that we made. Everything about the moment heightened my senses. I was quickly reminded why I'd been caught up in her bliss for years and years. From the age of eleven when we finally admitted to wanting to be boyfriend and girlfriend to the age of twenty-three when I finally decided to end our twelve-year relationship, I'd been entrapped. Still was, secretly.

Homebase.

Walls surrounded me. Drowning me without remorse. Her floodgates had opened and were pouring nonstop. The holy water between her legs pounded against my flesh like crashing waves.

"Fuck, I've missed this shit," I admitted, dropping my head between her shoulder and chin. "Urgh!"

"Laike," she cried out, "Laike!"

The sound of her voice, so sultry and sexy in my ear, was summoning something from within me that I wasn't familiar with. It was as if my heart and soul intertwined, holding on to one another, as they both prepared for their undertaking. I could feel a tightness in my chest and a lump in my throat that coupled with the churning of my stomach.

There was no doubt in my mind that this girl was the one for me. However, I couldn't bring myself to face her or myself for what I'd done to us. It had been over ten years since we'd been in a relationship or intimate in any way, but the way my complete existence gravitated toward hers was all the proof I needed to back up my claims.

It was as if she owned me. When in her presence, I wasn't in control of anything that I said and did. She was. I was all ears, hands, tongue, and lips. Whatever she needed, I was willing to give. Whatever she wanted, I was willing to make it happen. I'd spare no expense and leave no stone unturned when it came to Baisleigh. I knew. She knew. Hell, we all knew.

Truth was, though. The chance I knew that I wasn't deserving of, she wouldn't give me anyway. Baisleigh was on her shit and made it clear every chance that she got that I wasn't welcomed in her world as anything more than a friend. In an effort to respect her wishes and protect her heart, I stayed away. I couldn't break it again, and I knew deep down there was a chance that I would.

Slowly, methodically I slid into homebase, steadily and repeatedly. Her pussy had a death's grip on my dick, locking it in as if it was afraid it would disappear, again. For now, it wasn't going anywhere. I could promise that much.

The natural lubrication that she produced was music to my ears as I listened through labored breathing and a pummeling heart. It was the sweetest sound from what used to be the sweetest girl. Though she still was, in my opinion, life had hardened her. *I* had hardened her.

"Remind a nigga who this shit belongs to."

The request was from left field but felt most genuine. I truly wanted to hear her profess what I already knew. It didn't matter how far she traveled, who she fucked, or where either of us ended up, Baisleigh belonged to me. Heart, soul, body, pussy, mind... everything. Not in a possessive way, but more of the inevitable. We were synced, souls mated. There was nothing either of us could do about it. I hadn't made the rules so I couldn't change them. She was forever mine, and I was forever hers.

"It's yours," she confessed, lowly, and breathlessly.

I watched as her eyes closed, and she tucked her lip between her teeth. She was nearing her peak, again, and losing her mind. However, I needed her to be lucid with a clear understanding of everything that was happening between us. To acquire her attention, I slowed my strokes to a creep. Her eyes popped open and met me with a menacing glare.

"Hmmm? Who's pussy is this, again, B? I can't hear you."

"Yours." She huffed, frustrated with my change in pace that knocked her off the climb to her peak.

I immediately picked up the pace as I lifted my body in the upright position. Baisleigh's legs were already in the air, but I bent them back as far as they'd go so that I could get a clear shot of her glistening pussy as I slid in and out of it. I also wanted to stretch her ass out to remind *her* why the pussy belonged to me, anyhow.

"Laike. Oh my God. Wait. Waaaaaait. Oh Laike."

She struggled to accommodate me. Her body slid backward a bit more with each stroke, eventually forcing her to end her climb at the headboard. Any further and she'd be climbing the fucking wall. It didn't matter though because I was right behind her. Every move she made in the opposite direction, I followed.

"Ummmm. Shit. Laike. Please."

Her hand went up in protest, pushing at my chest. I slapped it away and continued to dig into her guts. I wanted her fully gutted and unconscious by the time the sun rose. She'd been needing a good dick down and something to cackle with her friends about. I'd give her that and more.

Only when I felt like she'd had enough, I snatched away from her. I left a gaping hole in the center of her body that I watched close, slowly. *Snapback.* She had the best of that shit. Feeling as if she'd had enough time to catch her breath, I flipped her over onto her stomach and then lifted her body up until she was on all fours.

I didn't waste a second of her precious time. The beauty of her pussy drew me in closer. I French kissed her pinkness from behind, focusing mainly on her clit. Remembering every detail of our experiences and exactly what sent her over the edge, I massaged her wetness with my thumb. Once fully lubricated, I plugged her asshole with it as I continued devouring her poor clit.

Mercilessly, I pounded against it with my tongue in

search of her peak, knowing that it wasn't penetration that helped her reach it. For Baisleigh, clitoral stimulation was paramount to the success of her orgasm. She'd never successfully sprouted without it involved in some manner. I knew her body and so did she.

That's why she didn't hold back at the realization of my mission. She came effortlessly on my face. Before she was able to fall forward, I caught her and pulled her back up on all fours. Her climax exhausted her, always had. It would put her in a coma for hours if I allowed it, but I wouldn't. Not now.

My dick found its resting place. I entered Baisleigh's contracting pussy and it served its purpose, immediately. I counted the three measly strokes that I managed before my nut rushed from the head of my dick. I felt utterly betrayed knowing that I wasn't even on the verge of cumming before I'd slid in. But the combination of her moistness, contractions, and the waves her ass made that crashed against me was my ending.

"Shiiiiiiiit!" I bellowed, releasing everything within me.

It felt like a decade worth of semen exited my body at once. Together, we fell onto the sheets. I remained inside of her as she pulled the comforter over us both.

As my dick began to deflate and the high of the moment subsided, reality hit me like a sack of bricks. I'd broken the promise I'd made to myself long ago. *Don't disrupt her world if you're not ready to give her a newer, safer one.* Regret crept in, forming a lump in my throat.

"I love you," she uttered, pouring salt on the open wound.

I've fucked up.

DEDICATION

to my dearest Tierra...

I dedicate this series.

It's been far too long since you left me.
It's been far too long since I've heard
your voice or seen your smile. I'm hurting
every day thinking about you not being here
to experience the beauty of my characters,
our friendship, your daughter, and life
itself.

You should still be here.
My God, you should still be here.

My heart breaks more often than I'd like
to admit thinking about how prematurely you

were snatched away from us all. A spirit like yours, I guess the world didn't deserve. I love you beyond words can express and I don't think this pain will ever subside. You're in my heart, in my head, and I won't ever stop loving and thinking of you.

You're forever with me. The tattoo on my arm is a daily reminder. But, it's never enough. Your presence is the only thing that would fill the hollowness of my heart... this abyss. Only your presence.

I wish you could've met Luca and Lyric and Laike. They're all beautiful, just like you!

I miss you forever, baby girl.

forevermore

GREYHUFFINGTON

THE **EINSENBERG EFFECT** BOOK THREE

ONE

baisleigh

TWO AND A HALF MONTHS LATER...

WAS THIS MY LIFE? I asked for the fifth time in the last ten minutes. The contentment that swelled in my chest wasn't to be taken lightly. After so many years of hurt, pain, and unhappiness, things for me were finally falling into place.

My jaws hurt from the excessive smiling I'd done over the hour. I could hardly believe that I was getting my happily ever after. Though I knew it was obtainable, I knew that I couldn't make it happen alone. I needed a partner to make my dreams come true and there he was, standing just a few feet away from me with his hands shoved into the pockets of his slacks. His piercing gaze only made my lips rise further and my cheeks burn with glee.

'*I love you,*' he mouthed, causing my center to throb.

'*I love you back,*' I mouthed.

My line of vision shifted as my head fell, and my emotions lumped in my chest. We were really doing this. I was really doing this. A wife. I'd be a wife soon. I'd waited patiently for my turn, and I was up next. This was a title I'd wanted to wear since I could remember. Before I even fully understood the role, requirements, and reality of being a wife, I wanted the responsibility. Forever, it had been a dream of mine and my man was finally making that happen for me.

Wow. My eyes settled on the ring, again. I'd been fixated on it the entire night. It was modest, yet, the most elegant piece I'd ever owned. The single, large diamond in the middle glistened along with my eyes. My moment had come and it was a glorious one, one that I couldn't wait to tell my children and grand-children.

"Awwwwww. Poor baby," Ditto teased, scooting her chair closer.

Though six years my junior, she was much more like a sibling than my cousin. We hadn't exactly grown up together but as we got older, we got so much closer. She and I were almost identical in spirits, ambition, energy, and self-awareness. However, we were so much different from one another, physically. While my skin was dark like chocolate candy, hers was closest to the color yellow. My hair was full of thick, fluffy kinks and coils while she rocked thick, fluffy spirals.

Ditto had left Channing for a while to pursue her college education and ended up staying a bit longer than she intended. She returned to Channing with, not only a bachelor's degree, but a master's as well. She specialized in product development and was helping me bring my ideas for my herbal tea line to life.

She preferred coffee. I guess that was another thing we didn't share, interest in coffee. Though I served hundreds of dollars a day worth of coffee at Baisleigh's House on a daily basis, it wasn't the best beverage in my opinion. It was never very pleasant to my body.

I'd consumed it for as long as I had because I didn't think there were any other alternatives. After digging a bit deeper, I discovered herbal teas and began making my own. I hadn't gone back to my sporadic cups of coffee since.

She handed me the napkin to catch the tears that nearly slipped from my eyes. The last thing I wanted to do was ruin my makeup. I didn't think it would be the case, however. Though I'd waited for this day almost all of my life, I didn't feel overcome by emotions or over-whelmed by them. I was handling the moment much better than I'd ever imagined.

It was beautiful. It was appreciated. It was everything that I could've dreamed and with the man that had promised me the world. I had no doubt in my mind that he'd give it to me, either. He hadn't broken a promise since the day that we agreed to make our thing work. I had no regrets choosing him. If I was given the chance, I'd choose him, again.

"Can you even believe this?" I asked her as I patted my eyes. "I'm getting married."

"You're getting married, Bais. I love that for you, mommas."

"Thank you so much for being a part of this day. It means the world to me. You really helped him put all of this together?"

I took another look around the venue. It was beau-tiful. The words Will You Marry Me? were created with roses of the deepest shades of red. I loved the display most. Above us was the prettiest display of greenery. What was supposed to be a private dinner at the botanical gardens had turned out to be my engage-ment. The attention to detail and the fact that he remembered how much I loved gardens and greenery were just... *everything*.

"Yes. I did, but not much. He handled 80% of it on his own. He really loves you, Bais."

"Yeah?" I nodded my head as I asked. Knowing that I wasn't the only one who believed it was refreshing. He was refreshing.

"Yes," she assured me.

"He's a good man, huh?"

"From as far as I can tell, he's a great man. You did good, babe."

"Mrs. Reeves," I said aloud, desperate to see how it sounded rolling off my tongue.

"Mrs. Nicholas Reeves," Ditto added.

"Mrs. Nicholas Reeves," I repeated.

"How does it feel?"

"It feels... satisfying."

"Good," she replied, "I'm so happy for you, babes."

My eyes left Ditto's tearful face and shifted in my fiancé's direction. In his chocolate suit, looking like the best piece of Hershey's I'd ever put my mouth on, he headed in my direction. Butterflies remained at the pit of my stomach when he approached, leaned down, and kissed the very top of my forehead.

"Is my fiancée ready to roll?"

Fiancée. It sounded swell coming from his lips. With legs long like stakes and a smile that could bring any woman to her knees, Nicholas was the ultimate catch. Luckily for me, I'd been the one who caught him. For two months, we dated before he finally asked me to be his woman two months ago.

Once we were exclusive to one another, things changed so rapidly. I was falling and I was falling fast.

While I wondered sometimes if I was falling alone, he showed me and assured me that I wasn't. That's why it was an easy *yes* when he asked if I'd be his wife. I was so tired of waiting for my happy ending by the time he'd come along. However, he made the wait well worth the time I'd spent dreaming of it and hoping it would come someday.

Nicholas had effortlessly swept me off my feet. There wasn't a time that I remember when he wasn't trying his hardest to make sure that I felt seen, heard, comfortable, appreciated, and adored. He was the ultimate romancer, which was why I hadn't expected all that came with tonight's dinner. I imagined it was just another extravagant date night for us. Although he'd retired four years ago, his professional basketball career had left him without a care in the world when finances were involved.

"I am."

"Ditto," Nicholas said as he turned to her, "I can't thank you enough. You made this a breeze. I know you've said a million times that compensation isn't needed, but if there's ever a way for me to repay you, don't hesitate to tell me."

"This wasn't a favor. This was just me... on sister duty. Please don't ever think you'll have to repay me for helping you make something happen for my favorite girl in the world. Just treat her right and continue making her happy. That's enough payment for me."

"That I can and will definitely do. You've met this woman," he chuckled, taking me by the hand, "she deserves nothing less."

"Nothing less. I'm going to let you guys get out of here. I'll make sure the staff knows we're all leaving and will clean this all up. The videographer and photographer promises to have your files ready within three business days. I know how much I hate waiting on files, so I made sure they prioritize you guy's special day."

"Thank you so much, Ditto. You're truly a godsend."

"You, too, my love. Go ahead and go enjoy the rest of your night."

"Love you, babes," I told her as I leaned forward and kissed her cheek.

"Love you back," she responded before prancing off toward the prettiest pink flowers.

I wasn't sure what they were called, but they were amazing and there were so many of them. I made a mental note to go online and grab the downloadable list of the wide range of plant life living inside each greenhouse in the gardens. We were in the second pod, and I definitely wanted the list of greenery that surrounded us. Everything was beautiful, serving as the perfect backdrop for us.

Hand-in-hand, my husband-to-be led me out of the

pod that he'd reserved for us and into the main building. There was a single line of employees smashing their palms together and whistling as we made our way through. My heart galloped like horses through the Kentucky Derby. *Another warm surprise.* I wasn't expecting this, any of it. When we finally reached Nicholas' Jaguar, my head was still spinning.

"How are you feeling?" he questioned once he was situated in the driver's seat.

"Loved," I admitted with a sigh, "I'm feeling loved."

"Because you are," he told me as he took my hand into his and kissed the back of it.

"To my place or yours?"

"Mine," he confirmed.

With one arm resting on the leather of the middle console to meet Nicholas', I used the other to recline my seat slightly. I'd had a very long, very eventful day. Though I wouldn't change one portion of it, exhaustion had finally hit me. I closed my eyes, hoping to rest them a least a few minutes on the twenty-five minute drive.

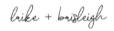

I'D GONE a step further than resting my eyes. I woke to Nicholas' nudging me awake.

"Hey," he called out as he rubbed the side of my face. "Hey. We've made it."

"Ummm?" Disoriented, I groaned. The cat nap I'd taken felt more like a brief coma that I was trying my hardest to wake up from.

"Are you okay to walk or would you rather me carry you inside?"

"I'm okay to walk. At least I will be. Just give me a few seconds, okay?"

"Of course. I'm going to run inside to put the bags from earlier away and then I'll be back."

"Ummm hmmm." I nodded, still trying to make sense of everything around me.

I wasn't sure how long passed before I felt alert and able to support my own weight. By the time I closed the car door behind me, Nicholas was out of the house and headed in my direction. I waved a hand to assure him that I was well and didn't need assistance. With a smile, he waited on the porch with both hands in front of him.

My husband. I imagined the same glorification that rested in his eyes as he watched me make my way to him would be displayed on our special day as he watched me carefully walk down the aisle. Even the thought caused those butterflies to swarm. *Me. Married?* Dreams really did come true.

When I stepped inside of his home, a trail of roses met me at the door. I turned toward Nicholas, who was casually locking the door behind us as if nothing was out of the ordinary. That's the thing that I loved about him most. This was who he truly was, the thoughtful gentleman. He didn't expect me to be jumping up and down or falling out about anything that he did for me because this was how he reciprocated his love.

The same way that I expressed my love for him through meals with time, effort, energy, and lots of meaning behind them, he did through surprises, thoughtful gifts, date nights, and acts of kindness. I knew his love language, and he knew mine. It was one of the reasons we worked so well together.

"Really?" I gushed.

"Really," he responded, wrapping his arms around me and swaying me from one side to another. "Just think about it. An entire lifetime of this... of me."

"I can hardly wait." I smiled. "Where does this lead?"

"I don't know. Why don't you follow it and find out."

I took him by the hand, making sure he was near, and followed the roses through his home, up the stairs, and into his bedroom. They ended at his bed and then began again on top of the bed, forming a heart. In the center was what must've been the sluttiest teddy I'd ever seen. It left nearly nothing to the imagination. On the tips of my toes, I turned to face the man responsible for the garment.

"What?" he asked with a shrug.

"Hmmm. You're just full of pleasant surprises."

"Is that a complaint?" His dimpled jaws rose to the occasion.

"Not at all."

"Good. Now, grab that motherfucker off the bed, head into the bathroom, and squeeze into it. I'm ready to take you to that special place that you showed me and that you love to visit so much."

He was a great learner and even better listener. After we'd made things official and I was exclusively his, Nicholas set out on a mission to please me wholly – mind, body, and soul. That included learning my fantasies and desires in the bedroom. My climax was always his priority. Once it was reached, and only then, did he seek his own. The selflessness he exercised in bed was almost as sexy as he was.

With tingling, hiked cheeks and a throbbing pussy, I snatched the teddy from the bed and headed for the bathroom. Its spaciousness allowed me to peel my skin-tight dress off comfortably upon entry. The thong that I removed from between my ass cheeks was drenched. The creaminess in the seat of them was evidence of the night I was looking forward to having.

Fiancé. I was still on the clouds, floating from the festivities of the night as I placed my panties in the clothing basket that was dedicated to my laundry. At the end of the week, any clothes I left over the few days that I stayed, I made sure to take home and wash.

With Nicholas' occupation, he was always in a different city for various reasons and working with various athletes. Most of our nights were spent alone. His in lonely hotels and mine in my bed. However, our hours-long conversation made it feel like we were only a few miles apart. The two or three nights that we slept in one another's arms were the best.

Once I was completely unclothed, my reflection stared back at me in the mirror. Perfection. As the years passed me by, it was as if my body was improving a bit more. At thirty-six, I was more in love with myself than I'd ever been. A year ago, at thirty-five, I thought the same thing. Thirty-four wasn't much different, I was in love with myself then, too.

Each year, I seemed to get better and better. My frame was filling out as beautifully as my mother's. My curves had settled and were proportioned perfectly over the length of my body. The slim-thick version of Baisleigh no longer existed. There was nothing slim about me now but my waist, arms, wrists, and ankles.

One foot after the other, I stepped into the confusing garment, silently praying that I was putting it on the right way. I'd hate to return to the bedroom looking crazy. Though it would be a good laugh for Nicholas and me, that wasn't in my plans. I loved the atmosphere we'd created for the night and didn't want to disrupt it with laughter. For once, I wanted to embrace the solemness of the night and allow it to lead us both to our final destination.

"Perfect."

My reflection revealed the accuracy of my decision. The red against my dark, glistening skin was astounding. Utterly in love with the entire look, I twirled to get a good look at the backside as well. The piece left little to the imagination. The side part and silk press that Fee had given me for the weekend paired well with everything into consideration.

Anxious to get back to Nicholas, I tidied up and gave it all a final glance. There wasn't even a strand of hair out of place. Completely satisfied, I stepped out of the bathroom with a smile on my face. It quickly faded and was replaced with a smirk as I caught sight of Nicholas' curved dick standing tall on the other side of the room.

I swallowed the lump in my throat as my mouth began to water. This man was beyond fine. His skin was the same color as mine. I knew we'd make the prettiest babies when the time came. Until then, I'd ride his dick in preparation for the day that we decided. Tonight, he'd have to pry my pussy lips from around his pole because after the way he'd shown out, I had every intention to return the favor.

"You going to just stand there or are you going to come suck this motherfucker?" He baited me in, knowing it was exactly what I planned to do.

Slowly, I made my way to him, giving him a chance to get a very good look at what he'd have in his possession for the rest of our lives. His lusty gaze never left my body as I placed one foot in front of the other. From the way his jaw locked and released every other second, I knew that tonight was one that would go down in the books for us both.

Though I should've been running in the other direction, I was headed for the tall, dark trouble that was beckoning for me. I wanted to be involved with whatever was on his mind as he clenched his teeth, flexing the muscles of his jawline. Whatever it was, I was with it.

Wasting little to no time, I lowered until I was on my knees in front of Nicholas. I was ready to worship him like the king that he was – in my life and in life in general. He was a man of a different stature, nothing like the men that came in and out of my life before him. He, in so many ways, was like me and that's what drew me much closer to him than the others.

In my favorite position, I spat a glob of spit onto his lengthy tool. *Puh!* I used it to lubricate his shaft, then began to massage it with one hand and his balls with the other. His neck rolled until his head fell backward and left hand landed on my head. I loved that, every bit of it.

Through the silence, sounds of my wet, moist mouth on his dick was the only thing heard. Up and down, I maneuvered on his curve, shoving it as deep down my throat as it would go. *All mine*, I thought, finding comfort in the fact.

"Get up," Nicholas demanded, startling me from my thoughts. "Get up."

As if I was moving too slow for his liking, he bent

down and placed a hand underneath both of my ass cheeks and lifted me into the air. Though he was headed toward the bed, I had other plans.

"Wait," I pleaded.

"Nah. You sucking my dick like that ain't fair. Let me get some of that," he said, referring to my pussy. He was ready to put his lips on me, but I was ready to bury him between them.

"Put it in," I requested, instead.

"Hmm?"

"Put it in, like this," I clarified.

"Oh yeah?" he asked, a smile registering on his face.

"Ummm hmmm." I nodded.

When I felt his fingertips against my center, my cream spilled out of me. He gently pushed the lace of the teddy to the side until my pussy was fully exposed. Without warning or hesitation, he mounted me on his dick and slid me down until my ass touched his balls. I clung to his body as if he'd vanish into thin air.

"Oh Godddddddd."

He was so perfect. His dick was just the right size and one I could handle for the rest of my days. It wasn't too big and it was far from small. It was a bit above average and one I could fuck and suck for hours without feeling as if my pussy had died in the process. The way he worked the deep curve in it should've been illegal.

"Shit so good, baby," he hissed, attempting to get his head on straight before slowly stroking me.

That's when the real magic began. I slid up and down his dick effortlessly. His long frame was perfect for the position. The weights that he lifted on a daily basis and his athletic abilities made handling me seem like such an easy task. He tossed me around like a ragdoll on any given day, making me feel as light as a feather although I knew that my 5'8, 165 pound frame was anything but a feather.

"Ummmmmmmm, yes. Just like that. Just like that."

The space he placed between us while leaning me backward made the muscles in his arms work overtime and the veins poke out. The sight of them, the sight of him turned me on tremendously.

"Damn, baby."

Evidence of my pleasurable experience could be heard throughout the room. My slipperiness was loud and it was flamboyant, announcing its presence. *Too good. Too good*, I repeated in my head, closing my eyes.

Light brown skin, thick curls on top of a perfect fade, pearly white teeth, a stunning frame, that contagious smile, and a dick so fucking thick that it should've been forbidden all appeared behind my lids, forming the man that I'd given my heart to all those years ago.

"Laiiiiiiiii... Like that. Yessssss," I moaned, forcefully, praying the correction concealed the truth of the moment.

I slammed my eyes together once again, determined to rid myself of the previous image behind them. Nicholas did. He didn't deserve to be there. He'd made his decision, again, and I wasn't part of it. The difference between this time and last, I knew it was the best decision he could've made, again.

Nicholas' incredible frame and addictive smile appeared behind my lids, causing me to cream on his dick a little more. I closed the gap between us, needing him nearer. The thudding of his heartbeat could be felt through his skin as ours touched. *All mine.* That was enough. That was all I knew and all I needed. All mine.

"I'm 'bout to cum," he announced as he pulled out of me.

I rushed to my knees and closed my eyes, waiting for him to bless me with his seeds.

laike + baisleigh

A FULL WEEK had passed since Nicholas had slid the precious diamond on my finger, and I still hadn't stopped smiling. We'd been living in pure bliss ever since. Aside from one night alone, we'd spent the rest together. He'd taken a quick leave of absence from his job to enjoy this stage of our engagement. That made me even happier, knowing that he'd strategically planned every aspect of this journey for us.

I'd decided to take a few days off from work myself, which was something I never did or really had a reason to do. Nicholas was a good enough reason, and according to him, I'd be taking a lot more time off. I didn't mind. My staff was ready and willing to step in and step up if I needed them to. For now, I was happy working. It was my therapy outside of Tiana's office.

That's why I could hardly wait to walk through the doors of Baisleigh's House this morning. Now, five hours into my workday, and I was just settling long enough to get something in my stomach. The simple salad I'd whipped up was nourishing to my soul. I had hardly gotten a chance to sit before I was clearing my bowl of its remains.

I reclined slightly in my chair with a sigh. Out of sheer habit and just like the other six days prior, my hand went out in front of me as I marveled at the ring on my finger. *A wife.* I was still in shock that the time had finally come. Everything that I'd hoped and dreamed for was at my feet. I had the perfect business, home, man, and was working toward so much more. For now, I was content with the things that I had in life. They were more than enough for the moment.

Sucking the lettuce from the sides of my jaws that it had hid in, I unlocked my cell. There weren't any missed calls from Nicholas, but there were two texts.

I love you.

See you tonight at eight. We're having dinner so be dressed to impress.

Hmmmm. Dinner at eight and dick briefly after? I started to text, but quickly erased it.

Okay, I love you, too

I replied, instead with a sinister smile on my face.

Instagram was my next stop. I'd drafted a post two days ago that I had yet to make public and share with the world. It was a carousel of Nicholas' and I's special day. The slide consisted of two videos and four images I loved most from the large files the photographer and videographers had sent me. This was their practice run, a chance to prove themselves worthy to shoot our wedding and they'd both made the cut.

I swiped my hand from one side of the screen to the other, going over the imagery and videos again. My heart was full. The happiness that bled from both was what I wanted the world to see that we were both full of. I rarely shared any personal details of my life on social media, especially concerning my love life. Since I'd gotten on the platforms, I'd never posted the face of a man, not even an inkling of who I was dating. I'd always promised to keep those details to myself until someone put a ring on my finger.

Well, Nicholas had and his time had come. His feature was pending. At the push of a button, my life would no longer be such a mystery to the public, nor would my man be. After little contemplation on whether or not I was ready to make that move, I pushed the button.

The post instantly appeared on my feed. As if I hadn't seen it a thousand times before, I replayed the video of Nicholas on one need and the red roses rising behind him. The images to follow were just as stunning. And, lastly, was the video of me agreeing to be his forever thing before flashing my diamond ring in Ditto's direction.

My emotions were all over the place. As the notifications began rolling in, I shut my screen down and placed my phone on my desk. Anxiety was squeezing the life out of me. Slowly, I breathed in and out.

My phone began vibrating before I was able to get myself together. I flipped the phone over, ready to ignore whoever the caller was, but when I saw Ever's name appear on the screen, I knew that I couldn't. I didn't have it in my heart to. She was my girl, and I'd never intentionally ignore her desires to reach me. She'd never do that to me, either. It wasn't the way our friendship worked.

"Hello?" I answered, finally gaining control over my breathing.

"Congratulations, doll. You deserve it. You look so happy and so good... so does he."

"Thank you, Ever. I truly appreciate it. My nerves are so bad right now. I'm just trying to wrap my head around it all. I'm really going to be a wife."

"You are! And not to make this about me, but I do have a request." She chuckled.

"Whatever for my Ever," I reminded her.

"Put me in the wedding party and in charge of the cake," she requested.

"You thought someone else was making my cake? Babe, I'm insulted," I replied with a hand on my chest.

"Just making sure you knew."

"Of course, I knew!"

"Anyway, my intentions aren't to hold you up. I'm about to get up and get in the kitchen before my man gets home from playing ball."

Silence grew on the line. The anxiety returned as my nerves endings split, realigned, and then split again. Now, the uncontrollable breathing made sense. It wasn't the public I was worried about witnessing my moment, it was *him*.

Laike. Though he was partially the reason I'd made the post, the thought of him seeing it was still slightly unsettling. My goal was to inform him, as well as everyone else, of my pending title. I was officially off the market. Because I didn't think he deserved a personal call or even a warning, I felt justified with the post. It would relay the message so I didn't have to. *Two birds, one stone.*

"Baisleigh?" Ever repeated.

I'd heard her the first time but I was too lost in my thoughts to respond.

"I'm here."

"I thought I'd lost you for a second." She chuckled.

"No. I was looking at something," I lied. Not completely, though. I was looking at something, thin air.

"I'm going to let you go. I'm so happy for you, babe. I'm down for some planning."

"Girl, you didn't even plan your own wedding," I reminded her.

"I didn't have one," she reminded me.

"Exactly."

"But, I did help Lyric and that turned out beautifully."

"It did, though. Maybe you and my cousin can form a little wedding committee or something. I don't know how this stuff works, but I'm sure you two can figure it out."

"Of course and which one?"

"Ditto, for sure," I told her.

"Yes. I'm down with that."

"I just don't want you guys to feel like you have to start right away. I'd like to enjoy my engagement for a few months before I get overwhelmed with wedding details," I explained.

"Of course. Of course. We'll start when you're ready. And, now you see why I didn't have a wedding. I just wanted my person. That's all. I had him and that was all that mattered to me."

"I know. But I'm my parents' only girl. I can't cheat him out of walking me down the aisle or my mother out of seeing me in a dress. My brother has been in the army since he turned eighteen. Hell, they barely even know what he looks like, now."

"I don't even know what he looks like." Ever laughed.

"Me."

"Alright. I'm hanging up for real this time. I have to start dinner. Call me tomorrow or next week or whenever. I'm here."

"I know you are," I admitted. "Talk to you later."

As soon as my phone hit the desk, I exhaled, releasing the stress of my thoughts along with it. I closed my eyes and rested my head in my hands. *Please, get out of my head.*

TWO

laike

THE SHOWER I'd just finished was like food to my soul. After three hours and several rounds of basketball with Luca and Ken, I smelled like I'd run a marathon and built half a house shortly after. With the towel swinging from my neck, I took a seat at the edge of the bed.

"Shit."

The phone stuffed into the side of my gym bag

sounded just as my ass touched the sheets. As much as I wanted to, I knew that I couldn't ignore the call coming through. I was waiting on an important one, which could only mean that the clock had struck six.

Sluggishly, I made my way to the opposite side of the room where my bag sat against the wall. I unzipped the side where the sound was coming from and retrieved the phone. Without checking the numbers dancing across the small screen on the front, I flipped the top up and placed it at my ear.

"Yeah?" I asked.

"3.5 is the best I can do," the man on the other line informed me.

"3.4," I countered.

There was a brief silence before he spoke again. A grunt led the way for his words.

"Wire the funds."

"Send the product."

I closed the phone, ending the conversation and the call. Then, I immediately popped the back open, removed the battery, and then removed the SIM card. It split in half with enough pressure from both of my thumbs. Without much thought, I made my way to the bathroom and tossed the pieces in the toilet. As I flushed it, I unlocked the phone that had been sitting on the counter. Luca's number was the first that came to mind.

"Yeah."

"Just saved three hundred thousand by switching to amigos," I informed him. "Have sis send that wire."

"3.5?"

"3.4, nigga. Do the math," I responded, sucking the skin of my teeth.

"Good shit. I'm about to call her."

"Bet. Hit me up tomorrow."

This time when I sat on the bed, there weren't any interruptions. I leaned backward until my head touched the sheets and my body stretched its length almost. Though I had no complaints, other than my mother's health, I felt the weight of the world on my shoulders. The heaviness in my chest couldn't be explained, but it was felt.

Lord, please do a nigga a solid. I need my ole lady around. I said a quick prayer to the Lord, hoping he heard it. Though small, I meant every word of it. *Amen.*

In an attempt to rid my thoughts of my mother and the relentless disease that was attacking her body, I opened my cell and tapped the multi-colored app that motherfuckers loved wasting time on – including me when there was nothing else on my to-do list. The second the application opened, I wished that I'd found something else to lend my time to. The heaviness in my chest was no longer a mystery. I knew exactly what was causing it.

The fuck? I thought, lifting up from the bed until I was sitting upright again. Aside from my loud, obnoxious thoughts, there was my loud, obnoxious heartbeat in my ear. *What the fuck, B?* I asked myself, again, knowing damn well I didn't see what I thought I'd seen.

"Nahhhhh," I said as I shut my screen off. "Nah."

I refused to believe that my eyes were being truthful. There was no way I was watching a nigga down on his knees proposing to *my* Baisleigh. There was no way!

Too obsessed with the idea and the fuckery surrounding it all, I unlocked my phone, again. There it was. The same post was sitting on my feed. It had amassed over three thousand likes and over a thousand comments. Of course everyone was happy for Baisleigh. The city loved her. She'd been feeding our hungry asses for years now. But, me, I was never one to agree with the majority.

"Naaaaah."

Denial was my refuge. Even as I watched her nod her head and agree to be the next nigga's forever when she knew damn well she was already spoken for, I didn't believe the shit. Not even the pictures that followed and the final video of her flashing her ring could convince me that this was real, that this was happening.

"And what the fuck is that?" I fumed, trying my hardest to get a good look at the premature rock on her finger.

For a woman of Baisleigh's stature, that motherfucker was embarrassing. She wasn't your average girl. Baisleigh was sitting on a stack. Her restaurant brought in over a million dollars in profit yearly and had been doing so for the last three years at minimum. That wasn't a secret in the Eisenberg household. Lyric helped her prepare her documents and taxes for the government each year.

So, it was baffling to see the pea-sized diamond on her finger that she was happily flaunting on film. The fact that the nigga who'd asked for her hand in marriage was a hooping ass nigga automatically raised red flags. *What that nigga's money running low?* I wondered, closing the screen down again.

Not even a second later, I'd unlocked it once more. The post had disappeared but it didn't take me long to find it. I searched the short list of people I followed. She was one of the first.

Maybe I'm missing something, I reasoned.

I'd never heard of this nigga being in her life or in her world. I kept enough tabs on her to know damn near everything about her. Shit, starting with the fact that I was just in her guts three months ago, so her having a nigga was news to me.

There wasn't any evidence of a man's presence on Baisleigh's Instagram page. *I knew I wasn't crazy,* I thought. However, I continued to scroll for the hell of it. Eventually, I ended up right back at the top of her feed and fixated on the last post she'd made. It was still garnering *congratulations* and hearts, making me ill. Mentally, physically, and emotionally, I felt sick.

Bitterness consumed me. It was a new, very foreign feeling that led my fingers to the keyboard. I, too, had something to say about the engagement. Maybe it wasn't in relation to what everyone else was saying, but my thoughts mattered, too.

You've got to zoom in, baby. We can't see that motherfucker. I hit send and waited patiently for a notification. Though Baisleigh wasn't one for drama, she didn't back down from it, either. She was very direct and could chew out the best of them if they tried her – including me. I didn't give a fuck, however. I was ready for all the smoke.

After staring at my phone for a few minutes, I didn't get a response as I was hoping. However, I noticed a few likes on my comment that suddenly disappeared. When I revisited the actual post, my comment had vanished, too. I tried to retype it but was unable to post it. That's when my new status was made apparent. *She blocked me.* I cringed.

I shut down my screen for the hundredth time. Silence ate away at my flesh. No matter how many scenarios I imagined for B and I, this one never surfaced. Her trying to have a happily ever after with another nigga never crossed my mind. How could she when she knew how I felt about her and how she felt about me? That shit was impossible.

"What the fuck, B?"

I tapped my phone against the side of my head as I let reality sink in. I'd given baby girl an inch, and she'd taken a fucking mile. The life she was envisioning with the nigga at her side wasn't the one for her. A life with me was. That's the only way I saw things for her. And, frankly, when it came down to B, it was my way or no way.

In my boxers, I headed downstairs. Too impatient for the elevator and needing to blow some steam, I took the set of stairs that led me directly to the first-floor kitchen. On the counter, in a tin, were four blunts that were rolled to perfection. With the news I'd just received, I had every intention of facing them all.

laike + baisleigh

SMOKE CLOUDED my lungs and the space I was in as I searched through the closet for something simple to step out in. I wasn't sure where I was headed, but I knew that I had to get out of the house before my brain exploded. Four blunts and three hours later, I was no closer to comprehending what I'd seen on Baisleigh's page.

The only thing I'd accomplished other than facing a few blunts was making a second Instagram page so that I kept my front row passes to Baisleigh's world.

She was one of the only reasons I was on the platform. Being blocked wasn't going to cut it for me.

"Turn his ass to a booty clapper," I rapped along to 21 Savage's verse while opening the glass case to choose a pair of sneakers that would match the fit I'd gathered.

A simple white Gucci shirt with dark blue denim to match would have to suffice. I laid one of the few pairs of fresh, new Air Force 1s beside the jeans and tee shirt. *Cartier watch, bracelet and a decent chain*, I finalized in my head.

Ping. The music paused momentarily and then restarted, again. Because I only ever hooked one particular phone up to my Bluetooth system, I knew which one of them was sounding off.

Kelsey. The name brought a smile to my face. With the day that I'd had, I was sure she could lighten a nigga's mood. Kelsey was always down for a good time. Just like me, she had a roster, so she wasn't ever tripping about the things I did and times that I went missing. Whenever we linked, it was a good time and that was the part most of the women in my phone couldn't grasp.

After a few times in my presence, they were ready to start clocking my moves and keeping tabs on me. I assume I was partially to blame. From day one, I introduced them all to a vibe they'd never had and showed them things they'd never seen. Money wasn't an issue so I spent it as fast as it came, especially when entertaining. I was always down for a good time and good company only made those moments better. That's why I didn't mind bringing them along.

> Hey, friend. Come buy me a drink

She texted.

> Where is the drink being bought?

I responded, already sliding into my clothes.

> Jilted. New spot on Lenox. I'm about to leave my house now.

> Grab a Carriage. Don't drive. You're coming home with me

I informed her before silencing my phone.

My night was already looking up, and I didn't want any more interruptions. The music was the only thing I wanted to hear. My thoughts were far too loud to turn it down or off.

It only took a few minutes to get dressed. I finished the minimalist look with a few pieces of jewelry and hit my body with a few sprays of cologne. When I stood in front of the mirror, I was rather pleased with myself. I debated on tossing a hat on for the hell of it, but remembered I was headed to a new spot.

Though dress codes rarely applied to me, I wasn't

in the mood to chin check a bouncer for playing his part far too well and forgetting who the fuck I was. So, the hat idea was quickly tossed for security's sake. With the day that I was having, not too many people were safe.

I removed three shoes from the glass case, being very strategic about the ones I chose. Once the third shoe was removed and the glass door was closed, the entire case began to descend. Behind it, the darkness evaporated as bright, blueish lighting illuminated the large room that was two stories high.

I stepped inside, wasting little time grabbing one of the many Glock 19s that lined the shelves. It was easily my favorite of any gun I'd ever pulled the trigger on. The grip was superior and so was the fire it spat.

Once it was secured on my waist, I started down the winding steps until I reached the bottom level of the two-story safe. The final level required more security. Aside from the stairs, there was only enough room for standing unless granted access to the safe within the safe.

I quickly stood tall with my eyes facing forward as my body was scanned from head to toe. Any detection of stress or fear would trigger an alarm that would alert one of two people – either my father or Luca. Video footage would automatically appear on their screens when they tapped the alert so that they were able to decipher what I had going on and if anyone was trying their luck before losing their life.

When the door opened, I stepped into the large, padded room that was vacuum sealed in my absence to preserve the precious bills that were inside. Upon my scan's completion, the seal was always removed and air flowed through the vents. Otherwise, I'd die upon entry from lack of oxygen. The door didn't open until air was flowing through and it wasn't a borderline suicide mission.

Bills piled to the ceiling in the padded room. Aside from the money Lyric had managed to clean up for me, this was my life's worth. I was making too much, far too fast and giving her a lot to deal with. To make her job easier, I stored a portion of my money in my home. Little by little, she funneled it through her system and got it washed.

However, business was booming. The more she cleaned, the more came through. It was a never-ending cycle that I wasn't complaining about at all. Neither was the nigga who shared the same issue as me. Luca, too, had a safe much like the one I was standing in at his home. No one knew it existed but my father, Lyric, and I.

When it came down to his business, he never involved his wife. We were both adamant about keeping some shit to ourselves. The less your partner knew, the better. It was for their safety and sometimes ours.

I grabbed six stacks and was out of the room just as fast as I'd entered. I wasn't sure what the night would bring, but I wanted to make sure that I was prepared. Fucking with Kelsey and we'd end up hitting every corner in the city. She knew how to have a damn good time, and she kept her feelings in check while doing so. It was as if she was my homegirl, but one with good pussy that I slid into a couple of times a year.

When I finally made it out of the house, it wasn't without a drink in my hand. Hennessy white filled my cup. The splash of pineapple soda did little to conceal the sting, but that's exactly what I was going for. Inside of my car as I waited for the gate to close behind me, I swirled the ice in my cup for the twentieth time, sure to mix my ingredients well before taking another sip.

"Out of body. That's just how I feel when I'm around you, shawty."

Drake's shit bounced through the speakers, heightening my mood. There was one thing, one person, on my mind. And, true to nature, the shit felt like teenage fever. I bobbed my head as I took another sip of my drinks while the flow continued.

"I should've stayed. You say the word, I'm on the way. This shit feels like teenage fever."

The words hit a lot harder in the situation that I was in. Baisleigh had really agreed to live the rest of her life with a nigga and that nigga wasn't me. I understood I'd taken a little too long to get back at her, but this wasn't the way to get my attention if that's what she was trying to do. A phone call would have sufficed.

After I'd left her crib the following morning after

I'd spent the night, I'd shared with her how selfish of it was for me to interrupt her world in the manner that I had. However, that night had put so much into perspective for me. I just needed a little more time to get my shit in line.

With a shake of the head, I found myself laughing hysterically. This had to be a joke. A sick one and I didn't want to play anymore. I wanted my woman back and if I had to die in the process of doing it, then so be it. When it came down to B, the entire city knew it was up and stuck about her.

"Aight, B. You really bout to bring out that side of me."

It didn't take long to reach Lenox. It was a twenty-two minute drive from my crib, but I made it in sixteen minutes. When I reached the secluded location, I was thoroughly impressed with what I was seeing. My only issue was parking my own shit. Luckily, there was VIP spots that were only $20 and were supervised by some young cats that were definitely from Dooley.

"I don't forget faces. If my shit missing when I come out, I'm knocking on your door. And, trust me, I'm the last motherfucker you want on your porch."

"We got you, big homie. Ain't nobody touching your shit while I'm out here," said the shorter one, slightly lifting his shirt to expose the decorations on his waist.

"Right on, young nigga," I responded with a nod as I peeled off another twenty to put in his pocket.

Though I'd expected one, there wasn't a line outside of the door. I was able to walk in and pay the cover fee within seconds. I headed straight to the bar where I knew I'd find Kelsey running my tab up as she waited for me. And, there she was, bobbing her head from side to side with a drink in her hand as she looked over her shoulder every few seconds. It was obvious she was waiting for someone... *for me*.

"What this shit hitting for?" I asked as I climbed into the chair next to her.

"It's a little vibe. It's like the second weekend it's been open. I say that it has some potential. I like it. Real chill shit," she responded.

"Yeah, real chill."

Though it wasn't empty, there was too much space and not enough people inside. I made a mental note to come back in a few months because just as Kelsey had stated, it had potential.

"Let me get a double shot of Hennessy," I told the bartender when her and her big ass wig swayed in my direction.

"Coming right up."

"Double shot?" Kelsey questioned, turning in her seat to face me. "Is it that bad?"

"Worse."

"Care to share?" she asked.

Though I knew I could talk to her about what was on my mind, I wouldn't. I'd never share details of my personal life with anyone that I was fucking unless it was *her*. And I surely wouldn't share any details about her with anyone I was fucking. That wasn't my thing and bitches didn't need to know any more about B than she shared herself.

"What brings you out tonight?" I redirected.

"Wow. Hard curve, huh?"

I shrugged, not responding to either of her questions, but posing one of my own.

"You crossed my mind and everyone on my roster is on ice. Sooooo... yeah."

"Seems like you need a new lineup, Kelsey."

"My star player is still in the game, though. So, that works."

Hopefully, not for long, my thoughts screamed as my drink was sat in front of me. I grabbed it and tossed it back without thinking twice.

"Another one," I yelled out to the bartender, "then a Hen and cranberry."

"Oh, yeah. I'm in for a treat tonight," Kelsey sang, dancing in her seat.

According to her, Hennessy dick was the best dick, which was why she loved having a drink with me before the festivities started. But, for once, fucking her wasn't on my mind. Baisleigh occupied every corner of it. I wasn't drinking for a night to remember with Kelsey. I was drinking to forget the shit I'd seen a few hours earlier on Instagram.

When the next round of shots sat before me, I downed them and replaced the glass in my hand with the one the bartender gave me that had cranberry juice and Hennessy inside of it. The liquid slightly burned my chest, but it served as the glue to keep my breaking heart from falling apart. At any minute, I knew it could fall from my chest.

erike + brisleigh

I WOBBLED out of the spot that Kelsey had invited me to on a completely different level than I'd entered it on. When I reached the parking lot and spotted Bumble, still sitting pretty in VIP, I searched for the young lot attendant I'd given a few extra dollars to.

"Told you," he said, walking from the opposite side of the lot.

"Appreciate you, little homie. Be safe out here."

Although I was trying my hardest not to display my lack of control or true level of intoxication, I found it extremely difficult to perform the simplest tasks such as walk or stand straight up. Driving, in my condition, would prove to be difficult.

"Keys," Kelsey insisted as if she'd heard my thoughts out loud.

Without hesitation, I dug into my pocket and handed them to her. The sooner we reached her crib, the sooner I could sleep my liquor off and possibly give her exactly what she'd come in search of. Either way, I needed a bed and some thick ass sheets to wait out the toll that the alcohol was taking on my system.

"Aye," I called out to Kelsey once we were settled in my whip. A bright idea had come to mind, and I wanted to see it through. I had to, or else I wouldn't be able to get that sleep that I needed desperately.

"I'm not going to wreck your shit, Laike. I promise."

"Nah. I wasn't about to say that. I know you're not that fucking stupid. I was going to tell you something else," I slurred, dragging my words as I spoke them.

"Then, what's up?"

"I have a really, really important stop... I... I need to make."

"Laike, you're over your limit, way over your limit. I promise the stop can wait."

"No. No it can't. I really have a stop to make. I need you to take me somewhere right quick. It won't take long. Then, we can go to your crib, aight? This is... This is important."

"Where do you want me to take you, Laike?"

"Here, let me punch in the address," I told her, slowly reaching for the navigation system in the dashboard.

I felt like I was moving like a sloth. Everything around me was going in slow motion, or maybe it was me. I wasn't sure but things seemed chopped and they seemed screwed. As my world began to spin, I punched in the address and then hit the green button beneath it once complete.

"There," I explained as I tapped the screen. "Take me there."

"Alright. Buckle up."

I waved Kelsey off. I'd hardly managed to punch the address in. Getting on my seatbelt would be impossible. However, reclining the seat was doable, so that's exactly what I did.

The car felt slightly stuffy, so I cracked the window to get some fresh air. The last thing I wanted to do was get overheated and end up with the contents of my stomach all over my carpet and seats. Even the thought of it had me lowering the window a bit more.

I closed my eyes for what felt like a brief moment but must've been much more. Kelsey's voice registered in the distance as I came to the realization that the car had stopped, and we'd made it to our first destination.

"Laike. Wake up. Wake up. We're here."

I lifted my seat as I scrubbed the exhaustion from my eyes. My adrenaline had kept me going all evening long, and I was finally starting to crash. The liquor in my system didn't make it much better, either.

"Keep the engine running. I won't be long," I instructed.

When I climbed out of the car, I nearly lost my balance and busted my ass. I could hear Kelsey cackling from the driver's side, causing me to do the same. Those shots were on my ass and weren't letting up.

Nevertheless, I pushed forward until I was on the porch ringing the doorbell. Picking the locks or forcing entry wasn't in my deck of cards tonight. I was too plastered and knew that neither of those would end well. So, like a decent human being, I stood on the porch waiting for the owner to come to the door.

I could hear the lock as it twisted. Someone had made it to the door. Naturally, my hand went to my waist. For his own sake, I prayed it wasn't the nigga from the videos. I had every intention to pop his ass with a hot one and that was one thing I wouldn't blame on the alcohol.

"Laike," Baisleigh stirred, "what are you doing here?"

Even with a slightly blurred vision, I could see the beauty standing before me. She was everything – my everything. Why she couldn't see that, I didn't understand. Yes, I'd fucked up all those years ago by making her hurt heart, but it was for the best. Now that I'd explored the world, I was ready to come home. But, she'd already given another nigga permission to enter a space that only I should've had access to.

"You happy, B?"

"What?"

"You happy?"

"Laike, you're drunk."

She waved me off.

"That nigga in there?"

I pointed toward her house with one hand and

removed my Glock from my waist with the other. If he was, then it was time for him to see me. He'd successfully stolen the one thing in this world that I assumed was mine to keep, my heart. My Baisleigh. And, that shit, it cut me deep. I was bleeding all over the place and there was no one willing to help me. Not even B.

"No, he's not. He's at home, actually," she corrected, pissing me off even more.

She sounded so sure of herself, so sure of another nigga. That got me tight in the chest, causing my features to contort and steam to come from my nose. I wanted to jack her ass up and pin her against the house, but violence was never the resolution for me when it came to B. Love was. With her, love would always win and that's why it was the only thing I had for her when in her space.

"You been with that nigga, haven't you?"

"You don't want to know the answers to the questions you're asking, so stop asking them."

The answer was yes. I could tell by the look on her face. My chest ached and my eyes burned.

"You happy?"

"How'd you get here, Laike? I know you didn't drive like this. Why are you being so careless right now?"

"'Cause my fucking heart!" I yelled out to her, tossing my hands in the air. "My fucking heart is hurting like a bitch, B."

"Laike, please. Let's not do this, okay? You're drunk and obviously need to sleep this off."

"Do what? What the fuck am I doing, B? You really trying to marry that nigga?"

"Laike," she sighed, "come inside."

"Nah. My ride out there waiting. I just need you to answer the fucking question, B. You happy?"

I watched as she stepped down onto the porch and closed the door behind her. In the long robe that she wore around the house, she stalked down the driveway until she reached my driver's side window. Like a lost puppy, I followed behind her. When I made it to the whip, I wasn't surprised at the exchange she had with Kelsey as she opened my door and reached over her small frame.

"He's not going anywhere tonight, unfortunately. Thanks for your services, but you have to figure it out from here."

"Figure out what?" Kelsey sassed.

"Kelsey, not this one," I barked, putting an end to that shit rather swiftly.

Kelsey quickly gathered what was being advised of her and sealed her lips.

"You're welcome to wait on my porch for a ride, but he's staying put."

"B, answer my fucking question," I demanded.

There was so much happening at once. Too much happening at once. My world began spinning as I clutched the side of my face briefly, closing my eyes until it stopped. When I opened my eyes again, I felt Baisleigh's fingernails pressing up against my skin as she dragged me behind her and into the house.

"What the fuck, B? Marriage? You want to marry this nigga? For real? We doing that now?"

The questions came flying out of my mouth the second the door was closed and we were alone again. She remained silent, pacing the floor with her cell in her hand. I wasn't sure when she'd gotten it or where she'd gotten it from, but she was tapping the screen with enough force to nearly break it. She was seething. I could almost see the smoke coming from her ears.

"Laike. Seriously, just shut up right now. You're drunk and you're not thinking at all, bringing someone to my house? Really?"

"I had a question to ask you that you still haven't answered!" I reminded her, stepping to the side so that she could continue to pace the large area.

"I'm the only one that should be asking questions right now. Like, what the hell are you thinking? You're an Eisenberg. Have you forgotten it? You're out here intoxicated, not knowing what is going on. You could've easily been targeted tonight. What if she wouldn't have brought you to my house and taken you somewhere else? Huh? Your mother and father would be devastated. What are you thinking?"

"I'm thinking with a broken heart, B. I've never felt that before so I can't tell you why I'm on the shit I'm on. All this is new to me just like this fucking engagement shit is news to me. When the fuck you fall in love? And why the fuck is your ring so little?"

"My ring? Is that what you're worried about? My ring?"

"That nigga must ain't put up no bread? He running low? I can barely see that shit, baby girl. You deserve better than that."

"I'm assuming I deserve you," she snarled.

"Yes. In fact you do. I know it and so do you." I stepped closer, halting her movements.

"You don't get to do this, Laike. You don't get to play the victim. I'm not playing it, so neither can you. When you broke my fucking heart, stepped on my shit, and left me to rot in my sorrow, did I show up to your door in my feelings?"

"No. I took that shit with a grain of salt, kissed my wounds, cried myself to sleep every night, and eventually got over it. That's my advice for you. Get the fuck over it. If you never let me go, then another man wouldn't have had the chance to capture me."

"I waited year after year after year after year for you to save me from the hell I was in. I've watched you run the city with woman after woman, never offering my opinion, getting jealous, or bringing any drama to your door. I respected your decision because I respected you. If you made it, then I knew it was because you had to and not because you wanted to. It was something you needed to do for yourself and that's all that mattered. I know that some decisions we make will have to be selfish, so I'm expecting the same courtesy from you."

"Three months ago, I was single and after you came to me, laid your head on my chest and then made love to me, I thought that maybe our time had come. It was the best night of my life. I thought that maybe for once you could see what you'd left behind and mend what had been broken between us."

"But, no. What did you do? You chose to run, again. And, then send me some lousy ass text about how sorry you were for disrupting my world. Laike, you were my fucking world. How could you ever disrupt it? Hmm? How come you never saw that?"

"Like, were you fucking blind or just plain ole stupid? I don't understand. But, that's in the past. I quickly came to the realization that I'll never understand, and I don't have to. Waiting around for you was getting me nowhere. I had to take charge and seek my own happiness. Nicholas is the best thing that has happened to me since I can remember."

"Who gives a shit if you don't like it. I'm not asking for your permission. I don't need it. Never have. You don't get to dictate what happens in a world that you had the chance to be a part of. It doesn't work like that. Now sit the fuck down and shut up while I call your brother to come pick your dramatic ass up."

I'd never heard Baisleigh use so much profanity in one setting. She wasn't a saint but she wasn't like the rest of the sinners, either. She had this thing about herself, though, that didn't allow her to put much negative energy into the universe and to see her completely out of her shell made me do exactly what she'd told me to. I sat the fuck down and shut up while she got Luca on the line.

I rested my head in my hands as I tried to get my world to stop spinning, again. Baisleigh left the room, leaving me alone with my thoughts. She didn't return for a few minutes, and when she did, she had on a pair of pajama pants and a shirt to match. It didn't matter if she was wearing muddy boots and a raincoat, she was pure beauty.

"Luca is pulling up with Ken in a second," she informed me.

I took a second to admire her resilience. She was right. When I broke her heart, she cried in her corner and never disrupted me. Most times that shit bothered me, too. I wondered why she didn't at least try to fight for us, have any objections, or tell me to sit my ass down when I said that I wanted to openly date during my twenties. Though knew she was still vexed, I could no longer hold onto the questions that surfaced year after year.

"Why didn't you stop me?"

"Stop you from doing what?"

"Making the most regrettable mistake of my life by leaving you."

"Because, Laike, I'm not into keeping a nigga that

doesn't want to be kept. No matter how much I love them, I'll always love myself more."

I nodded, appreciating her honesty. However, it didn't stop there.

"And, let's face it. Though the decision was regrettable, you had your reasons and they were valid. We were too much, too soon. We were both young and so serious about one another. If you didn't have the chance to explore the world, date, and fuck up in your twenties, then you would've done so in our marriage. That was heartache I wasn't willing to put myself through. So, I respected your decision. Although I wanted you to choose us instead, I knew that it would ruin us. I never wanted my views of you to change. That's why I let you go on your way. That's why I didn't try to stop you. I just never imagined you'd take this long to come back to me. Now that you're here, I'm already happy."

Just as she finalized her statement by answering my question, there was a knock at the door. However, I was stuck. Immobile. Unable to think straight. I felt as if Baisleigh had reached in my chest, fisted my heart, and twisted it until she was able to pull it from my chest. And, when she did, she smashed it against the floor, placed her foot on top of it, and applied so much pressure that it busted.

"LAIKE!" Luca called out to me. The rigidness in his voice let me know that it wasn't his first time calling my name in the last few seconds and that he wasn't very happy about the visit he was making.

"Nigga, I heard you the first time," I lied, gathering my bearings.

"Then get the fuck up and let's go," he fussed.

"Nigga, you might look like Liam but you ain't him. I'm not one of your fucking kids so keep your voice down when you talking to me."

"Mention my kids again, and I'm going to give you the ass whooping Baisleigh should've."

"I'm with that," I assured him, removing my gun from my waistline and laying it on the couch.

"Nigga, you won't even stand a chance tonight. Try that shit tomorrow. You can barely stand the fuck up," Ken added, shrugging in the process.

I hadn't even noticed he'd entered.

"Nigga, you can get it, too," I belted.

"Then, you might want to pick your Glock back up. I'm not fighting no nigga. Not even you. I'll shoot the shit out of a motherfucker, though."

"Laike, put your gun back up and go home to sleep this off." Baisleigh sighed.

She picked the Glock up and handed it to me. Not wanting to cause her any more trouble than I already had, I accepted it. Once it was tucked, I headed for the door as if I was suddenly in a rush. I pushed through the front door and slightly missed the step that led to the porch. That miscalculation landed me on my ass.

"Fuck!" I grunted.

My back was on fire from making unrestricted contact with the threshold of her door. The laughter from behind came from all three of the motherfuckers who were observing the scene. Because no one was trying to help, I was forced to find a way myself. Once I was upright and standing, again, I fixed my clothing and headed for Luca's truck. For the first time during the entire night, I knew I needed to chill the fuck out.

Luca climbed into the truck shortly after. It was still running and his music was still going. When I heard the volume lower, a stream of air rushed through my nose. My ears were already preparing for the shit that was about to come from his lips. He pulled out of the driveway as he began to speak.

"I don't give a fuck about you sighing. You're wrong, Laike. I'm riding with you 'til the wheels fall off and you know it, but I'm going to let you know when you're wrong. You were ignorant, tonight. Aside from the danger you put yourself and the organization in, you should've never ended up on Baisleigh's doorstep."

"My nigga, you've had over a fucking decade to snatch this woman up. All of a sudden, a nigga has realized how much of a prize she is and you're hot. You don't have the right, my nigga. You fumbled her. That's your fuck-up."

"You think I'd ever give Ever a chance to be single out here, knowing the good she has to offer? You think I'd ever give a nigga a chance to push up on what I know is mine? Nah. That nigga would surely die 'bout that and I'd never forgive myself for the fumble. But, I'm not that stupid. You are. And, I've been telling your stupid ass to get your girl back since you left her. 'Cause let's be real. What have you gained from these hoes out here, Laike? Hmmm?"

"That dating and fucking other bitches you broke Baisleigh's heart to do, what the fuck has it done for you? Did it elevate your life or your bank account in any way?" he barked.

I didn't have a proper response, so I remained silent. We both knew the answer to his question.

"Nigga, when I'm talking to you, speak up. You got a whole lot of shit to say any other time. Don't be quiet now! Did that shit elevate your account?"

"You asking questions you already know the fucking answer to."

"You made a choice that you already knew the outcome of, too, didn't you? What you expected her to get old and gray waiting on you to claim her? Nah. Baisleigh is a fucking bag. Any nigga would be happy to have her. She's 'bout her shit, stays out of shit, and is actually a decent fucking human being – unlike the nigga she's in love with. Well, was in love with."

"Still is," I corrected.

"Maybe so, but that shit ain't 'bout shit right now. She's about to get her happily ever after, even if it doesn't involve you."

"I'm not letting her marry that nigga, Luca. I'll go

to my grave before I let another nigga walk away with what's mine."

"She's not an object. You do not own her, nigga."

"I'm not saying that I do. I'm just saying... that's my heart, Luca."

"And I know this. I'm with whatever you're with, Laike, but not like this. Don't disrupt her peace, create more peace for her. I'm all for you getting your girl back, nigga. Ain't no way I'm watching Ever walk down the aisle with no nigga if it ain't me or Lucas. You feel me? But, will I cause her hell? Nah. Do what you need to do but find another way to do it. This ain't it. You'll only piss her off more and make her hate your ugly ass. Then, it won't be shit you can do to get her back."

"I know. That shit just took me there today."

"Get your shit together. Take a few days to get your head right and you'll figure it out. I wouldn't be telling you this shit if I didn't know if for sure, but... you've still got a chance. She loves you. I don't know why, but she loves you more than she'll ever love another nigga. That's your only advantage... I mean besides the fact that you're a fucking Eisenberg. We're not easily forgotten."

Luca increased the volume on his stereo as I zoned out. He was right. Tonight wasn't a good look on my end, and I'd try my best to make that shit up to Baisleigh. She didn't deserve what I was willing to put her through to secure my spot in her world, again. So, it was necessary for me to take a step back and make sure that when I stepped to her it was with peace, love, and some fucking sense. Until then, I'd stay at a distance.

When I made it inside of my crib, I began emptying my pockets and undressing. It had been a long night, and I was exhausted beyond belief. The talk I'd had with Luca slightly sobered me up. I had to get my shit together and that started with a hot shower. However, I needed to apologize to B before I did anything else.

I unlocked my phone in search of her number. However, something led me to the browser window. I googled 'flower delivery services' and waited for the search results to pop up. It didn't take long. I clicked on the first result that popped up, scrolled their selection of roses, and chose the biggest, brightest bouquet. According to the description, they lasted for up to a year. By the time I got my girl back, they'd still be alive. Once that was squared away and I knew she'd be getting roses delivered to her door, I shot her a text.

> I apologize for any trouble or frustration I caused you tonight. In no way am I happy about the news that I got today, but it's your life. Live it to the fullest. Love you... too much.

> Your forever nigga.

THREE

baisleigh

"YOU LOOK PERFECT. Don't stand in that mirror a second longer," with a hand around my waist, Nicholas told me.

The thing was, I wasn't staring in the mirror. My eyes kept finding their way to the flowers that sat behind the mirror. I'd received them four days ago and had yet to build up the courage to throw them away. Not only were they beautiful, but they were from

Laike, and I knew he meant well when he sent them. It was his way of making peace, peace that I wanted him to maintain throughout the course of my engagement and marriage with Nicholas.

"I'm ready. I promise," I admitted.

If I stayed any longer, staring at those damn flowers, I'd scream. We had dinner reservations and guests that were possibly already waiting for us at Dolce. It was the first night we'd get to share time with our loved ones since the engagement. That made me much happier than I imagined it would.

The only thing I wished about this night was that it involved my parents. However, they no longer lived in the United States and with everything surrounding my engagement happening by surprise and so fast, they weren't able to make it.

However, I would take it slow when it came to planning my wedding so that they would be able to be a part of everything from helping me pick out my dress to helping me choose a venue. This was a milestone that I refused to leave them out of. They were part of the equation or there wouldn't be a wedding. I'd, instead, drag Nicholas to the courthouse and call it a day. But, because I refused to rob my parents of this opportunity, I had no other choice but to take my time with wedding plans.

"Good, because we're running a few minutes behind."

Before stepping off, Nicholas kissed the side of my neck and slapped my right cheek.

"Are you trying to make us even later?" I asked.

"Nah. My bad. My bad." He chuckled, holding his hands in the air while stepping away.

"Okay. Because, if you keep playing then we won't make it at all," I warned.

"Yes, ma'am," he joked.

I followed him toward the door of my home and grabbed the YSL clutch on the way out. The mid-September weather was perfect for the occasion. The smell of rain lingered in the air from the last two days of thunderstorms. They'd subsided and left their beautiful residue on the city's sky. The gloom of the night hugged me like a bear would her cub as I made my way to Nicholas' passenger seat.

"Comfortable?" he asked once he settled in his seat.

"I am. I'm just hoping the mugginess doesn't puff up my hair. Fee will be in there trying to hot comb it in the restroom." I chuckled, lightly, placing my hands in front of me.

"You're nervous."

Nicholas noticed. He noticed everything. He was a man of detail and hardly missed any. The cracking of my voice and my trembling hands must've been the giveaways. Or, maybe it was the chuckling and continuous smiling for no apparent reason at all.

Nervousness swelled my throat and inflated my chest. There was something resting heavily on my heart, applying unnecessary pressure. I hated feeling this way. Feeling uneasy and confused when I was my happiest and most vibrant. A double entendre, the moment was.

"A little," I confirmed.

His suspicions were spot on.

"Don't be. Tonight will be great. I know it can be scary, finally welcoming everyone into our world, but we've been in our bubble long enough. I want everyone to know just how great you are and how blessed I am to have you in my life."

"I know. It's just that... I haven't been this serious in so long. It feels so good. Too good. I almost want to hold onto the secrecy of it a little longer."

"You've made it public, already, Baisleigh," he laughed, "there's no going back."

"I forgot about that," I replied, rolling my eyes. "You're right."

I'd forgotten all about the famous Instagram post that was now the talk of Channing. Everywhere I went, people were congratulating me. And, according to Nicholas, he was getting the same reaction. It was hilarious every time he called to tell me he'd encountered another one of my restaurant guests. He joked that the Instagram post had made him more famous than his entire basketball career.

"So, chill. Everything is fine. There's no need to be nervous. You've got this. We've got this, aight? You're not alone anymore. Your battles are mine, now, and this one is pointless. Get out of your head and let's go eat some good food."

"Yes. I'm starving."

Just like that, the nerves subsided. I resumed my role as the passenger seat princess as Nicholas hit corner after corner. The sound of H.E.R. playing in the background was soothing to my soul. He knew just how to get me back on the right track, and I loved that for me.

We arrived at Dolce ten minutes after seven. We weren't as late as I assumed we'd be. Hadn't Nicholas pulled me out of the house and out of my head, we would've been, though. When we walked into the private room, all of our loved ones were sitting around the table. Just as my parents were missing, so was Nicholas'.

His mother had died the year after he was drafted and his father had never shown his face in his life. His grandmother had raised him, but she'd died six years ago. The only people he had left in his world were his aunt and her two daughters. They were all in atten-dance. The rest were his friends and associates. As for my people, they filled nearly the entire room. Ditto, of course, was in attendance, as well as friends and family.

Everyone stood from their seats, applauding us as we walked in. My eyes burned from the tears that threatened to fall. This moment was so far-fetched just six months ago. I wouldn't have fathomed I'd be here today, and with Nicholas, nonetheless. We'd just met and had only enjoyed one another's company maybe twice six months ago. Yet, here we were, engaged to be married.

"You can have this seat," Nicholas said, stepping to the side.

He wanted me closest to the side where all of my family and friends were. The entire dinner was segregated, but I wasn't complaining. It made it easier for me to communicate with my people when necessary.

Just as I got situated, the applause came to a halt. When I was finally seated, I had the chance to really get a good look at everyone who's shown up to celebrate Nicholas and me. Everyone had pulled out their best and gotten to Dolce on time.

"Welcome. Can I get you started with something to drink?" our host asked. "I'm Brittany, by the way."

"I'll start with water," I replied, "Babe, what are you having?"

"I'll start with water, too. Once the food is delivered to our table, I'll be having something a bit more suitable for the occasion."

"Are you guys ready to get your order started?" she asked.

Everything had been pre-ordered. Guests would be having the same dishes. The only thing that wasn't set in stone was the number of plates we needed. Though everyone had RSVP'd, I knew that things came up last minute and it was possible someone wouldn't have been able to make it. In this case, Ricky, my older cousin, and his wife had to cancel.

"Yes. We're missing two guests. Everyone else is here."

She leaned in a little closer so that she could hear what I was saying. Everyone was chatting and filling the room with joyous laughter.

"Wine was also ordered, would you like me to grab your bottle?"

"Right before the food arrives. I'm working with an empty stomach right now."

"Got it. I did a head count before you guys stepped in. Would you like to include the gentleman that just walked in?"

I followed the direction her pen was pointing in. My heart rate increased tremendously as my entire body began to shut down. As if I was seeing a ghost, my eyes widened and fear crept up my bones. Not only was our newest guest uninvited, but he looked as if he'd just stepped off the runway in Paris.

Fuck, Laike. I crumbled inside.

The right side of the table, where my loved ones were seated, silenced at once. All eyes were on him. I wrecked my brain, trying my hardest in that very moment to remember him being so fucking handsome. I didn't. I imagined it was the black-on-black dress shirt and blazer combination.

Or maybe it was the dark colors highlighting his

gleaming jewels. Or, maybe it was the fresh haircut. Or, maybe it was the open-faced gold teeth that glistened when he smiled. Or, maybe it was the fact that he wasn't welcomed that made me soil my panties and lose all self-control.

"Uh, yes," I answered Brittany, trying my hardest not to alarm Nicholas.

"Alright. I'll get your order started and be back with that wine in about twenty minutes."

I'd tuned her out almost completely as my eyes wandered the table until they landed on Luca. He and Ever had blessed me with their presence and it was such a relief to have them there. With the canon on the loose, I'd need his assistance.

I was positive no one else at the table could handle the unruly guest. Luca was the only one who had a chance. With a nod of the head, he silently assured me that he had things under control. Ever's sad eyes met mine, causing me to tilt my head in response.

"Sounds good to us," Nicholas replied.

"Hey," I said, turning toward him, "I need to go to the ladies' room. Do you think you can hold it down for us until I get back?"

"Did you even have to ask?" He chuckled. "Go handle your business. I'll be right here."

"Thanks, babe."

I stood, carefully, refusing to let my nerves get the best of me and embarrass me in front of our guests. My eyes shifted downward where they remained until I managed to escape the private dinner room that we'd reserved for our dinner.

Once I was around the corner and out of view, I held onto the wall, hunched over as I tried catching my breath. I felt as if I was suffocating. My anxiety had spun a web, and I had gotten caught right in the center of it.

Breathe. Breathe. Breathe, Baisleigh, I coached.

I slammed my back against the wall, thanking God that our private room was around the corner from the restroom. Hadn't it been, then I doubted I'd made it without losing my balance. I rested my head on the cold, stiff wall and closed my eyes, desperate to catch my breath because I was afraid I'd pass out at any moment if I didn't. My lungs had been drained of oxygen and my chest hurt from the constant pulling with little to no results.

"Breathe."

The familiar baritone was, simultaneously, a breath of fresh air and a punch to the gut. When my eyes slowly reopened, there he stood with weary lines across his handsome face.

"What are you doing here, Laike?" I managed to get out. "Why are you here?"

I had questions and they needed answers. Answers that would possibly help me understand why this man had such a hold on me. Answers that would possibly help me understand why I couldn't let go of him, no matter how hard I tried.

Answers that would make all of this make sense for me.

"I come in peace, B. *For now*. I'm a little hurt that I wasn't invited," he admitted with a hand to his chest for emphasis. "But, I come in peace, unless you give me any reason to believe that you'd prefer it was me at the head of that table with you instead. Then, I can't promise you what will happen. As long as you're happy like you say you are, then we shouldn't have an issue, right?"

I said nothing. It was as if time had frozen. My heart and my head both betrayed me. Images of Laike heading the table with me surfaced. I squeezed my eyes together, desperate to get rid of them. As if he was privy to the internal battle I was facing, Laike chuckled.

When I opened my eyes, he quickly closed the gap between us. I sighed, eyes focused, as I waited for his next move. He was always and would forever be unpredictable. I'd always loved that about him, but tonight it was more of a curse than a gift.

His hand cupped my chin as he lifted my head. Like a lost puppy, my orbs glossed and heart pounded against my chest, unsure of what he was preparing to say. However, it wasn't his words that took me by storm. It was his next move. His paper sack brown lips lowered until they were pressed against mine.

Covered in defeat, I sighed as I felt his tongue exit his mouth and enter mine. Instinctively, my hands landed on his chest as I accepted him, all of him. Our tongues danced briefly to the interlude before rationality sat in and I found the strength to pull away. The only issue was, he'd already done so. I hadn't noticed I'd closed my eyes until I opened them and found Laike standing less than two feet away, licking remnants of me from his lips with a sinister smirk on his face.

Shit, Baisleigh.

"Happy, yeah?" he asked.

There were no words in my vocabulary that would justify my actions, so I didn't even bother with them. I simply watched as Laike ran both hands down the sides of his face and spun on the back of his feet. I prayed he'd continue out of the door, but that prayer went unanswered the second he turned the corner. He'd made his way back to the room where our friends and family were waiting for my return.

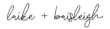

THE DINNER CONTINUED WITHOUT FLAW. Laike was on his best behavior, choosing to remain quiet for the most part. Every few seconds, his eyes found mine. With each drink that he consumed, I grew a bit more concerned. The episode he'd had a few nights ago was still fresh on my mind. I just hoped he was able to handle the liquor that he was consuming.

"This is really good," Nicholas complimented, swirling his fork over his entire plate.

It was almost empty. So was mine and everyone's around the table. Dolce never disappointed. The last-minute dinner reservations was a favor from Don, himself. After getting word of my pending nuptials, he insisted I have one of his larger, private rooms to celebrate. I was appreciative because everyone knew reservations at Dolce were as hard to come by as a new lung or a kidney.

"It always is. I'm getting us a plate to go. We ordered for Ricky and his wife, but they couldn't make it. That leaves an extra plate," I explained.

"Oh, yeah."

"For the bride-to-be," Brittany appeared with a bottle of Ace of Space.

"I'm sorry, we didn't order Ace."

"I know. The gentleman at the end of the table did," she informed me, pointing toward Laike, who held his glass in the air.

I cringed as I tallied the drinks he'd had altogether. He was on his fifth. Before I could decline, Nicholas grabbed the bottle and held it toward Laike with a nod. Sighing, I shook my head. Nicholas had always been great at reading the room, but suddenly he didn't have a fucking clue and it was making me nauseous.

Without hesitation, he unraveled the wire that

encased the cork. Once it was loose enough, he pulled it off and slid the cork up with the tip of his thumb. There was a loud pop before the liquid came rushing out, spilling on the white tablecloth. Everyone erupted with cheer.

While they rejoiced, I was unmoved. Both Laike and I only had eyes for one another, attempting to read each other's thoughts. I wasn't sure what he was thinking or where his head was, but I'd pay any amount of money in the world to find out. Still fixated on me, he held the index finger of his right hand in the air and twirled it around, signaling for the dinner party host to open the other two bottles that were in each of her hands. He'd purchased enough to quench the thirst of every dinner guest.

"To the future Mrs. Reeves!" Nicholas shouted, excitement spilling over and into the room.

"To the future Mrs. Reeves," everyone joined, except me. Except him.

Our eyes remained locked, saying so much while we said nothing. I hoped he understood my stance and why my decision to marry Nicholas was as easy as it was. He was a great guy, one that I didn't see myself getting tired of, bored with, or outgrowing. He was my happy ending, and I couldn't wait to see it unfold.

"I'd like to propose a toast," Ditto said, standing from her chair with her drink in her hand. She pulled me from the trance Laike's pretty brown eyes had me in, forcing me to remain present in the moment and not get too lost in his world.

"I'd just like to congratulate you, Baisleigh, on your success thus far. I've watched you grow from afar and it has been such a pleasure. I'm the little cousin who has had the perfect role model within arm's reach. Not everyone can say that. I've seen you succeed at so many things and have patiently waited for you to succeed at that one thing I've always known you've desired... love."

"You pour so much of it into everyone... anyone... I've always wanted to see that reciprocated. So, to see Nicholas showering you with just that on a daily basis is just... it's beautiful. I wish you two nothing but the best. I can't wait to plan the wedding! Cheers to you two!"

"Cheers to Nicholas and Baisleigh." Ever lifted her glass.

"To Nicholas and Baisleigh," almost everyone joined in.

Glasses clinked, but before anyone could take a sip, the sound of metal hitting glass caused us all to look toward the end of the table. The air left my body as I watched Laike stand to his feet. He tapped his glass until the top of it fell completely off.

"Aw shit," he chuckled, "didn't mean to do that."

I shuddered, laying my head in my right palm.

"Uh ummm." He cleared his throat as he fixed his black blazer.

My eyes scanned the room for Luca. His eyes were closed as he shook his head.

"I want to start by thanking everyone for coming. You all look nice. You look good," he started.

By the slurring of his words, I could tell that he was intoxicated and in his feelings. I knew that no matter how much I prayed over the moment, it wouldn't end well. The timer was ticking on the bomb and it would explode at any second.

"I just feel like you've all wasted some good... like really good fits. Especially you, Ever. And, Lyric," he said, sarcastically, looking at his sister with a snarl. "Got real fancy for the night, huh?"

We all knew that he was salty about their invitations. I'd even invited Ken, but he made it abundantly clear that he wasn't coming. I knew it was out of respect for Laike, so I wasn't offended. The two were loyal to a fault. When Luca secured his reservation with Ever, I was partly surprised.

"And this nigga," he scoffed, pointing at Luca, "dressed to fucking impress. I never took you for a snake, my nigga."

"Laike," Luca gritted his teeth.

"I'll get straight to the point. Consider this dinner covered. I'm going to take that hefty bill off your hands. From the looks of B's ring, you could use the money, my nigga."

Gasps were heard around the room. Other than the

hiked breaths, you could hear the dropping of a needle in the space.

"So, consider it a favor. I'd advise you to come to me for a loan to make sure she has the wedding of her dreams, but y'all not making it that far, my nigga. No hard feelings, but I'd die before I let that shit happen. This, this was just a rehearsal... yeah. Let's call it that. This was practice. Because, B and I both know that she's only marrying this nigga because her forever nigga was dragging his feet. But, I'm ready, now, baby girl."

"Aight," Luca grunted, pushing his chair backward and standing to his feet.

"I know I took my precious time, and I apologize for that. You know. Niggas be stupid sometimes. It's me. I'm niggas."

"Aight, my nigga," Luca told Laike, finally reaching his side.

With a hand on his chest, he began pushing him toward the door.

"Let's go, Laike."

"What?" he asked, "I'm just trying to explain this shit to everybody, Luca. This shit was cute, but it's time to prepare for the real thing."

"That's enough, Laike!" he yelled at his younger brother.

"You see that fucking ring, bro? Where this nigga get that motherfucker from? The bubble gum machine? That nigga's jeweler needs to be fired. The

AP she's rocking... That's a lot of fucking bricks on her wrist. I got that."

Nicholas' head dropped as his eyes focused on the watch that was on my wrist. I'd worn it for every special occasion since Laike had gotten it for my birthday almost two years ago. Now, I was regretting even pulling it out of its case.

"Who the fuck is that, Baisleigh?" he asked, "and what is he talking about?"

"He's a bitter ex, baby. A very bitter ex that is nothing to worry about."

"Why the fuck you still wearing his watch?"

"Because it's mine and it wasn't gifted during our relationship. We haven't been together in over a decade. There's really nothing, absolutely nothing, to worry about."

"Uhhhh, anyway," Ditto said as she stood, again, "before we were rudely interrupted we were toasting to such a beautiful couple. Let's focus on that and pick up right where we left off!"

"Cheers!"

While everyone tried to get past the Laike fiasco, both Nicholas and I were stuck. He couldn't believe what had just happened or the new bits of information he'd just learned. Me, on the other hand, couldn't wait to chew into Laike the minute we were alone. I'd assumed he was ready to make peace, but I should've known better. Laike didn't know peace.

laike + braisleigh

NICHOLAS WAS STILL FUMING when he sped out of my driveway. My plans of spending the night wrapped in his arms were quickly canceled thanks to Laike. Instead of going into the house, I let up the garage door and hopped into my truck. Before it was even closed, I was already out of the driveway and burning rubber down the street.

What I had to say to Laike couldn't wait. He didn't deserve the peace he wouldn't let me have tonight. Although I had never been to his new residence, I knew exactly where he lived. The Hills was a tight-knit community. I didn't live there, but I knew almost everyone who did and where they rested their heads. Laike wasn't the exception.

I made it from the cusp of Huffington Mills and Edgewood to The Hills, at the very top of Huffington Mills, in minutes. When I pulled up to the security gate outside of his home, I began honking the horn to get his attention. I didn't know the code, so I knew that I wouldn't be getting in. I also knew that if I blew the horn loud enough and long enough, it would get him up and to the door where I wanted him.

Hooooonk.

Honk.

Honk.

Hooooooooonk.

I laid on the horn, waiting for him to appear from behind his door. When he didn't after a few seconds, I began honking again. I could feel my temperature rising. There wasn't a time in my life that I recalled feeling so much negative energy consumed me. I hated giving Laike so much power over me, but the truth was I had no control when it came to him. Whenever he was involved, I was out of body. As scary as it was, now, it was once exhilarating and as addictive as him.

Hoooonk.

Hoooonk.

Honk.

Hooooooonk.

Mad at him. Mad at the world. Mad at myself, I opened the door to my truck and stepped out.

Hoooonk.

Hoooonk.

Honk.

Hooonk.

"Laike Eisenberg, I know you hear me!" I screamed at the top of my lungs.

Hooooonk.

Honk.

Honk.

Hooooooooonk.

"Laike!"

"If you'd quiet the fucking horn and pay attention

to your surroundings, then you would've heard me pull up," he spoke, so close that I could feel his breath on my neck.

A chill ran down my spine as the tiny hairs on my neck and arms stood straight up. When I turned around, his hand smothered the one closest to him as he pushed my body against my truck. Words, the ones that I'd been thinking of the entire ride over, were stuck in my throat.

The smell of marijuana was heavy on his body, but his breath smelled like the peppermint that he was sucking on. The thought of him sucking on me made me shudder and close my eyes simultaneously. I felt like I couldn't win for losing when it came to this man. He was a disease that I simply couldn't rid my mind or my body of. To say it was frustrating would be an understatement.

"Whatever you came over here to say, you might as well save that shit, B," he warned, "'cause a nigga not listening. I told you I'd behave if you proved to me that you were indeed happy with that nigga. You ain't. I could see it in your eyes. It's me. I'm the nigga for you. Until you figure that out and act accordingly, then I'm on your ass. Literally and figuratively."

"And, I'm not apologizing for nothing I do no more because I'm not fucking sorry. I'm standing ten toes behind every move I make when it comes to you from now on. I walked away once... I'm not doing that shit again. So, get your fine ass back in the truck and take your ass home before I fuck the shit out of you. Right here. Right now. And really give your ass something to shout about."

Before I could gather my bearings, he'd disappeared. I heard the engine of his car roaring as he took off down the street. Still, I was left gasping for air and praying I didn't collapse from overstimulation.

FOUR

laike

"LIKE, A WHOLE BABY!" Ken emphasized as I hit the blunt again while scrolling my timeline.

There wasn't much of anything going on with the short list of people I followed, so I decided to switch to the most recent profile I'd created. Since Baisleigh had blocked me, she left me no choice but to watch her from a profile that I created out of desperation. I wanted to keep a close eye on her.

Though I'd given her time to collect her thoughts after so much chaos, I was still on her ass. At the first sign that the nigga she was fucking with was slipping, I would sweep in and save her from her misery. Before I could switch profiles, a text came through.

> Get more napkins. Do not get pink. Brown or tan. Last resort, white.

Lyric texted in the group she'd created for Ken and me. She'd sent us to the store for a few last-minute items for the shower. Everything was set up and everyone was at the venue. The shower was starting in less than thirty minutes.

> And, get more ice

She sent.

"Like, really. A whole baby, dog. Like, what the fuck I'm about to do with a whole baby?"

"Same thing you do with Elle. Shit, you been had a whole baby if you ask me."

"That's different, though. We give them back when our time with them is over. I can't give this little motherfucker back. She's mine. Like, forever."

"Most definitely that. She's even going to have your name. The shit dope, but another Keanu... I don't know, man."

"Her mother loves my name. Wasn't shit I could do to change it. She barely wanted me to choose the middle name. She wanted her to have my whole shit."

"I know. I tried to talk some sense into her."

"Don't get me wrong, I love that she chose Keanu, but I at least wanted her to give our baby a middle name that wasn't related to mine."

"Jade, nigga. That is related to yours. Your middle name is Jaylen," I reminded him.

"So, nigga, it ain't Jade."

"Might as well been, ya soft ass."

"Soft? Not Mr. Crybaby ass drunk in love ass calling me soft. Nigga you've been sensitive to the touch since you found out Baisleigh ass was getting married."

"'Cause, that's my bitc... that's my woman. Damn right I'm in my feelings. Same way you were in your feelings with that Collin nigga. You didn't even know that motherfucker and wasn't feeling him off the rip. That's because you were trying to slide in and get your chance with Lyric. Same shit, different day. Don't act brand new."

"True. True. True."

"And, Laura's nosey ass forbid me from fucking with that girl. So, I've got to chill. I haven't fucked with her in over a week. I'm telling you, my nigga, it's been a struggle to keep from pulling up, snatching her ass up, and locking her in my house until she comes to her senses. I'm pissed because she seems to be getting finer and finer every time that she cross my feed. Like, you been this fine or what, B?"

"Nigga, she's not crossing your timeline. You already told us she blocked you. You're actively going and searching for her from another page. You're on some stalker ass shit, but I don't blame you. If it was Lyric... I don't even have to say the rest."

"Exactly. Luca knows the deal, too, so I don't even know why that nigga snitched to moms. Like, nigga, we're not teenagers. Why the fuck you snitching? At my appointment with her last week, all she wanted to talk about was my behavior and how embarrassing I am like I give a fuck."

"You haven't did shit else, so you must do."

"That's beside the point," I explained.

"Oh," he chuckled, tapping the steering wheel, "then, what's the point."

"That nigga too grown to be snitching. I should just sneak his ass one day when he's not paying attention and take off."

"Please don't do that. I'm not getting between you motherfuckers, and I'm not answering any calls pertaining to that shit either. I don't want to be in the middle."

"You the only nigga they're calling. Pops too old. He might shoot one of us to get us off each other."

"I'm with Pops on that."

"Who you think he's going to shoot?" I asked, already knowing the answer.

"You."

"Where you think he's going to hit me at?"

"I don't know, nigga, why?"

"I'm trying to see if it's still worth it."

Instead of responding, Ken hiked the volume on his radio to tune me out, simultaneously cackling. He thought I was joking, but I was as serious as a heart attack. Luca had to see me. I didn't give a damn when, but I'd pay him back.

laike + baisleigh

BY THE TIME we made it back to the shower, it was in full swing. The guests had arrived and everyone was mingling. The area that was reserved for KJ's gifts was in shambles. There were gifts spilling over into the area designated for food and the makeshift bar. It was a shame how everyone was secretly competing with each other on buying the most expensive gifts and plenty of them. That had resulted in a room full of neatly, possibly professionally wrapped presents and gift bags from the top designers in the world.

Definitely an Eisenberg shower, I thought with a shake of my head.

"Laike, go help your brother in the kitchen. He needs that ice," my mother said as soon as we came into contact.

"With all due respect, Momma, I'm not helping that nigga. Forget your son. Ken, go give your brother this ice."

"Laike, if you don't go do what I told you, today is the day that I'm going to put my foot up your ass."

"You can barely lift your leg," I reminded her.

She closed the gap between us, gathered all the strength that chemo hadn't taken from her, and popped me in the arm.

"Ouch. Keep putting your hands on me woman, and I'm pressing charges."

"Do it!" she challenged.

"Aight. Keep acting bad. I'm going to pull that wig right off your head," I teased.

Making light of her condition was my personal way of coping. Luckily, she was made of stone and hard to bruise. My humor was food for her soul during such a trying time. It was the reason I had two days a week with her at her chemo sessions and everyone else had alternating days.

"Aw. You low down and dirty for that one," she tittered, waving me off and heading in the other direction.

"Yeah, I thought so."

"Don't make me have Luca and your father jump you, Laike. You know they will."

"Tell them I'm ready when they are. Put something hot in both them niggas. I feel like they've been wanting to jump me for a few years now, anyway."

"Oh, they have. I've even heard them talking about it," she joked, but I knew it was all a lie.

"Say no more."

144

"Boy, I'm just playing. Go give your brother that ice!"

"Man, whatever."

She walked off, leaving me with the task she'd given me to handle. Though I didn't want to, I made my way to the kitchen where Luca was packing a second cooler with ice.

"Here," I warned before tossing the two bags of ice in my hand in his direction.

He managed to catch one but the other fell to the ground. Before he would announce his frustrations, I was out of the door. I didn't make it far before my body collided with another. The familiar aroma traveled up my nose, through my system, and landed on my thudding heart.

"Sorry," Baisleigh apologized.

"Nah, my bad," I said. "Not watching where I'm going."

Before taking her in, completely, my eyes searched the large room. I wanted to make sure that she hadn't brought along her boy toy. That shit wouldn't fly, today. Because my mother was around, I knew I'd be on my best behavior, but he wasn't welcomed, regardless. After realizing he wasn't in attendance, I gave Baisleigh my undivided attention.

"You need help with that?"

She was holding a large silver pan in her hand that smelled like it held something delicious. Just like me, cooking was therapy for her, and she did it well. I couldn't wait to dig into whatever was underneath the foil.

"Uh. No. I just want to sit it down on the counter behind you."

Though she'd made it clear that she needed me to move, I couldn't. The sadness in her eyes as she tried to avoid mine had crippled me. I wanted, badly, to ask if she was good, but I knew it wasn't the time for our shit. However, I made a mental note to check on her when this was all over. There was a gloom surrounding her bright, bubbliness that I despised. If there was anything I could do to lift it, I wanted to.

"Laike," she called out to me, "behind you."

"Oh yeah. Right."

Finally, I moved out of her way and allowed her to sit the dish on the counter. I held the door open for her and waited until she exited to let it go. As I did, I heard Luca mumbling.

"Sucker ass nigga."

"Treat me like one," I tossed over my shoulder.

From a short distance, I watched Baisleigh in the black leggings and black top to match. Though she was completely covered, every curve on her body was revealed. My mouth watered at the thought of putting my lips on hers, both sets. Before I could advance, Lyric stepped in front of me.

"Leave her alone and stay away from the bar. If you fuck up my day, I'll never forgive you. I won't even talk to you or let you see your niece for an entire month after she's born. And, I'll pawn all the jewelry you've ever gifted me."

"Damn, what the jewelry got to do with this?" I asked, scorned with her idea of retaliation.

"Just behave yourself, Laike."

"Lyric, the fact that you think I'd fuck up your day hurts a little."

"Well, you never know with you," she admitted, scanning me with those big eyes of hers.

"I wouldn't do that, baby girl. Not when I can catch her in the parking lot right after." I shrugged with a smile.

"I can't stand you sometimes. Stay away from the bar!"

"I haven't had anything to drink in a week, Lyric. Stop acting like I'm an alcoholic. I was fucked up and drinking my sorrows for what, like a few days?"

"Ummm hmmm. And it led you to some crazy decisions."

"I know. Which is why I've been chilling on that shit. I want to make sure my head is clear and y'all not blaming the liquor the next time I pull up on Baisleigh. 'Cause, I'm after her whether I'm drunk or sober. That shit ain't changing."

"You need help," she laughed, "but aight. As long as you play nice today, I don't care about the rest of the days."

"I'm good. I promise."

"Cool. Now, please tell me why your brother is

looking over here with those eyes... like he is seconds away from attacking one of us?"

"'Cause he's a bitch and he knows it. Don't worry about him. It's your day, baby girl."

I turned in Luca's direction and lifted my middle finger.

"You two are childish." Lyric chuckled.

"He started it."

"Come on. I think it's game time. Get to your seat."

"If it ain't by B, I'm not taking it," I warned her.

"Well, luckily, you're at the same table. I knew you'd pitch a fit otherwise, so I saved us both the headache."

laike + baisleigh

LYRIC WAS ALWAYS on my side. As I watched Baisleigh from the other side of the table, I silently thanked my little sister for thinking of me when making the seating arrangements. She'd put me exactly where I wanted to be.

The hired staff had served our plates to the table. Lyric had obviously advised them to pack on my helpings because they delivered two plates to my seat. I wasn't complaining. As I looked down at the assortment of food, I automatically knew what Baisleigh had prepared. The ultimate pasta. It contained chicken, salmon, shrimp, scallops, and steak. I'd loved it since she'd come up with the recipe.

I pierced the pile with my fork, anxious to get even a bite of it in my mouth. As I closed my eyes and praised the savory taste in my mouth, I could feel her staring at me. It wasn't a secret that I loved when she threw down in the kitchen. Though pasta was a common dish, hers wasn't. She just did shit differently.

After the first bite, I took another one. Baisleigh, on the other hand, had yet to touch her plate. She was too busy watching me enjoy the fruit of her labor. Wanting her to enjoy them too, I managed to pick up a healthy serving of pasta and guided it toward her. I stopped just before her lips and watched her cheeks flush with red hues.

"Open up," I told her.

"Laike."

"Taste it."

"I did. I made it," she reminded me.

"Well, taste it, again. For me."

Obliging, she opened up and allowed me to feed her what was on my fork. Her left hand appeared from underneath the table and covered her mouth as she chewed. Her eyes were closed, just like mine had been with the first bite. However, mine was wide open and the fact that the tiny ass engagement ring she'd been wearing was missing didn't go unnoticed.

Although I was silently rejoicing because the opportunity I'd been waiting for had finally presented itself, I was a bit saddened by the news. The empty ring finger explained the gloominess. Shit wasn't working in her favor. It didn't matter how much I wanted her, the last thing I wanted was to see her hurting and that's exactly what was happening.

"Can I ask you something, B?"

"I'm afraid to answer that, Laike, especially right now. It's your sister's baby shower."

"It's nothing like that.'

"Okay, then sure." She shrugged, finally digging into her plate.

I could see that she was nervous. Her hands were shaking, and her eyes dropped from my face into her plate. However, she had nothing to worry about. I was truly at peace for once. I just needed to know one thing.

"Did he hurt you?"

Baisleigh dropped her fork and placed her hands back in her lap, where she'd been hiding them all along. She hadn't even noticed I'd seen the missing ring until I asked the question. Silently, I waited on an answer. However, she simply stared back at me and began nodding. The tears that glossed her eyes let me know that the pain she was feeling wasn't pleasant. That tugged at my heartstrings.

"How?" I needed to know more.

She cleared her throat as she patted her eyes dry with a napkin. I leaned closer so that I didn't miss a word that she said. I knew she wouldn't give me all the details and specifics, but a few words would suffice.

"I didn't check my messages after I made the post on Instagram..." she began, "not until two days ago when I finally had the time. Well, let's just say that there were two women in my direct messages with the same ring and engagement stories as mine. We even had the same fiancé," she tittered, sarcastically and on the verge of tears.

"Bet," I responded, letting her know that there was no more that needed to be said.

With food in front of everyone, there was a little less chatter. Everyone was too busy stuffing them-selves. Baisleigh, on the other hand, was quiet for other reasons. Although I wanted to know what was going on in that head of hers, I didn't pry. Now wasn't the time. However, I did make it my mission to get her out of the sunken place she'd fallen into and back to the bright, bubbly girl that we all loved so much.

"You know what I'm craving, though?" I asked her.

"I don't," she responded, "but, I know you're going to tell me."

"That crusted parmesan chicken you used to make."

"Oh yeah. It's been so long since I've made that. I forgot all about it."

"I haven't. Eating this pasta got me wanting that and one of those stuffed bell peppers."

"Now, those, I've made recently," she revealed.

"Invite me to your dinner table the next time they're on the menu. I promise to behave." I smiled at her, knowing that she didn't believe a word I was saying. Neither did I.

"You're a terrible liar." She sniggered.

"Okay. I'll admit that it might be a bit of a lie. But, I figure the worst that could happen is me having you for dinner instead. What's so bad about that?" I challenged her with the question.

Flustered and unsure of a valid response, Baisleigh remained silent. She simply looked in my direction, rolling her eyes with a shake of her head.

"What?"

"You're not entitled to me or my body because he's no longer in my life, Laike."

"He ain't got nothing to do with this entitlement. I felt like you were mine before him and after. Don't even mention that nigga and me in the same sentence."

"You two surely share some things in common, so..." she emphasized.

"We don't have shit in common, so nothing," I responded, offended in the worst way.

"Well, me, for starters. And, the fact that you both managed to break my heart. Sounds common enough. The only difference is, you had two chances to do it and you used them both." She laughed as if she'd told a joke.

I didn't find the shit funny.

"They say the third time's a charm."

With a shrug, I stuffed my mouth and hiked my brows. If she wanted to play, then it was fine by me. However, I didn't play fair. She knew it.

"You won't get a third chance, Laike," she swore.

"Ummm hmmm." I nodded, opening the can of soda in front of me before turning it up.

Baisleigh was unmoving, simply staring at me with a mixture of lust and disgust. Either way, she knew that her words were untrue. I'd get the third chance and it would be the charm people had claimed it to be. Because, this time, I wouldn't break her heart. This time, I wouldn't run. This time would be the last time. This time, she'd get her happy ending.

laike + baisleigh

FOUR VEHICLES, and we were still wondering how we'd managed to fit everything inside. Lyric's shower provided her with everything she'd need for the baby for the first few years of her life, at least. If she and Ken bought anything else, it would be because they were desperate to spend some money. Keanu was covered, for sure. Family and friends had made sure of it.

"That's everything?" Ken asked, checking the back of all the vehicles parked out front.

"Yeah," Luca responded as he hopped into his truck. "We're out."

"Appreciate you. Tell Elle I'm coming to get them next weekend, and I'm sorry I didn't see her today."

"Elle gone be aight," Luca assured Ken. "Especially once you stop spoiling her."

"He will, once Keanu gets here," Ever added.

"Nah. Then, she's going to just move up to Big Sister status," Ken explained.

"She's already a big sister," Ever reminded him.

"Not to a little girl. They're about to be inseparable."

"This, I do believe," Ever agreed.

"See y'all later, though, let me get my black ass in this house."

Luca and Ever continued waving as they pulled off, leaving Ken and I alone.

"Nigga, what? I know that look. You must want something," he sighed, "what?"

"I need you to take me somewhere before you duck off in the house," I shared.

"Nigga, I'm exhausted and you talking about taking you somewhere?"

"Yes. Now, hop in and come on. You know you're riding, exhausted or not."

Because we both knew it to be true, Ken didn't fight the urge with more words. He rushed to my driver's side and slid in. That's what I loved about him. He was down to ride first and ask questions later.

Whatever shit I was with, he was with it times ten. That's why I wasn't surprised not to see him at

Baisleigh's engagement dinner. He'd been the one to give me the drop on the location and time. Shit, I hadn't even known there would be a dinner until he called and told me. Unlike Luca, he was invested in my fuckery and wanted to see me win my girl by any means necessary.

"Where to?"

"That nigga's crib."

I didn't have to explain who I was referring to or give any directions. When we discovered who was knocking Baisleigh down and had convinced her to marry him, we acquired his location. In the event that anything ever happened to her, I wanted to know exactly where I was heading to catch a case.

"Bet. Roll up," he insisted, preparing for the ride.

No more words were exchanged between us. Ken controlled the wheel while I rolled a blunt. Once it was perfected, I lit it and immediately passed it off to him. I was far too busy getting my thoughts in line and wanted no distractions. This nigga had hurt my baby. Not even I was an exception when it came to hurting her. That's why I'd been kicking my own ass since the day I broke her heart all those years ago.

In twenty minutes flat, we were in front of Baisleigh's ex's house. For a nigga who'd been in the league just a few years ago, it wasn't anything worth bragging about. His spot was tiny, just like the ring he'd put on her finger. I'd seen niggas like him and they didn't last long, no matter what game you put them in because they didn't save for rainy days. They spent their money as fast as it came and when it stopped coming, they were left scraping pennies together.

"When the fuck you do all that?" Ken asked when he finally gazed in my direction.

He was referring to the removal of my shirt and replacing it with a tee that I had laying in the back of my car. The button down was far too restricting. I needed elbow room and the shirt I'd worn to the baby shower wasn't flexible enough.

"Leave the engine running," I told him, hopping out of the car instead of answering the question he'd asked.

As I made my way up the driveway, I wrapped the button down around my knuckles for protection. Barely a second after I'd reached the front door, I'd hauled back and rammed my fist into the glass. It shattered, falling into the home that I was forcefully entering. I reached in and unlocked the door before pushing it open.

Two by two, I took the squeaky stairs until I reached what I believed to be the master bedroom. I tossed all caution to the wind and entered it, not knowing what was waiting for me behind the door. However, I was sure of who was waiting for me. A pussy. A pussy ass nigga who was sound asleep with sounds of chirping birds and ocean water serving as background music for his sweet dreams.

This nigga is a bitch, I concluded, anger pushing

me forward and through his personal space. I dropped the shirt that was wrapped around my wrist, needing to feel his flesh against my bones. When I was close enough, I drew back and landed a blow to his throat.

"Wake up, bitch!"

The nigga's eyes popped open, instantaneously. His hands flew up in the air and landed on his throat. While he tried to catch his breath, I cut on the lamp beside his bed. The glow from the television was enough for me to see him, but I wanted to make sure that he saw me.

Because I wanted to be somewhat fair, I waited until his coughing subsided. This visit would've been pointless if I didn't get the chance to share my thoughts. I wanted him quiet, and I wanted him comprehensive before I moved forward.

"Listen, this is a courtesy visit. I won't make another. This time, I'm going to put my foot up your ass, but next time, next time I'm going to send you to the operating table and have your family praying that you make it. However, the bullets won't be able to be removed and you won't ever see the light of day, again. To save your life and the tears of your loved ones, I'm letting you know to stay away from Baisleigh. That's mine. Aight? Don't call her. Don't text her. Don't come through. And, if you see her in public, nigga look the other way. Understand?"

He nodded.

"Good. Now that we've gotten that out of the way,

let's address the bullshit you pulled. Breaking her heart... not even I'm safe from myself when it comes to that thing in her chest. If it's one thing I don't play about in this world, it's my girls. B happens to be one of them. Fucking with her is like fucking with bread and then here I come like a thief in the night to steal your life."

"Man, it's not like that. I told her that it's not like that. I was going to break it off with them. I just needed her to listen. To hear me out. Man, you know how this shit goes," he tried explaining.

"Nah, nigga, but now you know how this shit goes."

WHAM!

One blow to the chin and it was lights out. The covers had fallen slightly off his frame. Like the sucker he was, I tucked his lanky ass back in bed and flipped the switch on the lamp that I'd turned on. I picked up my button down and did a two-step out of the room. It was such a joyous occasion that I danced all the way down the stairs and out of the door.

"Nigga, is you humming?" Ken asked when I got back into the car.

Paying him no mind, I lowered my seat with a silly smile on my face. As I massaged my knuckles, I began to document the details of my plan to win Baisleigh over. It was game time.

When I finally made it home, a shower and some slow tunes put me in my zone. I was deep in my feelings, wondering what Baisleigh was doing and if she was alright. As much as I wanted to call her, I didn't. I knew she needed the time to continue processing everything that was happening in her world.

When I laid down, I couldn't shake the urge to reach out. She was heavy on my mind and heavy on my heart. Before I closed my eyes, I decided that it wouldn't hurt to send her a text.

> Thinking about you. I love you.

Now wasn't the time to sit on my feelings or conceal my thoughts. I wanted to be as open and honest with her as possible. That started now rather than later. I'd kept her in the dark far too long and concealed my true feelings even longer. It was time I began showing and telling her just how much she meant to me, *still*.

Gray dots appeared and then disappeared, starting and stopping my beating heart. When they reappeared, a smile crossed my face.

Too much, she responded. It was all the confirmation I needed. I closed my eyes, happily, and waited for sleep to come.

FIVE

baisleigh

DELETE.
>Delete.
>Ugh.
>Delete.
>Delete.
>This is ridiculous.
>Delete.
>Delete.

Every photo I'd taken or he'd sent, I deleted a week ago when I ended the engagement. However, I held on to the actual engagement photos and videos for some reason that I didn't care admitting to out loud. I didn't want it to actually be over. Him and I, yes, but the thought of my happiness and my forever after being over left a void in my belly that I didn't think would ever be filled.

There were only two men in my life that I'd grown to love and they'd both treated me like the joke I must've been. While one of them tried to save me from a broken heart, he broke it in the process. The other, he just didn't give a damn. His intentions weren't good and neither was his explanation.

According to him, he was trying to determine which option suited him better. Unfortunately, I'd been the chosen one and everyone else, he had dropped or was planning to. The sickening part about it all was that he expected me to continue the engagement that was built on an entire lie.

The nights I thought he was out of the city, working with his athletes, he was at one of the other women's houses. When he wasn't in my bed, he was in someone else's. To make matters worse, he was supposedly in between jobs.

At my big age, I wasn't welcoming any man in my life who was between jobs or without a job for more than a month or two. It just wasn't practical. As a woman who didn't have a worry in the world and was financially stable, a man that wasn't didn't fit the mold.

Ping.

My phone sounded, pulling me out of my head and back into the moment. When Laike's name flashed on top of the screen inside the notification banner, a loaded sigh left my body. It didn't matter how much time got between us, he still brought the young, bashful Baisleigh out of hiding. He still made butter-flies... *no.* He made the entire zoo stampede my stomach.

He'd been quiet for far too long, making me wonder exactly what he was up to. I quickly tapped the screen to open his message. The words caught me off guard and piqued my interest, however, I wasn't so easily swayed. Laike was full of shit, and I refused to give him free reign over my world, again. He'd fucked up. That was the end of the story.

Be ready at 8

He requested.

No

I responded before pulling my finger down the screen, starting at the top. I, then, enabled the *Do Not Disturb* feature so that his message didn't come through whenever he replied. I imagined he'd be talking slick at the mouth, but I didn't give a damn. It was starting to get cold in Channing, and I was in for the night. My silk pajamas felt good against my skin, and I wasn't getting out of them for no one. Not even Laike.

Ping.

I'll be there at 8.

He responded to my text. It didn't matter that I'd placed my phone on *Do Not Disturb*. He chose to notify me anyway.

I didn't bother replying. I'd given him the heads-up. When 8 p.m. rolled around, I would still be in bed, in my pajamas, watching whatever movie I found on Netflix. I'd worked doubles all week long to keep my thoughts occupied. It was Sunday, my night off, and I simply wanted to enjoy my own company.

However, that didn't stop me from tapping my dark screen to see exactly what time it was. The clock read 6:00p. My eyes grew tired simply looking at the numbers. Every day this week around this time, I was pushing hot plates and tending to guests. The yawn I felt coming on was massive, pushing me deeper in my bed and under my sheets.

With the covers pulled up to my chin, I powered on the television. I scanned the channels until I stumbled upon *Colombiana*. It had just begun. I was right on time. With it being in my top three greatest movies of all time, my eyes were glued to the screen.

laike + baisleigh

"AYE, B."

I heard through clogged ears and fogginess.

"Baisleigh, get ya ass up, baby girl."

"Laike?" I groaned, still trying to come out of the coma that I'd fallen into while watching television.

"Who else is it supposed to be?"

"What are you doing here?" I asked, wiping the sleep from my eyes.

"I told you to be ready at 8. It's 8 so I'm here."

The fogginess subsided and everything began to come back to me. I remembered the text he'd sent, but I also remembered declining his invitation.

"I'm not going anywhere, Laike. I told you that."

"I know what you said, but you also know that you're going with me... even if I have to toss you over my shoulder kicking and screaming."

"Are you serious right now?" I laughed, knowing that it was a rhetorical question. Of course he was serious as a heart attack.

"Dead ass," he told me as he began searching the room.

"What are you looking for?"

"Your shoes."

"Laike, I'm not going anywhere. I told you that."

"Bingo," he called out upon finding a pair of my work shoes.

When he flipped the covers back and saw that I was wearing socks, he smiled.

"What are you doing?"

"Quit asking questions you already know the answer to, baby girl."

"Laike, are you seriously putting on my shoes right now?"

Now, my stomach was in knots as I laughed, watching him maneuver as if he was in a rush. I was furious inside, but I couldn't express that. Not with his movements being so damn comical. He was serious about going out, yet I wasn't going anywhere.

"Another question you know the answer to. Help me out. Push or something. These ugly ass shoes."

"I'm not going anywhere, Laike," I repeated, but somehow managed to help him get my shoe on my feet.

"Whatever, B."

Once he'd secured them, he leaned down and placed both arms underneath my armpits. When he lifted me from the bed and tossed me over his shoulder, I nearly lost it. All jokes had been casted aside.

"Laike, put me down."

"You think I'm about to let you sit in the house and sulk over a broke nigga when your new nigga already available? Nah. We're moving on, baby girl. Consider this our first date."

"I don't have on any fucking clothes. This is not a first date."

He took the stairs two by two, making my breast rise and fall. The descend down the stairs was chaotic, making me feel a little sick. When we finally made it downstairs and to his car, he slowed his pace and placed me on my feet.

"In my defense, I told you to be ready at 8. You chose to ignore me, knowing what's up with me. Now, fix your pretty face and get ready to act like you have some sense in this restaurant. Aight? I hope you're hungry."

"My door." I sighed, pointing in the direction of my door. He'd closed it, but I hadn't locked it.

He rushed over to the door, pulled out a key that I definitely hadn't given him, and locked my door.

"Laike, I've never given you a key."

"You never have to, either. I'll always provide my own."

"That's borderline stalker behavior."

"Have you seen you? Shit, I doubt if anyone would blame me."

He rounded the car and opened the passenger door.

"You ready to roll, mommas?" Laike toyed.

"Do I have a choice?" I groaned.

"Nah. Not really."

Slowly, I lowered my body and then slid into the passenger seat. He ran around to the other side of the car and got in. He wasted no time getting out of my driveway and then burning the rubber from his tires on the way down the street. I braced myself for the wild ride by buckling my seatbelt and holding onto the handle on the door.

laike + baisleigh

CRUSHED PEPPER. I'd heard great things about the prestigious restaurant, but I'd never had a chance to visit. With my work schedule, I hardly had the chance to do much of anything. In fact, one of my New Year's resolutions was to hire a team of leaders who could run Baisleigh's House just as I would, especially in my absence. I was exhausted and wanted to shift my focus to my new herbal tea venture, Baisleigh's Brews. If everything panned out the way I expected them to, I'd be opening a tiny tea house within six months of introducing the world to my brews.

"I feel so underdressed," I complained.

Nervously, I pulled on the end of my top. Everyone around us was dressed impeccably. Even Laike had pulled out all the stops. He wore navy blue from head to toe and looked like he belonged on a runway. He'd decided to tease me with those teeth that he put in his mouth ever so often. They made a mess of my panties. And, his scent. He smelled like good dick and money. It was the only way to describe the aroma. To his credit, he had plenty of both.

"It's probably because you are," he replied. "Why didn't you get dressed, Baisleigh?"

"Because, Laike."

"You didn't want to come out with me?" he asked, his eyes softening while doing so.

"I just... I just feel like my life is falling apart, Laike. I'm one who always has her shit together but lately my life has been a shit show. I just wanted to take a second to gather myself."

"And, avoid me."

"No. Not really. I'm not afraid of you, Laike. We both know this."

"Me, nah. The shit I do to you, yeah. Most definitely."

"How do you figure?" I challenged.

"'Cause I've always been afraid of the shit you do to me."

His words silenced me.

"And from your reaction to me, whenever I'm around, I know that you feel the same way. Out of body, that's the only way to describe the experience when you're around. It's like, I can't think straight or some shit. Either I'm losing my mind, or I got my head on straight when it comes to you. There's no in between."

"I've never felt pain like the pain that you caused

me," I blurted, unsure of where the words had come from.

I just needed him to know. I'd never admitted that, though I was sure he knew it. Laike had broken me into so many pieces. I never thought I'd get me back. It took years, plenty of them, but I managed. And, now that I had my shit together, here he was. The fact that I knew he was a mistake I was willing to make again frightened me.

"I know," he admitted, lowering his head. "I know. I've been fucked-up 'bout it, fucked-up 'bout you since. I do my thing and it brings me some sort of thrill, but I haven't experienced happiness since you. I should've been back. Shit, I should've never left, but the way that pride shit set up. Plus, I've been loving watching you do your thing. I felt like you just were better off without me. You feel me?"

"I'm not," I confessed.

It was true.

"I can sit here and try to convince you that I am, but I'm not. Have I created a better life since you haven't been in mine? Yes. But, it's a direct result of me trying to avoid the truth of it all. Burying myself in work helped me build a million dollar business. I can give myself all the credit. It was the pain that you caused that made that happen. However, I know that you're bad news for me, Laike. Everything I've built, only you have the power to tear down. I know that you're expecting us to start something or whatever, but

I can't risk that for you. I took a chance on you once. I don't have the capacity to do it, again. The fear of waking up one day and you not wanting me anymore is too real. I know what that feels like. I'm not willing to put myself through that again."

"I've never not wanted you. I want you each and every day."

"You couldn't have because I've always been right there. You might have wanted me, but you wanted the streets more. Choosing other women over me is something I'll never forget. Not when you'd been telling me for years and years that I was everything you ever wanted."

"You are, B. That hasn't changed."

"Then why break my heart?"

"I left so I wouldn't do irreparable damage, baby girl. You have to understand that shit. We were young and we were in love. I had no objections to that. However, I was a young nigga, getting his money and temptation was knocking at my door every day. I got curious and wanted to see what was out there, and it was only to prove that I had something better at home. However, once I got out there, it got a little harder to come back."

"Especially after seeing what our breakup had done to you. I wanted you to live your life to the fullest and say fuck me. I just didn't think you'd actually do it. To see that shit happening, even all these years later, still fucked me up as if we'd broken up yesterday.

Because, in some sick and twisted way, I feel like I'm the only nigga for you. Is it just me or do you feel like you're the only one for me, too? Be honest, B. Neither of us have anything to lose here."

I hesitated before nodding.

"I've always felt that way, but I just never knew. Sometimes, I feel like I'm not enough for you anymore. You know. I'm boring. I work, and I go home. I'm not in the mix. I'm out of the way and just focused. I hate everything that you love. We're just nothing alike. That keeps my head on straight. Like, whenever I see you and get deep in my feelings about what could've been, I remind myself of the Laike that you've grown to be. I don't know him."

"He's not the man that I was in love with all those years ago. Though my love for you has remained and has never changed, I feel like I don't know you now. Like, I don't know the man sitting across the table from me. So, honestly, I'm just in love with the man I know you can be... not the man you are. Maybe I was the one for him, but that doesn't mean I'm the one for you."

"I'm still the same nigga, B. I'm still your nigga. Ain't nobody ever had access to my heart. It's been reserved for you all these years. It's yours. You've got that on lock for life. That's why I'm ready to quit my bullshit and do what the fuck I need to solidify my place in your life. I want you in my world, B. Only you."

"No you don't, Laike." I sighed, waving him off.

"Don't insult me."

"Hadn't Nicholas proposed, I'd still be hoping and wishing that you opened your eyes."

"Nah. After the night I came to your crib after my moms told us what she told us, I knew I had to get my shit together. She's made it clear that if she leaves this earth and I haven't made you part of the family, officially, she's going to haunt me from the grave. I've just been dealing with her shit and making sure she's good. When she got well, I was coming to get you. That fuck nigga just sped up the process. I'm sorry it took me so long. You didn't need to go through that."

"Yeah, well... that's life."

"I need you, B."

"You don't need me."

"Stop trying to convince yourself that I don't need you or don't want you or that I'm not good for you. We both know none of that shit is true. I don't give a fuck what I have to do. I'm tearing down all these walls you've built. You don't have to protect yourself from me. I fucked up once. I'm not doing that shit again. That's on my mom. So, tell me, what the fuck I got to do to prove it?"

"For starters," I began before reaching over to his side of the table and grabbing the phone that I knew was reserved for his booty calls. I slowly lifted it and inserted it in the large glass of water that had been placed in front of him.

"Okay, and what else?"

He didn't flinch when the phone hit the water. In fact, he pushed it down a bit further to make sure that it was submerged.

"Therapy. I want couples therapy."

"Done. What else?"

"Time, effort, and communication. I don't want to get to the point where we did last time. You allowed those thoughts to build and fester instead of letting me in on them. We could've worked out a plan or something. Instead, you left me in the dark and then ran off on me."

"I'm sorry. I'll spend a lifetime paying for that shit, and I don't mind. I deserve it."

"And, I want a ring. Not now, but I'm letting you know that I'm not going to be arm candy for years and years without you committing to me for life. I want a wedding. The biggest, best wedding Channing has ever seen. But, not until you prove yourself to me."

"Where do I start?"

"On your knees... You can start there. I want to see you beg for your woman back."

Without hesitation, Laike was on his knees and in front of me.

"Baisleigh Carmichael, please give a nigga another chance. Just one more to prove that he's off the bullshit and ready for forever."

"Laike, get up!"

"No."

"Get up!"

Gasps could be heard around the dining room.

"Say yes!" someone shouted.

My body overheated as my cheeks flushed with embarrassment. Laike knew how much I hated the spotlight. Him, on the other hand, thrived in it.

"He's not proposing," I bellowed and then turned back to Laike. "Please get up."

"I'm not proposing, y'all. Just begging for my girl back."

"Get up," I gritted.

"You said for me to beg, so that's what I'm doing. Baisleigh, will you please be mine, again?"

"Laike, I don't mean with your words. I mean with your actions. In order for this to work between us, I need you to show me that you're ready to give me my happily ever after. Because, this time, I'm not the one who will be leaving with a broken heart."

"Neither of us will."

"Then, show me better than you can tell me."

"I will. I promise I will," he claimed.

As much as I hated to, I believed him, wholeheartedly. Besides that one time, Laike had never let me down. Even after that, he continued to show up for me and that's why my love for him never wavered.

"Alright, then get up and start right now."

The smile on his handsome face was as beautiful as it was hilarious. The corners of his lips nearly touched his ears. I'd missed that smile. I'd missed him.

"When the waitress comes, can you order for me? I

need to go call my moms really quickly," he announced, glee bouncing around in his orbs.

"Sure, Laike."

"You know what I want?"

"Not exactly, but I'm sure I will once I've had a better look at the menu."

"I love you, B," he told me as he stood, fully.

"Too much," I mumbled as he walked away with his personal cell in his hand.

That's my motherfucking man, I danced in my seat, feeling utterly giddy and equally scared.

Secretly, I'd waited for the moment that he came to me with stretched arms and an open heart, ready to confess his love and plead for another chance. I'd been waiting on this day since the day that he walked away. Because, to tell the truth, he was my happily ever after. I knew it, even when I tried to fill his spot with Nicholas.

laike + braisleigh

EVEN IN MY PAJAMAS, I felt as if I was right where I belonged. For two hours, we dined on food, wine, desserts, love, and laughter. For once, I was able to shed my skin and be exactly who I'd always wanted to be – the girl that Laike gazed at from the opposite side of the room with nothing but pure adoration and love in his eyes. By the time he pulled into my driveway, I could feel the twinge of bitterness tugging at my body.

"What are you doing?" I turned and asked when he shut his engine off.

"What you mean what I'm doing? We're going in the house."

"Noooooo. I'm going in the house. I know the others might have let you fuck on the first date, but I'm not going out sad. You have to do a little more work before you get this pussy."

"Who said I wanted some pussy?" he asked, licking his lips with a smirk on her face.

"For one, those lips of yours. I know the thought crossed your mind. I can tell by the way you licked your lips. Two, you know like I know that's what's going down if you come in my house. Three, you think your dick will help plead your case and get me to go a little easy on you. I'm here to tell you, it won't. It'll only piss me off at the thought of you giving it away for all these years while I killed toy after toy. Motor after motor just quitting on me."

"Yo, you serious right now?" He cackled, finding my misery a little too funny.

"You know what, goodnight Laike Eisenberg. I'm full and I'm ready for bed. It was nice having dinner with you. I will text you with details and the location of my therapist. I'm going to see if she can fit us in this week. Please give me a day and time that works best for you."

He sucked the skin of his teeth before nodding, "Aight. Can a nigga at least get a kiss?"

"Ummm hmmm."

I leaned over, closing the gap between us, and puckered my lips. He lifted, slightly, from the seat and met me somewhere in the middle. Our lips collided, making my entire body tingle. Before he could get carried away and convince me with his tongue to let him inside, I pulled away.

I walked into my house feeling like a teenage schoolgirl who'd gone on a date with her crush. Once the door was shut and secured, I slid down the back of it with my hands covering my mouth. A squeal, unlike anything else I'd ever heard, came from my mouth. As soon as my ass hit the floor, I remembered my cell had been left upstairs along with the rest of my belongings. I beelined for my bedroom and made it in only a few seconds.

Just as I did, a call from Laike was coming through. I contemplated ignoring it just for the hell of it, but I knew he'd turn his car around and come back. That would only set us both up for a night of hip thrusting and wet thighs.

"Hello."

"You could've let a nigga hit the first night. I already sampled the shit. It's hitting, too."

"Goodbye, Laike." I laughed, ready to end the call.

"Don't hang up, B. The least you can do is talk to me until I get home."

"Okay," I agreed.

"Get out of them pajamas. Don't get under the cover with them clothes on."

"I'm not. I'm getting out of them, now. They're officially outside clothes, thanks to you."

"Nah. If you weren't so hardheaded, then, you would've been dressed for the occasion."

"Well, I'll know next time."

"Baisleigh," he called my name. From the seriousness in his voice, I knew that the conversation was about to take a turn.

"Yes."

"Do I really have to spend another night without you?"

It took plenty of restraint, but I managed to answer the question with what I thought was the best solution for us both. Closing my eyes to suppress the urge to give into him, I delivered the bad news.

"Yes. We can't start like this. If we do, things will never get resolved. We have some work to do. Lots of it. Sex isn't going to solve the issues we have."

"I feel you." He sighed.

"Any other questions?" I tried to lighten the mood.

"Yeah. What do you think about a winter wedding?"

laike

I STRETCHED my limbs until they popped. It had been two days since my first date with Baisleigh and that shit was working wonders for me. According to the mirror, having her in my life again even had my skin looking clearer. My shit was glowing, looking silky and smooth just like hers.

It was partially because she kept a nigga smiling. Her laughter was food for my soul. And, the other part was due to the new skin care regime she had me on. She'd shown up at my crib around nine the next morning, fresh after the nap I liked to take after my one-hour run, with all types of products in a bag. She'd gone out and tore the shelves down.

She replaced damn near everything in my bathroom with new shit and even added the things that she loved and needed to the mix. I assumed she was marking her territory, but according to her, she was simply preparing my space for her presence. That shit made my dick stand and my heart swell, because that meant that sooner than later she'd be in my arms again.

Baisleigh was acting hard for the moment, but she was a ball of fur. She loved being all in a nigga space and couldn't help herself when I was involved. That was the main reason for her visit the following morning of our date. She was missing me and needed an excuse to breathe the same air as me. It was cool though, because I was missing her, too.

Just as the thought crossed my mind, my cell buzzed beside me. *Speaking of the angel*, I smiled. She knew that it was my day with mom at her chemotherapy treatment. I'd shared that bit of information over the duration of our two-hour call last night. We stayed on the phone until we both fell asleep. Baisleigh was first. Her light snores lulled me into a deep slumber. When I woke up around three for a glass of water, the line was still connected.

"Good morning," I answered.

"Hi. Are you awake?"

"Yeah. I'm up."

"Good. I wanted to make sure."

"You already at work?" I yawned, listening to the ruckus in her background.

"Yes. I've been here for about an hour."

"You sound tired, already."

"It's because I am. Don't forget that we have therapy today. When you leave your mother's appointment, come to the address that I sent you, okay?"

"Okay. I will."

"Promise?" she asked. Though I couldn't see her, I knew she'd paused to put her hand on her hip and stick out her lips.

"I promise, baby."

"Okay," she cheered. "You think you can stop by and grab you guys something to eat before you go to the doctor?"

"Nah. She eats light before she goes and when she's there, the smell of food makes her stomach turn. It's not pleasant... at all."

"Awwww. Poor baby. Well, maybe I can take her something over later. You think she'll feel well enough to eat?"

"Not really. She mostly sleeps the day away after chemo. It exhausts her."

"Got it. Got it. I don't know. Everyone has their hand in helping. I guess I feel so useless now. I want to help, too."

"Come keep me company some days when we're doing treatments. We're there for six hours. She'd love to have some company."

"Now, that, I can do. I'll plan for it the week after next. Yeah?"

"Sounds good to me."

"I'm going to let you go. Don't forget therapy, okay?"

"I got you, B."

"Alright. And, don't forget to take those vitamins I left you, okay?"

"I'm not."

"Good. I love you."

Baisleigh was such a lover girl. She was completely and utterly in love with the idea and the act of love. It was her motivation. That's why she poured so much into the world. It was one of the reasons I couldn't wait to show her so much of it. If she'd let me, I'd love her ass down until she couldn't take anymore. I wanted her heart to explode from the overflow that I created within her.

"Too much," I told her before ending the call.

Shit, she was sounding like my mother already. Maybe that's why I fucked with her so tough. She was a caretaker, and she took her job very seriously. I didn't have a face routine other than washing my shit and coming on out of the bathroom. But, suddenly, I couldn't wait to spend ten minutes of my morning tending to my face while listening to niggas spit about guns, drugs, hoes, and money that they probably never even touched. It got me going for the day, especially after the daily runs I took Monday through Friday.

After that call from Baisleigh, I was up on my feet and headed for the bathroom to empty my bladder. If I wanted to be on time for my mother's appointment, then I needed to be out of the house in thirty minutes. It was doable, but with my new morning routine, I'd be pushing it. Laying in bed for even an extra few minutes wasn't an option.

laike + baisleigh

"BOY, either you're getting taller or I'm getting smaller," my mother said the second she saw me walk through the door.

My father was still at her side, waiting to be relieved. He refused to leave her before one of us made it to her side because if anything came up, he wanted to make sure that she wasn't alone. We hated for her to be alone at any stage of the process. That's why we were all on a schedule and rotated when she had actual doctor's appointments, scans, and tests.

It was important that we all played vital roles in her care so that no one felt too burnt out and the weight of her condition wasn't resting any heavier on one's shoulder than it was another. We split the tasks evenly. However, I was lucky enough to get two days with her at chemotherapy.

With me, she would always put on a smile, and we refused to talk about her condition. I was the joy she needed to push through. I took on the beginning of the week and the middle. These were the hardest days for her. Plenty of laughter was the cure for her exhaustion on those days.

Chemotherapy was a thorn in our sides, but cancer was a knife. We knew that in order to keep her alive, we'd have to deal with the frustration of the treatment. It took a toll on my mother's body, stripping her of her health before rebuilding it. When going through chemo, everything was up for grabs, especially the thing that she loved most – her hair.

That was always the first to go for her. Then, it was her strength and her energy. It was poison being pumped into her system to kill the weeds of cancer that continued to sprout and grow. Though harmful, it was necessary. In the end, it did more good than harm.

"Well, I ain't growing, so we both know what that means," I told her, tilting my head for emphasis.

"Oh, hush!" She waved me off.

"You said it. I didn't. What's good, Pops?"

"Shit. Shit. Chilling on it. You got this, now. I guess I'd better get on up out of here. They're waiting on me down at the course. I'll be back to get you when I'm done."

"You don't want to ride with me?" I snuffed.

"She said you drive like a bat out of hell and if cancer doesn't kill her then you will," my father revealed.

"First of all, ain't nobody dying no time soon. Secondly, why you telling this nigga? You could've told me."

"For what? You can drive faster and crazier? No sir. I told my husband. He's the solution."

"I told my husband. He's the solution," I mimicked, taking the seat that my father had raised up from.

"Let me go before I have to put my foot in your boy's ass. I'll see you in a few hours, honey."

I watched as he leaned over and kissed my mother's forehead, then her lips, and then her forehead again. The combination of kisses was one that I remembered well. He'd always used it for as long as I could remember. It wasn't until he walked off that I turned my nose up.

"Does he even be brushing his teeth?" I inquired.

"Laike, sometimes you ought to just hush. Make no damn sense how stupid you are." She giggled, tucking her tiny pillow underneath her arm for elevation.

After so long, the right one always numbed. She hated the feeling and kept it elevated for preventive purposes.

"I'm just saying. The nigga be all up in your grill. I'm just trying to make sure his hygiene in check."

"Is yours?" she sassed, obviously ready for me to back up off her husband.

187

"If it wasn't before, it sure is now. Baisleigh making sure I step out my best self so when I'm all up in her grill like that, my shit on point."

"Baisleigh, huh?"

"Ummm hmmm."

"You done wore the poor child down, finally?"

"Wore her down? Do you remember who we're talking about? This B, moms. She wore me down. Like so dramatic. 'Cause, why she have to act like she was about to marry another nigga like that? Knowing that wasn't going down. If she wanted my attention, all she had to do was pop out on me. Accepting another nigga's ring, that's overkill," I expressed.

"It got you off your ass and at her beck and call, I see. If you ask me, it was just the wakeup call you needed. If you would've let that girl marry that man and messed up the chances of her being an official Eisenberg, boy I would've disowned you."

"I don't know why I feel like you do that anyway." I sniggered.

"And do. Depends on who I'm talking to."

"Luca."

"Hush!" she warned.

"I'm for real. Your son really a punk."

"You still haven't gotten over him telling me about your foolishness? I hope you stay mad if that's the case. Someone had to talk some sense into you. You were being reckless."

"Ma, this B we talking about. Ain't no sense when it comes to her. That goes out the window."

"Well, luckily, all of this is coming to an end and you won't have to worry about acting a damn fool about her. You've got her. Well, almost. I hope she gives you hell to secure your spot. You put her through all of that just to come back?"

"I had to spin the block, ma. She had to know I would. She's the only woman that can make me do right and a nigga 'bout ready to do right."

"You better because if not... you'll be mad at me and Luca 'cause I'm snitching. I don't care."

"You won't have anything to tell. I'm done with all of that."

"Good. How does she feel about all of this?"

"She's putting up a front, but she's as happy as I am. I can tell. She won't leave a nigga alone for too long. The other day, she at my crib at like eight in the morning, changing out soaps, adding feminine products, putting all her shit in my cabinets, and putting me on this strict facial routine. Then, she bounced. She's been working her butt off. I want her to take a break so we can spend some time together soon."

"Whatever she's got you using on your skin is working. I can see that glow from a mile away."

"Yeah?" I smiled, rubbing my face, subconsciously.

"Ummm hmmmm."

"She wants to get married," I shared.

"I don't blame her. You've played around long enough. Sit down somewhere. You and her will live a good life together. I can feel it. I know marriage and all of that wasn't in your plans, but that's because Baisleigh wasn't involved. Give her what she wants, Laike. Don't fuck this up for us. We need her in our unit."

"I'm not. I'm going to give B whatever her heart desires. Whatever she wants, it's hers. But, this marriage thing, I'm not giving it to her only because she wants it. Seeing Luca and Ever, Keanu and Lyric, you and Pops... I'm starting to feel like I can do that. Ya know? Like, what's the worst that could happen if I lock in for life with B? Neither of us are going anywhere, so we might as well."

"Yeah. That's a way to think of it. I wish I had my phone. I need to record this because your father wouldn't believe his son is actually making sense for once. He'd be proud. Extra proud if he could get a few babies out of you."

"Now you pushing it."

"Baisleigh wants to be a mother. She's been very vocal about this for as long as I can remember. Besides, she has so much going for herself. She wants someone to pass all of that down to. You see how well you and your siblings are taking care of me in my time of need? Your father can't do it all alone although he'd try."

"Yeah."

"That's why it's good to have children, Laike. In old age, if you've been good to them, they'll be good to you. Don't toss the idea out of the window. Consider it. I'm not saying build a farm like Luca, but have you a child or two. I'd love to see you father before I leave this earth."

"You're not leaving any time soon."

"I know, especially if it means seeing you walk down the aisle. You damn right. This cancer has got to get the hell on about its business."

"Then, it better get going, then, 'cause your boy will be suited up as soon as this is all over. I even have a few rings in mind. Check 'em out and tell me which one you think I should get her."

I reached in my pocket and retrieved my phone. It felt so weird only carrying one phone around. The temporary business line was switched out weekly and never came inside of the doctor's office with me. All calls went to Luca and vice versa when it was his day with our mother. I unlocked the phone, went to my notes app, and began clicking the links I'd saved with the rings I was feeling that I'd found online.

Just like the rest of the chemo sessions, time passed us by far too fast. After the two movies we watched, the food break I took, ring shopping online, and FaceTime visits with the girls, it was finally time for our nap. I fell asleep on my mother's lap as I did at the end of each session. And, per usual, my father came to ruin our moment with his jealous ass.

"Boy, wake up and get your big head ass off my woman," he fussed, pulling me up by the shoulder.

"What time is it?" I yawned, trying to gather my thoughts.

"Just after four," he informed me, "I was stuck in traffic getting here."

Shit.

"You got this, Pops? I've got to get across the city before five."

"Yeah. I've got this, but good luck with that."

My mother was still asleep, exhausted from the day's treatment. I made a mental note to call and check on her before I went to bed later. For now, I had to get my ass downstairs and across town to meet Baisleigh for our first therapy session.

Though I'd rather not, I didn't have a choice. If she wanted me in therapy, then my ass would be there front and center. There was obviously some shit she either needed to work out or get off her chest and needed professional help doing so. I wasn't sure what was swarming in that pretty little head of hers, but I was about to find out.

I made it downstairs and into the parking garage in record time. My engine bellowed, echoing throughout when I started it from a few feet away. The second I was settled inside, I peeled out of the parking lot leaving behind nothing but smoke.

Just as the clock struck five, my navigation was instructing me to pull into the parking lot. The first vehicle I saw was Baisleigh's Maserati SUV. She'd had it for about three years now. I couldn't wait to upgrade her. When I stepped out of my car, I noticed that she wasn't in hers. I peeked through the tinted windows to find her truck empty.

Ping. My phone sounded off.

That's her, I thought, removing it from my pocket. I wasn't surprised to learn that it was.

> Laike, we can't start like this. You promised.

I didn't bother with a reply. Baisleigh knew me, and she knew that I didn't break promises. Ever. It wasn't something that I could do. Pride, or whatever the fuck it was, wouldn't allow me to. I rushed through the doors of the practice and didn't stop until I was in front of the door that read the same suite number on the text she'd sent earlier.

Tiana Wiggins Suite 110.

Gently, I knocked on the door and stepped aside. *She's dead ass about this therapy shit.* I ran my hand down my face and watched as the door handle twisted. A second later, the door cracked open. When Baisleigh's therapist peeked her head around it, the oxygen left my body.

Titi?

"Can I help you?" she asked in a voice much lighter and much softer than I remembered.

"Uh... Tell Baisleigh to let me holler at her really quick," I replied, still trying to digest my latest discovery.

"Come in, Laike," Baisleigh demanded from the other side of the door.

Titi opened the door wider so that I could see her. Baisleigh was seated on an emerald couch, at the very edge, gripping the ends of it until her knuckles turned white. From the look on her face, I knew that there was no convincing her to leave, but I had to give it a shot. Because for me, this wouldn't work out.

"B, let me talk to you," I begged, waving her over.

"Come inside and talk to me in here," she suggested.

"Nah." I stood my ground.

"If she closes the door and you're not sitting beside me, you can forget anything I said about giving you another chance. You asked what you needed to do and this is where we start. It's either this or nothing at all."

Knowing that she wasn't fucking around, I exhaled deeply and stepped into the room. Titi closed the door behind me with a low, tittering of her own. I wanted to turn my ass around and go home, but I knew it would upset Baisleigh. I sat down next to her, garnering a smile from that pretty face of hers. At the end of the day, I knew that it was all that mattered anyway. I'd deal with the rest.

"So, Laike, it is?" Titi asked as if she didn't already know.

"Yeah," I answered as I cleared my throat.

"Nice to meet you, Laike. Baisleigh tells me that you two were an item since the tender age of eleven and after over a decade of separation have decided to give this thing another shot."

"Ummm hmmm," I responded, keeping it short.

I felt an elbow to my side. Baisleigh immediately noticed my disinterest and wanted me to dead it quickly. Unfortunately, that wasn't possible.

"What brings that about?"

"She ain't tell you that shit already?" I asked, sucking the skin of my teeth as I got a little more comfortable on the sofa. I widened my legs and leaned backward to give my limbs a bit more stretch. I was a long ass nigga and hated feeling crammed.

"Laike," Baisleigh interjected.

"She did tell me, but I'm asking you."

"I'm saying, we paying for this shit by the hour, right? I'm not about to pay for you to ask me the same shit you've already asked her. Next question." I shrugged.

"I knew this was a bad idea." Baisleigh sighed.

"Me, too," I admitted.

"No. It's fine. He's right. I have an entire list of questions we can go with. We'll leave that one alone for now."

"Aight, what's next?"

"Baisleigh, is there anything you have to ask Laike? I'll let you go first."

"There are a few things I want to ask and a few things that I just want to say."

"Go ahead," Titi encouraged her.

"Well, first," she started and then swallowed a lump in her throat, "I just want to say that I'm not the same person you loved all those years ago. The fear that you won't be head over heels for the woman I am today keeps me up at night. Everything about me is different. I just want to know if you're ready to fall in love with the new version of me?"

"Maybe you aren't the same, B. I get that. I'm not the same nigga, either. I expect that. But, what I do know is that your heart is unchanging. That's the only thing that I need to remain the same for me to love the fuck out of you."

"Is there anything you need to ask Baisleigh, Laike? We can take turns here."

"Yeah."

"Go ahead."

"B, why the fuck we need a moderator? We can talk about this shit amongst us two. I'm not shying away from these types of conversations and you know it. I'm an inquisitive ass nigga, so I need to know what's going on in that head of yours at all times, anyway?"

"Laike, you're being rude," she warned.

"And, honest."

"Well, though it's easy for you, it's not for me. Communication is what landed us in the boat we're in now. If you'd been more open with me, then maybe I wouldn't have spiraled the way that I did."

"You've told me that, and I've made it clear that I will be. I'm not fucking up this time, B. We both know this though. I know you do. If you need to make a list of shit that's worrying you, stressing you, eating away at you then I'll read that motherfucker from front to back a hundred times until I get it through my thick ass skull. Aside from ending our relationship with the hopes of not breaking your heart, I was good to you or else it wouldn't have hurt so bad. Ain't shit change. Not that part, at least."

"I know. I just thought we needed this."

"Baby girl, if you need this then I'm all for it. But, us, we're good. Give me a chance first. Then, let's let this be first on my to-do list if you feel like I'm not getting you, improving, or making this shit work between us. Give a nigga a chance, first."

"One chance," she clarified, "that's all you get."

"Trust me, B, that's all I need."

"I'm sorry to waste your time, Tiana," she said to her therapist, "I'm still set for my regular at the end of the week, right?"

"Of course and it's fine. It looks like you two have an open line of communication, now. I think he might be right. You guys have nothing to worry about here."

"Well, this is his only chance, so I assume he'd better get it right."

"Trust me, girl. I've been around enough men to know which ones will survive the relationship, and he's one of them." Titi chuckled, putting on that fake ass professional voice that sounded like nails on a chalkboard.

"Meet me outside," I whispered to Baisleigh, pointing toward the door.

Without as much as a *goodbye*, I exited the suite and made my way down the long hallway that led to the exit. My stomach was touching my back, and I was praying that Baisleigh was hungry, too. Grabbing a bite to eat was the next thing on my agenda, but until then I decided to stop at the vending machine that was near the exit.

I shoved a hand in my pocket and pulled out the dollars I had left from my mother's chemotherapy session. I always kept a few just in case she got the strength to snack during her appointment. It was rare that she did because she knew that it would all end up in a bag that they provided in case patients had an upset stomach or got nauseous enough to vomit. My mother hated vomiting, especially in front of us. She hated the idea of being sick altogether, but there was nothing any of us could do about it or else we would've.

"You just can't help it, can you?" Baisleigh asked.

She was a few feet away from me, but I could still smell her perfume. I didn't understand how she managed to not smell like bacon, fried eggs, and syrup. As much breakfast she sold during the day, I imagined she'd smell like a meal leaving her place of business. However, she smelled like she'd just stepped out of the shower.

"Did you go home and shower before coming?" I

chuckled, realizing I probably wasn't wrong about the assumption.

"I asked you a question first," she sassed, putting a hand on her hip.

"I don't understand the question. Be more specific."

"You're pretty fucking ignorant, Laike. That's what I mean. You can't help being an asshole, can you?"

"We calling each other names now? Let me know because I'm not with that shit. Deal breaker." I scoffed.

My dollar went into the machine with ease. I immediately followed up with another one.

"I'm just saying... you could've had a bit of decency back there. You're so embarrassing sometimes," she whined.

"Nothing I said or did back there was embarrassing, baby girl. Being an asshole and being honest tend to sound the same. It just depends on who you're referring to. In my case, I'm blunt. Always have been. You've never had an issue with it before, B."

I chose the bag of pretzels from the machine. It was something to hold me over until I got some real food in my system. I wasn't a fan of the snack, but I knew they'd only make me get something to eat sooner than putting it off for later.

"I don't know. I guess it's going to take some getting used to, again." She sighed, frustration all over her beautiful face when I turned around.

"You're blunt, too, Baisleigh. We both are. A little

more reserved than me, yeah, but you're not afraid to let me or anyone else have it when the time comes. You're a ball of fire and that's something I've always admired about you. You give me push back and you're not a pushover. If you need me to tone it down for you, then that's no issue. But, then, I wouldn't be myself and I don't think you want that."

"I don't," she admitted, "I'm okay with how you are. I love it. I can handle it. It's just that sometimes it might be a little too much for other people."

"When did you start caring about other people so much, B?"

Baisleigh followed me as we headed out of the door.

"I guess working in hospitality. I don't know."

"If it's a big deal, I'll chill."

We made it to her truck first. I opened the door and let her slide in.

"It's not. Really. I love that part of you. I guess I just feel bad for my therapist today."

"Titi the last motherfucker you should feel bad for," I assured her before realizing I'd just mentioned Tiana's nickname.

"Laike!" She gasped.

I remained silent, wanting to kick my own ass for letting that slip. Some shit I was willing to take to my grave.

"You fucked her, didn't you?"

She knew me like the back of her hand. Of course

I'd knocked Tiana down. Shit, me and every other nigga with some change in his pocket. After our second hookup, I discovered Ken and I were both hitting that shit on damn near the same days, so we invited her for a ride on the Polar Express. For nearly two hours, she blew our whistles and hopped from one trailer to the other. When the train ride ended, we were both drained of our engine's fluids. That was the last day either of us mentioned her name.

"Of course you did," she sneered, sarcastically. "Of course."

My silence was revealing.

"She's famous around these parts, B. Everybody done hit her."

"Like that makes me feel any better!"

"It shouldn't, especially knowing the woman you're trusting with your mental health running through every nigga with a few figures in search of her own validation."

"Now I have to find a new therapist. Why didn't you say anything?"

"I tried to, but you wouldn't come out and talk to me."

"Fuck. I thought you were trying to get out of doing therapy."

"Not therapy. I'm down with that if it's going to help us. I just wasn't trying to sit there with Titi, pouring my heart out and shit. And, I didn't want you doing that either."

"That lady has been my therapist for three years now. Ugh."

"I'll go to a hundred sessions with you until you find your new person, aight? It's no biggie. She just ain't it."

"No. This is something I have to do alone. Maybe I need to search for a male. That way I know for sure my man hasn't been in her guts." She laughed.

"Your man?"

I didn't miss that. When she realized she'd said the words, she smiled and shook her head.

"Move."

She attempted to close the door on me.

"Stop playing, B. I'm with that shit."

My hand wrapped around her neck as I leaned her forward, in my direction, and stuck my tongue down her throat. She accepted it without question, sucking on it before allowing it to roam the hollowness of her mouth.

"Shit, B," I said as I pulled back, adjusting my dick in the process.

I stumbled back on my feet a bit, intoxicated from the kiss we'd just shared. That was the thing about Baisleigh, she always put my ass in a fucking daze and kept me walking around looking stupid. I didn't give a fuck, though. I loved every second of that shit. I loved every bit of her.

"You're not my man... yet," she teased, wiping her lips with her index finger.

"Officially or unofficially, let your man feed you."

"I am not in the mood for dick, Laike, especially not after the news I just got. Maybe tomorrow."

"I wasn't referring to dick, but I'm with that tomorrow shit. What time so I can block off my schedule?"

"I hate you so bad." She blushed, her cheeks attempting to reach her eyes.

"Ummm hmmm. But, what's up? You going to let me feed you?"

"I have to be back at work in like... thirty minutes."

"Then, feed me."

"I can do that. Follow me there, and we can have dinner in my office."

"Say less."

SEVEN

baisleigh

"THIS IS ALL I could come up with, with what I have in the kitchen," I explained as I placed the plate in front of Laike.

To keep his appetite from overwhelming him, I'd kept him busy with a Caesar salad and an in-house lemon-garlic ranch dressing that I'd created a few years ago. It was my customers' favorite. With two more recipes in the works, I was close to deleting ranch, Caesar, and all the other dressings from my menu. No one ordered them anymore, not unless they were new to Baisleigh's House. Even then, once they realized there were better options, they ended up with my lemon-garlic ranch in their hands.

"Baby, you're saying this is all as if this plate is underdressed," he replied. "This is more than enough to fill what little space the salad left in my stomach."

We were having brunch for dinner. On his plate was blackened chicken, shrimp, and grits, mixed in a creamy, buttery sauce. On the side was breakfast potatoes and scrambled eggs with lots of cheese. I was having the same thing. However, I'd opted for shrimp and grits, only, leaving the blackened chicken for Laike.

"Good, because I was hoping it was enough. I didn't want to keep you waiting too long to eat."

"Sit down," he demanded.

"I am. I am."

"You've been ripping and running all day, it seems. I know your fucking feet hurt," he teased, reaching over and propping my right leg up on his as soon as I was seated.

He removed my shoe and then placed it up to his nose. I chuckled as I watched his eyes roll and his head fall backward. The dramatics were his style.

"Liar."

"Sheesh."

He waved his nose before tossing my shoe to the

side. It felt so good to have it off my foot. And, it wasn't until I felt Laike's fingers kneading at the knots that I realized how much I could use a massage.

"Ummmmm," I moaned, rather intrigued by the pile of food I'd just stuffed in my mouth and the feeling of Laike caressing my foot.

He maintained the pressure with one hand and scooped up some grits from his plate using a spoon and his other hand.

"What's up with the food truck? What's the hold up on it?" he asked, referring to the truck that Luca and Ever had gotten me as a gift for my birthday almost two years ago.

"Honestly, I was so excited when I first got the truck. I went full force. But, then, I realized how much work it was right around the time when business picked up even more. I've been swamped and haven't been able to get back to it. I still need the buildout sketches completed, wrapping, new appliances, a simplified menu, and all that other stuff. I just feel like I have so much work to do. Not to mention I'm trying to start the herbal tea line. I guess I just need to focus on one thing at a time."

"You just need help, Baisleigh," he told me.

Help. Through the years I'd spent alone, it was something that I rarely asked for because I was too afraid of not receiving the answer or assistance I needed. Aside from my parents, when asking for help,

I'd always ended up disappointed with the outcome whether it was due to something being done incorrectly, not at all, or with a chip on the shoulder. I had no time for either, so I felt most comfortable doing it all on my own.

It wasn't until the very moment the words were spoken by Laike that I remembered when he was involved, I always had the help I needed. Even in the years that we weren't together, if I ever called, he'd come running. I just tried not to call because for Laike, I was a loss cause. With him, there were no barriers and no boundaries.

Though I put on a good front for the world, I'd never stopped wanting him. I never would. That's why it was so easy for him to walk back into my life. Because, my heart, he'd never truly left. Our love was put on pause while he frolicked the city with woman after woman, trying to find something within them that was only inside of me.

It wasn't fair, but it was the reality of it all. And, if I had to be honest, I was appreciative of his courtesy. He didn't have the guts to cheat on me, and I doubted he ever would. To make sure I didn't suffer through that heartbreak, he left. The hurt that I felt after was only a fraction of what I would've felt if we'd gone on to get married, have children, and then I found out he was unfaithful. It was pain that I wouldn't be able to come back from... that we wouldn't be able to come back from.

Our breakup was the only time Laike had ever caused me pain. We were perfect in every sense of the word. We had moments of despair, but nothing ever caused me pain. He was good to me. In fact, he was so good to me that it made it harder for any man after him to pull a wool over my head or even get close to me. Nicholas had been lucky.

The only reason I didn't see right through him was because I was still blinded by the one encounter I had with Laike. The night his mother shared the tragic news was the night I lost my center, again. After grounding myself and being as careful as I could be, Laike came into my world for one night and uprooted me.

So, when Nicholas told me he was ready to progress in our relationship two weeks later, I agreed. Two months later, after him being the perfect gentleman and giving me the closest thing to Laike's bedroom standards as I'd probably ever get, I agreed to be his wife. He was the next best thing, and I was willing to settle since I couldn't fathom waiting any longer for my truest love. However, now that he was in my world, again, I couldn't imagine settling for less.

"Maybe so," I agreed.

"Don't sweat it. Daddy's home."

Daddy's home. I smiled at the irony. He was. And, when he was around, shit got done. There wasn't any worrying or any concerns. Because he paid so much attention to detail and read me like a book, he almost always knew when something was wrong and how to find the solution.

With Laike, I could rest. With Laike, I didn't feel like an octopus. With Laike, less was best for me. With Laike, I could be gentle while he handled anything that was too hard, too heavy, too tough, too time consuming, and too much. He preferred me stretched out across his bed with my pussy on his lips or sliding down his dick, not worn out and stretched thin from life's obstacles.

"Other foot," he instructed. "And tell me what's on your plate. I'll clean it."

laike + baisleigh

IT FELT like a million hours had passed since I'd seen his face, although it had only been four. Because it was midnight when I was leaving Baisleigh's House, I decided to call and hear his voice. I was tempted to get into my truck and drive to his house, but I wasn't sure if I was ready for what came with that bold move.

Laike and I still had so much to figure out, and I was wondering if sex would interfere with that. The last thing I wanted was us to fall into the habit of sealing everything with a simple kiss. I wanted to work through our issues and grow even closer than we once were, but the more I thought about it, there weren't any real issues.

Our breakup wasn't one that was long overdue or happened because we were toxic. We were simply in over our heads, too young and too serious. Communication on Laike's part would've been appreciated, but he was performing well in that area so far.

In conclusion, I knew that it was my insecurities that was stopping me from going full force in this thing this time around. Yes, I still loved Laike unconditionally, but I was still scorned. I was still wondering if I was enough. Still wondering if any of it was my fault. Still wondering if he'd do to me the same thing he'd already done.

I was still dragging around the pain although I hardly felt it anymore. The scars it left still lingered, and with him in my life again, they were reminding me constantly that they were still there and his presence was triggering.

"I promise. I'm leaving now. I got caught up like I always do and lost track of time. My intentions weren't to leave after midnight."

"You said that the last few nights," he fussed. "Babe, that's why you have staff. It's not safe, neither is it okay for you to be working from morning to night."

"I knoooooooow, Laike. I'm working on hiring more staff to do the things that I don't trust my current staff to. Well, not that I don't trust them, but they've made it clear that they're good at their jobs and not mine time and time again."

"Aight. I'm going to be quiet so that you can pay

attention to your surroundings. You walked outside, yet?"

"Walking out, now," I confirmed.

"Put the phone in your pocket or something. Pay attention and make sure your hands are free."

"Alright. One second. You're going in my pocket." I laughed.

Maybe it was the hundredth thing or maybe it was the millionth, but his dedication to the protection of the people in his life that he loved was another aspect I loved about him. He was especially protective of the women. One would've assumed Lyric was the president's daughter before she married Keanu.

The only reason Laike slacked up on her security was because she had an in-house guard that was just as ruthless and unhinged as he was. They were one in the same and she'd married him, giving her brother a slight break.

I stuffed my phone into the back pocket of my jeans. I usually wore something much more comfortable to work, but the therapy session made me change up the attire a bit. Once Laike was in my pocket, probably listening a lot harder than he needed to, I grabbed my key fob from the zipped portion of my purse before stepping outside.

I hit the button to unlock the doors, but to my dismay, the lights didn't flicker. I tapped the button again, rushing toward my parking space. There were two cars and a truck on side of my spot, making it hard to see my vehicle.

"God, I've been meaning to change this battery," I groaned, praying it hadn't finally died on me after four months of tapping it against whatever was near.

However, when I reached my designated spot on the parking lot of Baisleigh's House, I realized I had a much bigger issue than a dead battery. My entire truck was missing. Panic-stricken, I snatched my phone from my pocket.

"Babe," I called out to Laike.

My hands and voice were both trembling as I tried my hardest to recall seeing anything remotely close to a towing truck of any kind in the parking lot all day. Aside from my usual towing company customers, there weren't any. And they always parked at the back because their trucks were too big to fit in the spots up front.

I'd been at the same location for years and no one had ever stolen anything from my lot that I could remember, so this was all baffling to me. Someone would've seen or heard something. I wasn't sure what was going on, but I knew that my truck was missing and needed to be found.

"Pay attention to your surroundings, B."

"I am! My truck is gone."

"Pay attention to your surroundings," he repeated.

"Laike, you keep telling me about my surroundings. I hear you but do you hear me?"

"Yes. And, see you. You're not paying attention to your surroundings, either."

I closed my mouth and scanned the parking lot with my eyes. The flickering lights from one of the vehicles I'd passed on the way to mine caught my attention. With a shake of my head, I headed in that direction.

"Is that you?"

"Yes, it's me," he confirmed.

I ended the call and made my way to the passenger side. It wasn't until I was inside and noticed the paper mat underneath my feet that I realized the sickeningly sweet Lamborghini truck was brand new. The new car smell hit me like a pound of weed.

"You got a new truck?" I asked, forgetting all about the fact that mine was missing.

"Nah. You got a new truck," he told me as he stuffed a blunt in his mouth.

"Me?" I asked, placing a hand on my chest.

"Did I stutter, baby girl?"

"Laike, are you serious right now? Did you take my truck?"

"Your truck has been gone since I left around seven."

"What? And, seven? I thought you left at eight?"

"Nah, my partner closes at seven. I had plans to meet him after closing hours to come scoop you something off the lot. You feeling this or you want something else?"

"Did I not just tell you I had my eye on this truck for next year?" I squealed, excitement pumping through my veins.

"Why wait?" he blew smoke from his nose, "that ain't an option with me. We're not eyeing shit. We're buying shit."

"Is this really mine?" I asked, getting closer to Laike.

I wasn't sure if it was the sight of him smoking his weed for the first time in forever, the fact that I knew he'd blown a fortune on the truck, the fact that he'd listened carefully and immediately acted, or the fact that he was all mine again that made my heart hurt and my center throb for him.

"Really yours, love. It's dark as hell out here, but it's sweet. You probably won't really be able to see the beauty in it until daylight. Tomorrow, I'm taking it for music and some new wheels. You can ride my whip until they get through with it or I can drive you around."

"I'll take your car. I have a few errands to run tomorrow."

"Bet. Either is fine with me. If you change your mind, just let me know."

"I can't believe you got me a freaking car!" I shrieked.

Unable to hold out any longer, I hugged his neck and pulled him closer to me. I planted kisses all over his face and forehead. The hoodie that he was wearing fell off as he submitted to my display of love and affection. When I was finally finished, he pulled his hoodie back over his head and gripped the steering wheel.

He had to have been the sexiest man alive, the way he whipped the truck out of the parking spot, reversing until he was clear to change gears. His skin was clear and free of blemishes, partially due to the new routine I'd put him on. I could tell he was following directions and it was doing his face justice. It was already top tier.

"I don't understand why you're surprised. It's almost insulting. Happy, cool. Surprised? Nah. Like I ain't the nigga to make shit happen for you. Ain't shit changed, B. Just got better."

"A whole car, Laike? On what? Day three or four? Bold move. You were hoping to make it official, huh? I see."

"Nah, I was hoping to get my dick sucked," he corrected, pulling on the blunt in his mouth.

The words that dripped from his mouth made me hot all over. Warmth surged through my body, stimulating me beyond explanation. All self-control flew out of the window at that very moment. If a sucked dick was what Laike wanted then a sucked dick was what he'd get.

"You wanna ride with me somewhere right quick?" he asked, but I was more concerned with the statement he'd just made.

"Ummm hmmm," I answered as I slid closer to his side of the SUV.

I tugged at the black joggers he'd changed into. When he left me earlier, he didn't have them on. More than likely, it meant he'd showered before coming to pick me up. The thought of his clean meat down my throat made my mouth water and my hands began to roam.

"What the fuck you doing, girl?"

Laike's eyes dropped from the road, momentarily, to see what I was doing.

"Eyes on the road before you kill us both."

"Don't be playing with my shit, B. if you ain't going to suck this motherfucker, then don't poke the beast."

"But, I am."

"Yeah?" he asked with cheer in his tone.

"Ummm hmmm. I'm ready to welcome daddy home," I confirmed, sticking my hand in his pants and pulling his dick from his briefs.

It was hard as a missile, greeting me with rigidness. Though we were in the dark, my fingers memorized every inch of his body. It had been mine for years and years and years. From the time I was fourteen years old, we'd begun exploring one another. The innocent touches and feels every now and then led to full blown kisses by fifteen.

By sixteen, we began sensual touches. And on my seventeenth birthday, Laike was given my virginity. While most girls regretted the man they'd first laid down with, I was proud to admit that it was Laike who'd dismantled my hymen. I'd been the first girl he'd entered, and I would be the last.

I knew him well. His thickness was my favorite. Though a challenge, it was one that I accepted. I remember nights with cracked lips and cuts in the creases that burned when I ate or licked them. Each shard of pain that ripped through my body was a reminder that he'd been there, in my mouth, and that always made me smile.

The space between us frustrated me because comfort was hard to come by. However, I was determined to make it work. A woman of my word, I wanted to welcome daddy home with an open mouth and wet pussy. He deserved it.

"Shit, B," Laike moaned as I pushed his dick down my throat, lowering my head until he couldn't go any further.

His hand, instantly, rested on my head. The sleek, low ponytail that I had mastered was perfect for the occasion. He managed to control my movements with ease.

Saliva coated his wood, making it glisten in the dark. I retracted, lifting my head until he was all the way out of my mouth. A trail of slob followed me. Anger did as well, mainly because I wanted, so desperately, to see his pretty brown skin wet and rock hard.

"You gone stare at this motherfucker or suck it?" Laike mumbled, lowly yet aggressively.

"I can't see."

"You ain't got to see it to suck it," he explained.

Casting my frustration with the darkness aside, I lowered my head until he was inside my jaws, again. This time, I didn't plan on letting up. I sucked the air from my mouth and let nothing but meatiness and skin.

Up. Down.

Up. Down.

Up. Down.

The tip of his dick touched parts of my throat that I'd forgotten were reachable, bringing buckets of saliva from the bottom of my mouth. The lubrication was necessary to maintain my rhythm.

"Shit, girl."

His moans set a fire ablaze between my legs. I felt as if I was burning alive in my own body. The heat that rose from my center paired with the anticipation of feeling his cum ooze down my throat sent me into overdrive. I reached inside of his pants and freed his balls.

My head dropped, welcoming them into my mouth. Careful not to leave his dick unattended, I used my right, and strongest hand, to massage him from mid-shaft to the very top. Simultaneously, my hands and mouth were at work, desperately trying to bring that thick, creamy cum to the surface.

"FUCK!" Laike howled just as the truck came to a complete stop.

As much as I wanted to look up and see what was

going on above me, I was too in the zone and aware that he was about to explode. He wouldn't be announcing it, but I didn't need him to. I could feel the bulge as it rose higher with each stroke. When it made it to his head, swelling it, I dropped his balls from my mouth and replaced them with his dick.

"Shit, B. Fuuuuuuuck."

Warm, thick semen squirted on the back of my tongue, nearest my throat. It had been so many years, but he still tasted familiar. I swallowed his cum and sucked him dry of any potential leftovers. It wasn't until he was forcing me up from between his legs that I left him go.

"Come 'er!" He grimaced.

Both hands were on both sides of my face, pulling me up to his. His tongue entered my mouth and met mine for a dance that I'd never forget. When I finally came up for air and managed to take my seat, I realized we were in the middle of the road.

"Did you really stop in the middle of the road, Laike?"

"It was either that or kill us both wrecking out."

"I swear," I chuckled, wiping my lips, "you're some kind of special."

"That's what they be saying."

He shrugged, fixing his clothes. Still, he was in no hurry to get out of the road.

"You should start believing them."

Relief consumed me when he turned off the emergency lights and switched gears.

"Now my top lip smells like dick." I chuckled, pushing my top lips up until it touched my nose.

"Dick doesn't smell, baby girl. It's just skin. Your top lip smells like breath. Yours. Not mine. So, what you trying to say?"

He was giggling a bit too hard for me.

"Just pull up to a gas station, Laike. I need some wipes or something."

"Or some gum, baby girl. Some gum." He cackled.

"I swear, I don't know if I'll survive a lifetime with you," I replied.

"You have no other choice. The way you just sucked my dick, you think I'm letting another nigga have that? Nah. You done sucked and slid down enough dicks, B. It's time to come home. Them niggas been practice and I must say, they've elevated your game baby girl. I ain't mad at em."

"You're sick!"

"About you, I am. I'll admit that."

"There should be some gas stations coming up on the right. If you're not in a rush, I'd like to stop at one to get myself together."

"Niggas can wait if I need them to. We're stopping by the gas station if that's what you want to do."

"Please. I can use the restroom."

"And get some gum." He sniggered.

"Fuck you, Laike."

"You ain't said nothing but a word, love. I plan to let you as soon as you wash them scrambled eggs off your body."

"You know what, forget it. I was going to play nice and come to your house tonight, but you can drop me off at home."

He didn't respond. He couldn't. He was too busy dying of laughter. His laugh was so infectious that I found myself smiling, trying to hold out. It didn't last, though. And, there I was, hysterically crying of laughter, too.

This. This was it. I couldn't quite articulate or pinpoint the exact feeling that this moment awarded me with but it was these kinds that I missed most. Laughter until the sunrise. Humor. And little pockets of conversation about nothing that made things make sense.

My person. I believed wholeheartedly that Laike was him. With everything in me, I was convinced that I was put on this earth for him and he was put here for me. We just fit together so easily, effortlessly, and naturally.

It was as if the only effort required when it came to us was staying apart. That had taken all my energy and all my time. *This,* however, took nothing from me. It only filled me with things – things like joy, happiness, love, peace, and harmony.

"Are we really doing this?" I found myself asking. "Are you really ready for forever with me?"

He reached over and took my hand into his. He pulled it upward and toward his mouth to kiss. He then rested his face against the back of it, before speaking.

"I'm ready, B. I know you're scared shitless, but this is nothing like last time. I ran. I'm not running again. Aight? I promise. I got you, and I know you got me. Shit going to end differently for us. We're growing gray and we're growing old together. Just wait and see."

"If you ever feel like you're getting cold feet on me, please talk to me. Don't leave me out of the loop. It's me."

"I know it's you and ain't no more cold feet, Baisleigh. I'm damn near forty. I'm not going anywhere. I'm here. You're here. Let's make some fucking magic."

"You have a few more years before forty, but let's do that!"

"You know what I mean. I'm getting too fucking old to be out here wilding like I have been since you let me off the leash."

"I did not let you off the leash, Laike. You ran away from home."

"And, I came back to that motherfucker, huh?"

"Ummm hmmm."

We pulled into the first gas station we saw. He parked in the spot closest to the door before hopping out of the truck with his blunt attached to his lips. I knew better than to advise him against it, so I didn't. Instead, I waited until he rounded the truck to open my door. After I stepped out, he closed it behind me and grabbed my hand. Together we walked into the store and toward the restroom signs.

"I'll be out here when you're finished," Laike told me as he posted up against the wall across from the bathroom door.

Suddenly, my bladder felt like it was about to cave in. I rushed into the bathroom and into the nearest stall. Fortunately, it was clean and smelled pretty good. My jeans didn't want to come off. They were hugging my skin, refusing to go down without a fight, but I still managed.

I pulled one of the toilet toppers down from the wall and split the tabs. It sat perfectly on the toilet but as soon as I turned around to sit down, I heard it flush. My body stiffened as I realized what had happened.

Fuck, I hate when it does that. I cringed. Completely peeved, I grabbed another one and repeated the same steps. This time, however, I held it in place as I turned around and sat down.

Once the mission was complete, I walked out of the restroom to find Laike standing against the wall with one hand in front of the other. If I didn't know before I walked into the restroom, I understood very well that he was the finest thing I'd laid my eyes on since the day my mother gave birth to me. His thick, rich curls, full beard, brown skin, and those oversized eyes. I loved every bit of him.

"You ready?"

"I am, but first I want a few snacks. I'm starting to get hungry again."

"Shit, I thought I was the only one."

Laike stood where he was, unmoving, and relit the blunt in his hand. I watched, amused, at his carelessness. Not by any means did he give a damn about much of anything. Rules hardly applied to him and it was partially because he was an Eisenberg. The other part of it was because he just didn't care.

I made a dash for the aisle I'd seen the pickles on in passing. It had been years since I'd had a sour one, but my taste buds started tingling the second I recognized the pouches lined up on the shelves. In addition to a sour pickle, I grabbed some Appleheads and a blue Airhead.

"Got everything you want?" Laike asked when I made it to the counter.

His eyes were low and heavy, his voice deep and lusty. I swallowed the lump in my throat as I nodded, taking a second to look at everything he had placed on the counter. Anywhere my eyes landed but on his face was fine with me. My God. This man had been created with precision and to perfection.

"I did."

He hadn't done too bad himself. There were two different bags of chips and two candy bars on the counter. He'd also managed to pick up the pack of gum that I'd forgotten. I'd expected much more from him.

When the munchies got ahold of him, he was a menace with snacks.

"Laike?" I heard behind us, causing me to whip my neck in the opposite direction.

I wasn't surprised to find a gorgeous woman behind the voice that had called out Laike's name. My eyes bounced between the two, waiting for Laike to acknowledge the woman. However, without haste, he placed a few bills on the counter to cover our things. Once they were bagged, he held them at his side and then grabbed my hand with his free hand.

"Now you're going to act like you don't see me," she scoffed, "I swear niggas are as fake as they come."

"Maybe they are, but not this nigga," Laike responded, stopping briefly to acknowledge her and then continuing.

"You, too," she reiterated.

"Grab some toothpaste while you in this bitch," he tossed over his shoulder as we stepped out of the store.

"I guess you didn't want to introduce me to your friend back there?" I joked as we neared the passenger side of the parking lot.

"I'm in a committed relationship and shit now. I don't have friends, baby girl."

Unfazed, he shrugged and opened the door behind me.

"Another one from your roster?"

"I don't have a roster, B. All them old news. We're not worried about them."

"Oh, I know. Just making sure I know who is who. I'd hate for one of your flings to let their jealousy rule their logic and try me. The last thing I want is to be caught off guard."

"You're good, but if you must know, her name is Ashlyn. I ain't touched her in a good five months or better. Shit, I don't know. Now, get your pretty ass in. I've got some moves to make."

EIGHT

laike

SURREAL. That's how it felt having Baisleigh in the theater room searching for something for us both to enjoy. It was the second night she'd agreed to stay over. And, to my surprise, we had yet to unclothe one another or tear each other to shreds in the bed. Last night and tonight, we'd spent time learning the newer versions of each other.

Baisleigh, I learned, had grown even more beautiful internally as she had externally. I learned that she was obsessed with herbal teas, start-up companies owned by Black women, food photography, pilates, and interior design. With my soft spot for architecture, the interior design obsession piqued my interest.

I was patiently waiting for my next project and hoping it came much sooner than later. With Luca, Ken, and my home being taken care of, I was without work. My hobby kept my head on straight and my hands occupied. The idea to completely remodel my parents' home came to mind often, but with my mother already having a difficult season, I didn't want to increase the amount of stress she was under. However, when her health improved, I'd get right on it.

Her new whip finally had custom wheels and a sound system that she could enjoy. It had taken two days instead of one, but she was up and rolling now. We'd picked up her truck before making our way to the house. I watched my rearview mirror steadily, making sure she followed me to our destination. If she ever cut out and tried to go home, I would follow her ass there.

Wherever she laid her head was where I wanted to be. Luckily, it was at my place. From the looks of it and the sound of her moans when she sat on anything in this bitch, she would be spending most of her nights here – if not all of them from now on. That, to me, was a win-win situation.

Right now, she was snuggled underneath the heated blankets that paired well with the reclining chairs in the theater room, waiting for my return. She'd chosen one of the few chairs that were wide enough to seat two and were great for movie night with couples. Baisleigh was keeping my spot warm until I returned.

In the meantime, I was pulling out fresh, hot brownies that I'd made from scratch, from the oven. I sat them on the cooling rack on top of the stove, marveling at their beauty. The perfect crisp on top and the visibly soft center that I could see through the glass. My mouth watered at the sight of it all, and, the smell, it was divine.

Just as much as Baisleigh enjoyed the kitchen, so did I. She was part of the reason I fell in love with cooking. It was a task that we both tackled together all those years ago, trying new recipes and even making some of our own. We'd created an entire recipe book of handwritten recipes for our future selves and child if we ever had one. I wasn't sure that we would because children simply weren't on my radar. Baisleigh, on the other hand, had made it clear that motherhood was in her future. And, for me, whatever she wanted she got.

Too anxious to get her reaction, I cut a huge square with the wide knife that was so unnecessary for the small treat. However, I knew it would serve its purpose. My hand rested on top of the brownie, holding it in place as I lifted it completely from the glass. It was steaming hot, just the way I liked it. The large knife, now flat, became a makeshift plate as I rushed through the kitchen, down the hallway, passed what felt like a hundred rooms, and then finally to where Baisleigh was still flipping through channels.

Her beauty was striking. Each time she appeared in my line of vision, I felt a jolt in my chest that left me breathless for a brief moment. She was the epitome of an enchantress, standing at 5'8 with legs that looked so damn good wrapped around my back as I dug into her or resting on my shoulders as I cleaned her plate. Her cocoa-colored skin was her greatest asset. It would be the death of me if I let it be.

The way her bright eyes popped on her dark skin made it hard to tear away from them. They commanded all your attention. Her breasts sat atop her chest, perfectly proportionate with the rest of her frame. Her hips expanded for miles, dazing me along the journey each time I caressed them.

They reserved room for her when she walked into any space and required everyone around her to give her more *personal* space. Her ass, it was as round as it was wide. Though Baisleigh never claimed to be, she was a fucking stallion. Not any man could handle her, but every inch of my 6'6 frame was equipped for handling the well-oiled machine.

I could smell the warm vanilla on her skin as I neared her. I couldn't help but wonder if it was from the shit she called body scrub that she'd made me use after her shower this morning or if it was the body cream that smelled the same. She'd rubbed her skin down, making it glow under the light. When we made it back, she'd complained about her dry hands due to washing them several times a day and disappeared upstairs. I was almost certain she'd dipped back into one of them.

My wife. Though we hadn't made shit official, yet, that's what I saw when I looked at Baisleigh. My center. My heart. My soul. Just the thought of seeing those umber cheeks rising made my heart flutter.

"They're finished?" she asked, sitting up in the reclined chair.

I got down on my knees in front of her, still holding the brownie in place. "I want you to taste this but before you do, I need to ask you something."

"What?" She panicked, "Is everything okay?"

"Everything is well, Baisleigh, as long as you're here," I explained to her.

"Then, what is it?" She smiled, visibly releasing the breath she was holding.

"Will you be mine? Forever this time?"

"Babe, I'm already yours," she responded, sliding up to the edge of the chair, "I've always been yours."

The cracking of her voice made me smile. She was such a softy. Her heart was as pure as they came and I loved her even more because of it.

"I know, but I'd like to solidify this moment. I know

women love anniversaries and shit. Mark this in your calendar as our first day being a couple."

"Again?" She chuckled, wiping her tearful eyes.

"Again. We can still celebrate the first one, too, if you'd like.

"No, I don't see a reason."

"We could get married on our first anniversary date so that we have a reason to celebrate it, again. I don't want to just let the years pass us by without recognizing it. I'll never forget December 21st. It changed my whole world, even at eleven."

I laughed, realizing how young and in love we were. It didn't matter that people called our thing puppy love. We knew it wasn't and us being together all these years later proved it.

"Gosh, we were just babies."

"But, we knew... even then."

"December 21st," she said.

"December 21st," I repeated, "That's the day I'll make you my wife."

"Well, you have to make me your fiancé first."

"Oh, it's coming. Just keep that finger warm for me and try doing some finger aerobics or something. The ice I'm about to put on that motherfucker is going to require some strengthening exercises. I don't want you breaking a finger carrying it around or whatever."

"Oh my God. You're so full of yourself." She giggled, popping my shoulder.

"You laughing, but you know what's up with me.

That AP still keeping your body cool on the summer days in Channing, ain't it? That was just a small gift. Imagine a forever gift."

Her silence was revealing.

"Yeah. That's what the fuck I thought."

"Put the brownie in my mouth and shut up," Baisleigh demanded, separating her lips.

"Keep playing and it'll be my dick in your mouth instead, B."

"I thought we were keeping our hands to ourselves?" she asked.

"You don't need your hands. I like it better when you don't use them, anyway."

"Brownie, sir. Please."

I pushed the brownie to the end of the knife so that she wouldn't mistakenly bite down on the edge of it. Cautiously, she bit into the hot piece of fudge. When her eyes rolled backward and her head went up and down, slowly, I knew that they'd hit the spot.

"Ummmmmm," she moaned.

"Yeah?"

"Yes, baby. Yes," she confirmed. "Give me more. Do you have ice cream?"

"Yeah. Homemade vanilla."

"Perfect. Oh my God."

"I'll be right back. Have a movie picked out by the time I return."

"I have one. I was just flipping through the channels for the hell of it."

"Oh, yeah? What we watching?"

"Premature. I've been wanting to watch it on Prime."

"Some sad ass love story?"

"I'm not sure if it's sad, but it is a love story. It's about young love. I thought it would be good for us to watch. I can remember those days like it was yesterday."

"Bet. I'll be right back."

erike + baisleigh

MY BABY WAS EXHAUSTED. She barely even got halfway through the movie before she was out. Work was kicking her ass and even the thought was fucking with me. I understood that it was her business and she'd worked her ass off to make it as successful as it was, but the long hours were going to be her downfall. I didn't want that to happen. In fact, I refused to watch it happen on my watch.

If it was left up to me, she'd be at home with her feet kicked up, but that wasn't Baisleigh. To be honest, I loved and respected that about her, too. She was a working woman, through and through. There was no changing that, and I wouldn't ever try. However, there needed to be some adjustments made to her schedule and the sooner, the better.

I pulled on the blunt in my hand as I stared out at the Channing skyline. It was beautiful from The Hills. Since moving in, it was the first time that I'd actually stepped out into my backyard and near the security gate that boarded my home. It was closest to the edge of my yard where a fall would be deadly. Over the gate, to the far right, I peered through squinted eyes, watching the lights of the house not too far from mine go off – one by one.

In the car, it would take a few minutes to cut the corners. On feet, it would take even longer. But, from my yard, I could see the beautiful home I'd built for a large family and a lifetime of memories. It was one of my first designs that I had full creative control over, so it was forever etched in my heart. I pulled out my phone at the thought of it and dialed the number I knew just as well as I knew my own. It rang twice before the line was picked up.

"Fuck you want," Luca answered.

"You still a bitch," I replied, exhaling smoke from my lungs.

"I'm just waiting for you to treat me like the bitch you think I am. Until then, nigga you're the bitch."

"I'm over here in my backyard, and I'm just think-ing... Nigga you living really comfortably in the house that I used my marbles to build."

"I'm afraid that architectural interests are the only time you use those marbles you speak of. Now, is there a reason you're calling me this late? My wife, kids, and I are in bed."

I pulled off the blunt again as reality smacked me dead in the chest. I didn't realize how much time had passed and just how silent I'd been until Luca called out to me.

"Laike!" he voiced, probably frustrated with me at this point. I didn't give a fuck. He was my big brother and it was his job to put up with my shit.

"I got her back," I told him, feeling like a huge weight had been lifted off my shoulders.

Luca remained silent, waiting for me to continue. He knew that I would.

"I just," I said, stopping mid-sentence to get my emotions in check. I didn't recognize my own voice. The cracking of it made my eyes tingle and my heart heavy.

"I... uh... I just wanted you to know I got her back and this time, I'm going to do right. A nigga be fucking up a lot, ya know. Just out here on some whatever shit. I just never gave a fuck about nothing really, not since her. I know I be getting on y'all fucking nerves and worrying y'all half to death, but I'm 'bout to get my shit straight."

"A nigga always felt like the disappointment in the family. Basketball didn't pan out for me. That knee still fucking with me 'til this day. I'd rather orchestrate a million-dollar drug deal than build million-dollar homes in Channing to make an honest living. I've probably fucked every single woman in the city and left my forever thing just to do it."

"I done fumbled the ball so many times in life that I want to get this one thing right. Ya feel me? Y'all deserve that and Baisleigh definitely deserves it. You should see her, Luca. She can't stop smiling at a nigga. Shit feels better than counting a few hundred thousand with my bare hands."

I cleared my throat to suppress the emotions that were ganging up against me.

"But, anyway, my nigga, I just wanted you to rest better tonight knowing that you don't have to worry about me no more."

"I'll always worry about you, Laike. It's my job. Lyric, too. It's just how it works. And, in my opinion, you've always had your shit together. A little stubborn, very bull-headed, and a pain in the fucking ass... yeah. But, you've never let me down, Laike. Well, that shit with Baisleigh, it was the only letdown. 'Til this day, I think you fucked up, but you're fixing it and that's all that matters. Not everyone gets that chance. Mom, she's fighting for her life, bro. You and Baisleigh are just giving her one more thing to fight for. We need that right now. She needs that right now."

"Yeah. I know. I know."

"Goodnight, Laike."

"Aight, man."

Before I ended the call, I heard him yell out to me.

"Aye."

"What's up?" I stopped to ask.

"I love you."

"Always... in all ways."

"Fa show."

This time, I managed to end the call. I watched his crib from afar a little while longer. Just as he'd said he would, he'd gone to bed. There weren't any lights on in the crib. It was officially their bedtime.

Ken and Lyric stayed a bit further around the bend. Their home was a bit too far to see in the dead of the night, but I could still see that they'd gone to bed, too. Everyone on their end had their lights out. On that note, I finished off my blunt so that I, too, could call it a night. I was ready to snuggle up against B until I fell asleep, too.

I stepped back inside my house after cutting through the grass, around the pool, and passing through the balcony. It felt like it took forever to get to the theater room, only to find out my sleeping beauty had risen. All that was left was the neatly folded blanket we'd been under together. I rushed through the house, toward the elevator. I knew that there was only one other place she could be and that's exactly where I wanted her. It was the cap to our night and where we'd end it.

When I made it to my bedroom, Baisleigh was nowhere to be seen. The dramatically large space made it quite easy to get lost. But, with shooting pains through my chest and the lingering of vanilla and sweet amber, I knew that I was in the right place. The anxiousness I felt was a dead giveaway. Baisleigh was near.

Settle down. I tried getting myself under control by sending a message to my neurons for distribution throughout the rest of me. I needed my heart and mind to quiet so that I could hear her because I already felt her. The lack of sound as my body completely quieted became my guide.

The sound of water molecules combining and then dropping on the floor of the shower make the hairs on the back of my neck stand. Her location was a bit more obvious. The only task in front of me was getting to her, now. The bathroom was on the opposite side of the room and seemingly too far. Eager to be in company with her once more, I trekked across the floor with speed and precision.

When I made it to the bathroom door and cracked it open, a cloud of steam brushed against my face. In the distance, I could see Baisleigh's chocolate skin, flowy hair, long limbs, and monstrous curves. My dick stood at attention as I watched the water drip down her skin.

Everything I'd mentioned to her about keeping my hands to myself went out the fucking window. There were five other showers in the house, totaling six, that she could've enjoyed. She'd chosen mine, which led me to believe that a hard dick was her intention.

I peeled my clothing off, one piece at a time.

Suddenly, I wasn't in a rush, anymore. Now that Baisleigh was in sight, she wasn't going anywhere. I wouldn't let her, especially not with the way my dick throbbed at the thought of climbing inside of her.

I stroked my meat as I got closer and closer to the shower. Her silhouette was hypnotic, demanding my presence. Like a moth to a flame, I was drawn to her body.

When I opened the door of the shower, she didn't even flinch. With her body dripping with water, Baisleigh stepped backward and welcomed me inside without words. I stepped forward and into the shower but didn't stop there. It wasn't until I was in her personal space with my right hand around her neck, her pushed against the marble of the shower, and my lips on hers that I planted my feet.

My fingertips roamed her body, revisiting familiar territory. Her pussy lips were so fat, forming a necessary gap between her legs. The fluffiness of the lips reminded me of the ones my tongue was lodged between. Patience failed me as I imagined my head between the second set, forcing me to pull away and retrieve the oxygen I needed to survive. So wrapped up into Baisleigh, I'd forgotten the most necessary and simplest task on earth.

Breathe.

"Turn around," I commanded, trying my hardest to settle my breathing.

Baisleigh slowly twirled her body, placing both hands on the wall.

"Bend the fuck over."

She deepened the small arch in her back and lowered her hands on the wall until her skin contacted mine. I maneuvered, giving us both enough room for free range of motion. When I dropped to my knees behind her, I could hear the gasp that came from her.

I spread both her cheeks, desperate for them to reveal what they were hiding and keeping warm on a daily basis. It was fire, literally and figuratively. Hot to the touch, her pussy had kept me warm many nights.

I arched my tongue upward as her pink valley came into view. The sweetness of her flesh was like sugar on my tongue, paired with the slight bitterness, and I was in heaven. She began to cream as soon as I put my mouth on her. I sucked her up like dessert after a full meal, leaving not even a crumb on the plate.

"Laike," she cried out as I tried my hardest to eat through her insides.

Swipe.

Swipe.

Swipe.

I showed Baisleigh no mercy and refused to leave even an inch of her pussy untouched. From one end to the other, I covered each centimeter with my saliva. Her clit was my main focus, but I wasn't ready for her to cum. Until I was, I'd continue to give the rest of her pussy the attention it craved and creamed for.

"Babbbbyyyyyy!"

The shakiness in her voice was like fuel to my fire. Her legs trembled, making it hard for her to stand straight. This was one of the reasons Baisleigh hated getting her pussy ate from the back. Balancing all that ass was a task for her. But, luckily, she didn't have to carry the weight alone. I used both of my hands to lift her ass cheeks and shift the weight from her to me. I wanted her fully engrossed in the moment without worrying if she would crash into the wall.

Front to back, I wrote my name in cursive on her pussy. Her shit tasted so good. The flavors of her food being the perfect seasoning I needed for the meal I was feasting on. The softness against my tongue was like heaven. My dick was so hard that it was beginning to ache. I needed to be inside of her, so making her cum was finally on my priority list. The act of teasing her eventually transformed into me teasing myself, and I couldn't resist sliding into her any longer.

I applied pressure to her swollenness. The bulb stuck out like a sore thumb, making it easy to suck into my mouth. My tongue glided across it, around it, and pressured it until I felt her legs shaking uncontrollably.

"I'm cumming. Baby, I'm cumming," she cried out to me. "I'm cuuuuummmmming."

Right on my fucking face, she came. When she locked her legs together, she secured my position, making it much easier to continue my assault on her pussy. When she finally released me, it was because she'd lost total control of her limbs and was releasing her feminine fluids simultaneously. Her river flowed, nearly drowning me as I tried swimming to shore.

"Fuck, B," I grunted.

I found my way to my feet and without hesitation or a second thought, I slid into her slipperiness. I wasn't sure what came over me, but I found myself bent forward in her ears, requesting something from her that I wasn't even sure I really wanted. But, in the moment, I did.

"Have my baby," I begged, knowing that the warmth of her pussy would leave me no choice but to send my minions swimming in her ocean.

I knew that Baisleigh was a planner. It was the way she went about life. She hated sporadic things and moments. She'd rather it all be written down in her planner, mainly because she managed a busy life. Not everything was at her fingertips, especially when it involved her time. So, I knew that having a baby would be something she wanted to plan for.

However, that wouldn't stop me from shooting up her club every chance I got. I wasn't sure, but most likely she was on birth control. That's the way Baisleigh rolled. She was careful, very cautious, and preferred strategizing every aspect of her life. With me, though, it would be almost impossible for her. I simply went with the flow of things, feeling out situations to better determine how to navigate them.

"Oh, Laike," she whimpered.

Long and slowly, I stroked her pussy. The sound of our skin touching every time our bodies met was driving me insane. I loved that shit. I tried my hardest to stuff her pretty insides with every bit of my dick that would fit.

I closed my eyes and picked up the pace, knowing that I didn't have long. No matter how many times I decided to stop or pull out, I'd only be prolonging the inevitable. So, the first round, I'd let her have. After our shower, she'd be in for the time of her life.

"I'm going to cum inside this pussy, B."

Her shit was so good. Too good. It had me wanting nothing more than to lay up in it all night, wake up to it, and then lay in it again.

"Cum inside of me," she agreed. "Please."

Her carelessness was exhilarating. This wasn't like Baisleigh, ever, to insist on my recklessness. If it happened, then it did. There was never influence or encouragement on her end. But her words extracted the nut right from my dick. It was my legs that shook next as my body stiffened behind her.

"Fuck, girl."

erike + baisleigh

AS BAISLEIGH PULLED one of my white tees from the drawer beneath my bed, I couldn't help but notice the healthy weight gain. She was rounder, fuller, and thicker than I'd ever seen her before. I didn't know that was possible, but she'd proven me wrong once again.

"You know you don't have to wear my shit every time you come over," I teased, pulling up the satin shorts I'd be sleeping in.

I didn't bother putting drawers underneath. They would only be in the way when it was time to slide back into Baisleigh. Round two was coming, certainly, so I was preparing for it.

"Unless you want me walking around here naked, then this is my only option."

"Naked is good," I assured her. "Shit, naked is great. But, I know it might not be as comfortable on some days as it is on others. That's why I made sure you were right."

"With fresh new tees ready for me to slip on. Thank you so very much," she responded, sarcastically. "I guess I should get me some clothes for when I'm over here."

"Handled."

Her neck whipped in my direction as her brows furrowed. Her glistening skin was extra smooth, much smoother than I remembered or maybe it was my new obsession with skincare that had me noticing it more. She'd officially sank her hooks into me and was about to transform me into her ideal husband. I could feel it in my bones, but I wasn't opposed.

"Handled?" She asked, "What does that mean?"

"It means what it sounds like. It's handled. You have shit here, already."

"No, I don't."

"But, you do. You haven't been in the closet to check, have you?"

"No. I haven't had a reason to go into the closet," she replied, taking strides toward the closet.

When she opened the door, she was smacked with the overwhelming scent of cedarwood and vanilla. Together, they made the perfect mix, just like Baisleigh and I. However, though she could smell hints of vanilla, its origins were nowhere in sight. She whipped her head around and tilted it for emphasis.

"This is all your stuff, babe. Why play with me?"

"Step inside, Baisleigh. Walk straight ahead and then turn to your left."

She followed orders as I instructed. When she noticed the French doors in front of her that led to the freshly painted and designed walk-in closet, her mouth stretched as her lips parted. The genuine appreciation on her face when she turned to me for the third time was like a warm hug on the worst of days.

I love this woman, I concluded as I watched her lips form a smile.

She's my heart. It was factual. She was and would always be.

I'm going to give her the world. Any of it that was in my grasp, she could have.

Please, Lord, help me get this right. Help me to be

the man that she needs me to be. Help me to release my selfish ways and become selfless for her. You've given me the only thing I've ever wanted in over a decade. I promise not to fuck it up. Amen.

"Baby?"

Her brief pause due to utter shock was so necessary. I needed that.

"Yeah?"

"Really? This wasn't here yesterday."

"Well, that's the beauty of having a man that does this shit and does it well."

"A full closet, though? It's bigger than yours!" She noticed. I'd made it that way, intentionally. I knew that she'd need the space.

"Yeah. You know how women are. Just got to get shit in every color and multiples of the same color. Not to mention your nigga loves to tear the stores down himself. On top of your shopping, I'm doing a bunch of that shit on my own. I'll probably build your collection faster than you will."

I just couldn't help myself when it came down to Baisleigh. I had the urge to empty my pockets, turning them inside out, just to see her smile. Though I knew she wasn't materialistic, it was still a good time when a few thousand dollars spent got her to show me those pretty teeth underneath those oversized, always-lined lips.

"My God, you already have so much in here. How?"

"You know who my mom and sister are, right? I gave them my card and didn't see them for hours while the crew worked on the closet. It was the bedroom next door that I wasn't doing anything with. They knocked the wall out, made the arches, put in the French doors, removed the carpet and put in wood, made the full-wall wardrobes, built custom purse and shoe holders, installed the jewelry cases, and all that good shit."

"Wow. How long did it take them? Did they do all of this while I was at work?"

"Yeah. They did."

"Dang, now it seems like I work too many damn hours because there's no way they did this in one workday."

"They did. They were on a ten-hour deadline. They arrived twenty minutes after you left and worked until the job was done. When they left, Lyric and my mother came in and did the rest."

"Your mom? Oh, now I feel awful. She needs to be home resting."

"Today was Lyric's day with her. She doesn't go home and somehow finds strength after chemo. Lyric days are the shorter ones, though. Treatment is only four hours. She takes a nap and then lets Lyric drag her around the city. Trust me, she'd rather be here than home. She'll rest today."

"I have to get over there and see her. I've just been so swamped with work."

"About that, B. I'm looking for some help for you. We can't have you working like this."

"I know. I'm in interviews with a manager, now. The night shift is the first one I want to cover. The night crew is great, but I need someone to cover for me after six. I at least want to be home by seven every day."

"That sounds much better than eleven and twelve every night."

"I know. I'm always so tired once I get home, but I never feel tired when I'm at work."

"Because you're doing what you love so it doesn't feel like work."

I closed the distance between us, wrapping my arms around her frame. When I leaned down to kiss her, she stood on the tips of her toes to meet me.

"Why are you being so damn good to me?" she wrapped her arms around my shoulders and posed.

"Because I'm begging with my actions and not my words. Am I doing a good enough job at it because I can do more?"

"You're doing a great job, baby, but more is always ideal."

"You like it?" Hearing her say it would feel the unfamiliar void that had developed as her closet was being created. I kept wondering if it would overwhelm her or show her just how welcomed she was at my place. It's where I wanted her to be and comfortably, making it both our home.

"I love it," she admitted.

"What about this?" I asked her as I slid two fingers into her piping-hot pussy.

The gasp that exited her body made my dick stand. She wanted clothes on, but I wanted her naked and riding my dick. Unfortunately for B, whatever I wanted, I got.

NINE

brisleigh

THE EMPTINESS of the side of the bed brought a smile to my face. I remembered his morning routine like the back of my hand. Though he hadn't played basketball seriously since his high school injury during the championship, his athleticism hadn't wavered.

He still maintained the build and that was due to his healthy proportions during mealtime, gym frequency, and morning cardio sessions. Running was his exercise of choice for cardio. He ran up to five miles each morning, depending on where his mind and heart were at the time of the run. Yesterday, he'd run two miles out and two miles back, starting at 4:30a.

"Headed out?" I yawned as I felt Laike re-enter his bedroom.

"Yeah. In a minute. It's a light day. A mile out and a mile back."

That was music to my ears, piquing my interest, instantly.

"Can I come?" I rushed out, sitting up in bed and pulling the cover over my naked body.

"You sure?" I could see his smile through the hazy, navy blue streak of light in his bedroom.

"If you don't mind. Yes. I'd love to."

"When have I ever minded, B? I loved when you ran with me, even though you slow me down. The conversation is always good and it helps me get through the run without even thinking about it for real."

"It's not always good," I reminded him as I tossed the cover from my body.

I didn't want him waiting for me. When he was ready to walk out of the door, I wanted to be right behind him.

"Baisleigh, I'd like to move forward, baby. We can't do that if we stay in the past."

The last time I decided to go on a run with Laike was the day that he broke my heart. We'd both had something to tell one another. I was so excited for the run and the news I had to share with him. However, I made the mistake of letting him share his news first. I thought it would be good news – like mine. But, it wasn't. It was the most devastating news I'd ever heard, and I was still somewhat recovering from it.

"I'm sorry, B. I'll tell you that a million times, but I don't want to keep being reminded of how I hurt you... at least not when I'm trying to make it right. I'm sorry. I'm sorry. I'm sorry. I'm sorry. I'm sorry."

He sat on the bed next to me, grabbing each side of my face as he stared into my eyes with those big, brown ones of his that every Eisenberg possessed – except his mother. Hers were a bit lighter with hues of olive sprinkled throughout.

"I'm sorry. I'm sorry. I'm sorry. I'm so fucking sorry."

With each word he spoke, he ripped another piece of the bandage off the parts of my heart that I'd tried to heal on my own.

"I'm sorry. Every day, I'm sorry. Every evening, I'm sorry. Every night, I'm sorry. Every time I look at you, I'm so sorry. Trust me when I tell you that I am truly, utterly sorry for the pain that I caused you. You didn't deserve that. Nobody does, but you especially. Let me make it up to you for the rest of our lives, but please don't keep reminding me.

"As I watch how much you've grown since our split, it's punishment enough. You did this without me. I've missed so much of your life, our lives, although we've always been right around. Being around and being there are totally different, and since you've been back in my life I'm noticing just how much of a difference it is. I'm sick to my stomach thinking about the time that we've missed because of my pride and selfishness.

"But, I can't change that now. All I can do is make better choices and better memories, ones that top those that are at the forefront of your mind... the ones that hurt you most."

"It wasn't all bad, Laike."

"Shit, it feels like it. One decision I made seems to have overpowered anything else in our relationship. I had a good time with you, B. I enjoyed every second of our time together. I just can't even remember half the good because that one memory is blocking the rest of them. The good ones. Got a nigga feeling like a villain."

"You're not. You're human. And, I'm sorry, too, for continuing to throw that in your face. I'm sorry."

The bandages were ripped off, leaving me exposed and vulnerable. But, I knew that it was the only way to truly heal from the hurt of our past. Laike was trying his hardest to assist, and I wanted to fully invest in the idea of giving him the chance to. I didn't owe it to him, but I thought he deserved it. Honestly. Truly. Deserved it.

"Put on some clothes before I get my cardio in without even leaving bed."

"No sir. Let me get up. I just hope my legs work after the night... morning we had."

I stood and was surprised that I managed my weight without falling on my ass. Laike had a chip on his shoulder and a point to prove it seemed. He didn't show any mercy on me throughout the night or during our wee hours of the morning session. I wasn't complaining, but I imagined I'd be stuck in bed until duty called this morning.

"Hmmmm. My legs work." I chuckled.

"Ummm hmmm. Barely," Laike replied as he reached over and pulled me between his legs. "Come 'er."

My hands, naturally, rose and caressed his cheeks. He was the most precious thing I'd ever seen. He was also the most misunderstood human I'd ever come across. To the world, he was an arrogant, self-centered asshole but to me he was perfection. His humor and filter-less words weren't everyone's cup of tea, but it was perfect for me. He was perfect for me.

Laike was the most loving being I'd ever met, though he had a way of concealing it for the most part. For eight years, I watched him suffer through Luca's sentence, yet still took care of him and Lyric during his time of incarceration. And, Lyric, she was his entire heart. It was surprising that he had any space left for me, but he managed us both and did a fantastic job at it. His parents, whom he loved dearly, had raised a fine gentleman and having him all to myself was a gift that I didn't take for granted.

"Listen, B. I'm deeply sorry. I know my words aren't enough so hopefully my actions are all the confirmation and validation you need that this is it for me. This is it for us. From here, we grow old and keep getting richer together. Nothing less than the best life for either of us. If you feel me slipping, reel me back in. If I feel you getting scared, I'll reel you back in. We both want this and that's what's going to make it work. I promise. I love you, baby girl."

"Too much," I replied.

"Sometimes, I wonder if it's even enough.

"But, it is. I know it and so do you."

"I'm going to put a ring on it and sit my ass down, Baisleigh. I just want you next to me when I do."

I rubbed my fingers through his soft hair.

"I'm right here, love. I'm not going anywhere."

"Thank you."

As the words left his mouth, he pulled me even closer, wrapped his arms around me, and rested his head on my stomach. He squeezed my body, tightly, before letting me go a few seconds later.

"Get dressed, B. I almost sucked your pussy right from between your legs just then. If I wait any longer, I won't be taking that run."

"Shit, I don't even have anything appropriate for running here."

"Did you forget about that big ass closet I just had built and filled for you?"

My memory came back, slowly, and with a smile. I nodded in response with a chuckle.

"Good dick tends to do that to you." I revealed.

"Ummm hmmmm. Go get dressed."

I turned around and headed for the closet. When I felt Laike's bare hands pulling my back into his embrace, I knew that I was in trouble – the good kind. A hard, pussy-pulsating slap caused my ass to jiggle. I could feel myself cream as I rubbed the spot that Laike had just assaulted.

"Ouucccch, baby," I whined.

"Let me kiss it," he suggested.

When his lips touched my skin, my fountain was activated. He sucked the pain right out, using his tongue to help patch the invisible wound. And, when I was least expecting it, I felt its wetness swipe my pussy.

"Baby, what are you doing?" I rushed out, gratitude filling me to the brim.

"What the fuck needs to be done. This pussy too wet to pass up."

"We're..." I stuttered as I felt him stand straight up behind me. "We're supposed to be running."

"Only person about to be running is you, B. Bend over the bed and shut the fuck up."

His words were stern, hard, and demanding. He didn't wait for me to take action. Instead, he twirled my body around and placed both of my hands on the bed. I tried preparing myself mentally for the damage that was about to be done, but nothing could prepare me for the moment he entered me. And, just as he'd assumed, I began my sprint up the bed in an attempt to get away from him. He was so deep in my stomach that I could almost feel him coming up through my rib cage.

"Laaaaaaaaaaaiiike."

"If you be a good girl and cum twice for me, I'll give this pussy a break tonight," he lied.

Through those perfectly aligned teeth of his, he flat out lied. There was no way he planned on giving me a break and there was no way I would let him. The night hadn't even come, yet, and I was already looking forward to having his dick down my throat and buried between my walls. He was addictive and as much as I could have him, I wanted to.

"Baby," I begged.

His strokes were lethal and his girth was maddening. With a hand on my shoulder and one on my waist, he made it impossible for me to find relief from his deadly blows to my backside. Our skin slapped against one another, assuring me that he was balls deep inside of me and giving me every possible inch of him. When I felt his fingers at the opening of my asshole, I knew that I was done for. Two, possibly three slid in with ease.

"Waaaaaiiit. Please."

"Ummmm. Hmmmm. Cum for daddy, baby. Make that pussy talk to me."

"Laaaaaaike, I'm cumming."

My center splintered and released a stream of liquid that forced him out of me. With his dick, he tapped my pussy until it was completely drained. My sensitivity increased to the point that even that was too much to handle. To give myself a chance to recuperate, I fell to my knees in front of Laike, ready to worship him for old, new, and next.

"That's right, big girl. On your knees. Open up and let me put this dick in."

I obliged, opening wide to accommodate him.

"Clean that dick off. You made a fucking mess."

Laike began stroking my throat just as he had my pussy, making me drip more and tingle even harder. I desperately wanted to close my eyes, but I refused to miss a moment of him. My orbs were locked in on him, loving every second of his performance. He never disappointed.

laike + baisleigh

"I'M sure that wasn't as effective as your run," I joked after we finally exited the shower.

My throat would surely be bruised by the end of the day. The way he'd fucked my mouth in the shower, again, I'd possibly need a splint just to help me hold my neck up and keep it from falling off my shoulders.

Nevertheless, the satisfaction on his face was well worth the injury.

"It sure as hell felt better than it, so I'm cool with that. If I come home early, I can get it in, then."

"I'm going to try my best to do the same."

My clothes were laid out neatly on the bed. I couldn't remember putting them there, so I imagined Laike had done so before joining me in the shower. Whatever the case was, I was thankful. The black top and jeans to match were perfect. He had even added a pair of Chanel tennis shoes that I was sure Lyric had picked up for me.

"We're getting each other's clothes out, now?"

"Whatever to make your morning easier," Laike nonchalantly said.

Acts of service and gift giving. Those were his love languages. It was a sure way to tell that he was into you and from the looks of it, he was very into me. Words of affirmation, that's what made my heart throb and when you knew I was feeling you.

"Well, now that I know, I'll make sure your threads are ironed and creased for you each day," I joked.

"For what? If I wanted a maid, I'd hire one. We're not doing that, B. I don't want a server. I want a partner – one who doesn't lift a finger unless she has to."

"You're turning into one of them ones, huh? You want me walking around here barefoot and pregnant?"

"Na. Not really, but barefoot will do."

"What's up with you and not caring to be a father?" I asked, truly wanting to know.

He was always on the fence about it. One minute he was considering it, the next it was a complete no, and then he was begging me to have his baby. This had gone on since we were in the late stages of our relationship. I never knew which was truly his preference, but he knew that I wanted to be a mother and was willing to give me what I wanted when I was ready. I wasn't, yet.

"Shit scary," he admitted, pulling his shirt over his head.

"What are you so afraid of?"

"You met my father before?" he asked, being sarcastic.

Of course, I'd met his father before.

"Don't play, Laike."

"Aight, then. That's the answer right there."

"I don't understand."

"He's a good man, Baisleigh. A damn good man. He's an even better father. Like, too fucking good of a father. And, to be quite honest, if I can't be that good then I don't want to do it. You know?"

His revelation stunned me into silence. The hesitancy to enter fatherhood all made sense to me now. Because his father was so damn good at his job, it made Laike afraid that he'd fall at being as good. And, if he couldn't be that good, he didn't want to do it at all.

"Have you met your sister?" I said to him as I

walked over to him, slowly, watching as he finished putting on his clothes.

"Shit. If I haven't, my pockets have."

"And your heart," I reminded him.

"What about it?"

"It knows her, too, and it has cared for her since she was just a baby. You've done such a good job with her that you've taken the weight off your father's shoulders... and Luca's for the eight years he was away."

"And, what about it?"

"That's fatherhood, Laike. It might not always look the same, but it's the same in the end. Your fears are valid. Your father is a very good man. But, so are you."

"Nah, that nigga ain't failed as nearly as much as me."

"You haven't failed. So what you injured your knee during the championship game. So what you made the decision to end a relationship that you didn't want to completely destroy. So what you haven't always made perfect decisions. You've never quite failed. You don't give yourself as nearly as much credit as you deserve, Laike, and it's time to stop that."

"I happen to think you'd be a great father and before you leave this earth, I'm going to show you how true it is. But, only if you want to. And, somewhere deep inside, I know you want to. I know you, baby. I know you want fatherhood. I see the way you look at Luca and his family. Now, Lyric and Ken. Don't strip yourself of that chance because you're afraid. I'm afraid, too. So, let's do it scared, together."

"Lucas... he was the one. He was the one that made me realize that maybe I could, ya know?"

"Yes. I do know. Ever's girls made me realize just how much I want that for me... and what's crazy is I always imagined it being your face that my child would have. It's insane, but a girl can dream."

"And her nigga can make it her reality."

"After we're married, I'm all in."

"All in," he agreed.

"Let's just be scared together." I sighed, wrapping my arms around his neck and pulling him down for a kiss.

laike + braisleigh

LEAVING Laike in the morning was getting harder and harder each day. As I pulled out of his driveway with him watching closely, I replayed our conversation this morning. He wanted me in the house with my feet propped up. Though I wasn't that girl, I could sometimes be for him. *Heck, for me, too.* Exhaustion was kicking my ass left and right.

It was just that I'd put so much blood and tears into my business that I refused to watch it crumble because I wanted to stay home and let others run it for me.

Laike was constantly drilling it in my head that once you got to my status in the restaurant industry, it was okay to disconnect a little and hire people who could handle things in my absence.

The only issue with that is, *Baisleigh's House* was my baby. No one loved her like I do, which made it difficult to hand her over to someone else knowing they didn't. Even the thought made my stomach turn.

I straightened my wheel and shifted my gears as my heart ached from the reality that the rest of my day would be spent without my man at my side. It was agonizing, the realization of it all. I wanted to crawl back in bed with him and cuddle my sorrows away, but I couldn't. I had to put on my big girl panties and tackle the day.

Everything about my truck was new to me. It felt weird driving a new vehicle after almost four years with my baby. However, the upgrade was everything I needed. I had a very hard time enjoying the money I was making or seeing it go. I was always at work and always saving as if I'd run out of money somehow. Splurging wasn't exactly my ministry, but I loved being spoiled, and I loved for Laike to be the one spoiling me.

As if on cue, H.E.R.'s song, *Exhausted,* blasted through my speakers when I turned up the volume. The list of things I had to do before the sun set began piling in my mind. It was never-ending and as much as it wore me down, it lifted me up. For so long, my job had been my escape and my therapy. Now that things for Laike and I were on the up and up, I still didn't know how to pull away from it.

Absent-mindedly, I traveled safely to my destination. When I arrived in the enormous parking lot, I found a spot closest to the door that I could. As I walked up to the door, I was secretly praying that I didn't have to wait long. My once-a-year visit to the office plagued me with anxiety that I couldn't shake no matter how empty or full the parking lot was.

The lobby was relatively empty when I walked in. *This has to be a good sign,* I thought as I made my way to the receptionist area. Bridgette, the receptionist, I was most familiar with wasn't the person who greeted me. I'd been looking forward to chatting about her last visit to Baisleigh's House.

"Good morning. Do you have an appointment with us today?"

"Yes. I do. I'm a few minutes early."

"That's fine. We don't mind, especially not with today's schedule."

"Swamped, huh?" I asked.

"Yes. In about an hour and a half, the lobby will be full. Be thankful you grabbed an early spot."

"I've learned my lesson over the years. The earlier, the better. That's why I'm here only thirty minutes after you guys opened the door."

"If you're all signed in, then have a seat for me. I'll call you back in just a second."

"Thank you. I didn't get your name," I mentioned before stepping off.

"I'm Sam."

"Is Bridgette out? Or sick? She's usually the one greeting me."

"No. Bridgette is actually shadowing our nurse. She's been promoted to our in-office medical assistant. Pretty soon, she'll be finishing up nursing school and making the big bucks."

"Yes. That's right. She did apply for the fast-track nursing program last year. She shouldn't have too much longer to go."

"Six more months."

"She'll be finished in no time."

I gathered my purse and phone from the counter so that I could find a seat in the lobby. Fortunately, there were plenty open and available for me to choose from. *One by the window,* I finalized and headed in that direction. The second I was comfortable, I pulled up my Instagram application. It wasn't often that I managed to get time to spend on the app, but when I did, I enjoyed myself.

I'd heard horror stories about people's time spent on the app, but I had only experienced good things. I imagined it depended on who you followed and who followed you. The app had even saved me from marrying a man that was not the one for me and helped me get back to my forever love. I was thankful for that, even though the experience was disheartening.

A slight chuckle escaped my lips as I thought about Nicholas and the fact that I actually hadn't thought about him at all since Laike rescued me from my bed – in my pajamas – that night. It was as if he'd recaptured my heart and created barriers around it that only he had access to.

Was I in love with him? I wondered. *Or, did I have love for him? Or was I trying to discover life outside of the one I'd imagined with Laike and settling for something just for the fuck of it?* The questions swarmed as I found Laike's Instagram page.

My heart drummed against my chest and eyes began to tingle at the sight of his last post and all the others as well. He hardly posted anything on social media. I knew because I always checked. However, he'd made at least five posts in the past few days, and they were all pictures of me or pertaining to me. The first was me at eleven when we finally decided to admit that we were more than crushes for each other.

Even then, I knew. Welcome home, baby.

His caption was simple, but there was so much meaning behind the words he'd posted. He'd made the post the night that he'd taken me on the first date. I still couldn't get over the pajamas inside *Crushed Pepper*.

The one that followed was a picture of our bathroom essentials, mine next to his just as I'd organized them the morning I came over and left in a hurry. There wasn't a caption underneath the photo, but it had garnered a lot of comments. Some from other men around Channing who I was familiar with, all advising him that it was a wrap now that I'd marked my territory. And, I had.

Those were my intentions when I went over, to leave my mark and make sure that it was known who the queen of his castle was. But, crazily, I wasn't worried about or leaving my things for another woman to find. I was solidifying my space as confirmation for Laike. There wasn't a doubt in my mind that I was the only woman, besides family, who'd stepped foot in his place. He didn't roll that way. There was an apartment, townhome, or loft somewhere that housed his women when he wanted to entertain them. That's just how he did things.

As for me, I'd never step foot on whatever property it was because I wasn't in the same category as them. Things between us were far beyond hookups and hideaways. It was home visits and lifetime arrangements for us.

The other posts were all pictures of me from the side or behind, where my face wasn't in the frame. I appreciated him protecting my privacy while simultaneously showcasing his infatuation with me. Those who needed to know already knew and that was enough for us both.

"Baisleigh Carmichael," my name was called.

I shut down my screen, looped my arm through my purse, and headed for the door that was being held open for me.

laike + brisleigh

AS I WAITED in the examination room with my legs cocked and Laike heavy on my mind, I wondered what we'd eat for dinner. Between the two of us, it would be delicious but that still didn't make deciding any easier. I made a mental note to give him a call once I left my appointment to see if he had any ideas. His enormous, walk-in fridge was always fully stocked, so the options were endless.

"Ms. Carmichael," Dr. O'Shea said as she walked into the room.

The nurse had gotten me prepped and ready for her arrival. It was always good seeing her. She was just as young as I was, having graduated school at fifteen and became a doctor by the time she was twenty-three. That type of genius was unheard of. So, her presence was always a gift.

"Dr. O'Shea. It's good to see you."

"Same. Same."

She pulled on a pair of gloves and sat in front of my cocked legs. I waited to feel the plastic enter me and spread my walls but the discomfort from them never came. It was actually her fingers that made me scoot up the bed slightly.

"Umm," she let out before standing again and removing the gloves from her hands.

When she walked around toward the side of the bed and grabbed the big gray machine on wheels that she'd never used during our exam before, my nerve endings split a million times. I was unsure of what was happening and as a woman of few words, O'Shea wasn't saying much, either. However, when she lifted my gown and squirted the warm gel on my stomach, I suddenly felt like I had to vomit.

"So, when was your last period?" she asked, confirming the suspicions that arose from the second she touched the gown I'd been given.

"My periods have been regular. I'm on the ring to keep them regulated. Is something wrong?"

"Babe, your ring is no longer there. From the looks of it, it hasn't been there for a few months, which means it hasn't been active. Right now, your body is taking its time to adjust to the baby. What you're experiencing might feel and look like a period, but it's not. When an egg isn't released, the body doesn't menstruate. It's rare, if not impossible, for a woman to have a period when carrying a child. You're as pregnant as pregnant gets, babe. And, we're not talking a few weeks, either." She placed the wand on my flat stomach and began swirling it around.

My heart sank into my stomach. *Nicholas. Fuck!* There were less than a handful of occasions that we'd been clumsy during our relationship, but I'd sworn by my birth control all these years and knew that I was safe from pregnancy until I was ready for children. I'd been on birth control for the last ten years and though I wasn't participating in risky behavior with the men I casually dated here and there, it was a lifesaver.

I hadn't even had as much of a scare since I'd started. Three times a year, I changed the ring out and got a new prescription that lasted the entire year during my annual appointments. Today was the day for a new prescription, but it seemed as if I'd be walking out with what looked like an ultrasound, instead.

"How far along am I?" I asked, voice trembling.

The room grew cold, brutally cold, at once.

"Well, with your abnormal bleeding, it'll be hard to tell. From the cervical exam, I'm guessing at least three months."

"Three months?" I scoffed.

My day had quickly gone from sugar to shit. However, when the whooshing sound settled and a loud, boisterous heartbeat could be heard throughout the room, I melted. I'd only remembered hearing that sound once in my lifetime, but it was one that I'd never forget. Tears stained my cheeks as I turned toward the monitor to see what my doctor was seeing.

"I can't be certain, Ms. Carmichael, but according to the measurements I'm taking," she said as she punched the machine over and over, "about fourteen and a half weeks, give or take a week."

"So, almost four months?" I did the math in my head.

"Not quite, but soon."

Fourteen weeks ago, Nicholas and I made things official. Our relationship was founded fourteen weeks ago and that very night, when he laid me to bed, we did things that we shouldn't have been doing had I known my birth control was inactive. My stomach knotted as she continued to probe, but the sweet sound of my baby's heartbeat kept pulling me back to the center of things.

"A healthy baby – do you want to know the sex of your baby?"

"You can see that already?"

"I can."

"I guess there's no reason to wait. I might as well get hit with it all at once."

"You're having a boy, Ms. Carmichael. A healthy baby boy from the looks of it."

"I don't understand, Dr. O'Shea. None of it makes any sense."

"The part where you had sex or the part where it resulted in a baby?"

"None of it. I was on birth control. If it's no longer in my vagina, then where is it? And, why am I still bleeding every month? Why haven't I felt any changes or movement? And, why isn't my stomach growing?"

"I see this all the time. Women coming in for chronic pains only to be rushed into labor and delivery at the hospital across the way to have a full-term, healthy baby. Periods in question, some light bleeding the first few months, stomach never grew, and never felt a thing. This happens, Baisleigh. You're not the first and you won't be the last. It's the craziest thing, how much of a mystery the woman's body still is. Now that you know, how are you feeling about it?"

I allowed her words and her question to sink in before answering. As beautiful as the heartbeat sounded in the distance, I couldn't deny the burden it immediately placed on my shoulders. A child with Nicholas meant a lifetime without Laike. Everything I'd been waiting for was finally happening for me, yet, simultaneously, it was all falling apart. My life, my world, was always in order and as of lately, I felt like I had no control over any of it. The thought drove me insane.

"Indifferent," I admitted, swiping the tears from my eyes.

"And, that's okay. You were taking preventive measures so this obviously wasn't in your deck of cards. Now that we're here, we have to make the best of the situation. Is there anything that I can do as your doctor to help?"

"Just help me understand how any of this is possible. I can't feel my baby moving. My stomach is still as flat as it's ever been. There isn't even a bulge.

"Some women carry in their backs – or at least that's what the public calls it – for the most part. You have a lot of room for a baby to grow between your back and your stomach combined. You might end up with a pudge or a tiny gut, but I don't see you getting a full, round stomach like most women."

"Will my baby be tiny?"

"No. I delivered a seven-pound baby from a nineteen-year-old about six weeks ago. She came in for her checkup last week. She never knew she was pregnant and barely weighs one-twenty in wet clothes. Her baby girl is healthy and thriving, eating everything in sight. Some women just carry differently. It doesn't mean your baby will be any less healthy. As of now, baby boy is on the right track. He'll be big and strong at term."

"Okay."

"The impromptu photoshoot that I'm printing the photos for will give you more details and show your measurements. It'll also detail your possible conception date, due date, and full-term date. Because we can't nail down when your last period was exactly, these dates aren't set in stone but they are as close to accuracy as possible. We can finish your annual, now, but things will be a little different."

"Alright," I answered, still stuck in place.

"Congratulations, Momma," she cheered, lowly, understanding my hesitation and astonishment at the news.

laike + braisleigh

"WHAT'S THE MATTER?"

Ditto answered the door right on time. If she'd left me standing out there even a second longer, I would've lost my balance and collapsed. The pregnancy news was so heavy on my heart that I felt like I was going into cardiac arrest.

I fell into her door, finding the first seat that was available while I got my thoughts together. Ditto rushed off and into the kitchen while I hyperventilated. The anxiety that swelled in my body was like nothing I'd ever felt.

When Ditto returned with a wine glass filled with plum-colored liquid inside, my mouth watered. I accepted the glass and placed it at my lips. But, before I could take the first sip, I remembered my new status and sat it down on the table beside me, further confusing my little cousin.

"My life has been a joke for the last what? Four months! First, my ex comes into my life and fucks me silly after revealing his mother's cancer has returned. Then, my anxious ass rushes into a relationship two weeks later, trying to fill the void he's left all those years ago. All I wanted to do was forget him. Two and a half months later, I'm engaged and seemingly happy."

"But, really, just masking my true desires and settling for what I could have versus what I really wanted. My ex acts an ass as if it wasn't him that I wanted literally the entire time. Then, social media does me a solid and sends several women to me wearing the same bubblegum machine ring that I have on my finger.

"I immediately call off the engagement and before I can fall, my ex is picking me up and whisking me away to finally shower me with the love and support I've been craving all these years without him. Our shit is going so good, like so damn good that it's scary. And, for once, since our breakup, I know that this is final for us. Like, this is our happy ending. At least it was until I went to the doctor today and found out I'm fourteen fucking weeks pregnant with Nicholas' baby!"

"WHAT?" Ditto yelled, dropping the cup in her hand.

I didn't have the words for her, so I replaced them with tears instead.

"Oh, baby. Pregnant?" she followed up with.

I nodded, unable to produce any words. Everything was caving around me and for once, I didn't know what to do about it. I was so accustomed to having my things in order that the chaos I was facing was foreign territory for me.

Ditto understood me well. Though I'd come over to vent, I appreciated space. She began cleaning the mess she'd made as she waited for me to settle my emotions.

Once we were both finished, I finally began speaking again. It wasn't easy. I could barely get a word out. My chest shook, and my eyes watered every time I tried to say something – say anything.

"Fourteen weeks pregnant, babe? Wow. And you don't even look like it."

"I know."

"Do you feel any different?"

"No."

"When was your last period?"

"They're regular, well at least it seems like it. Maybe they haven't been, and I've just imagined they were. There has been bleeding even though not the heaviest."

"My God. I've watched this on television. There was an entire show dedicated to women with phantom pregnancies. There are no signs but the babies are there, like little ghosts. Most didn't know until they were pushing them out on a bathroom floor or at the emergency room. There is just no way you're almost four months pregnant and you're not even bulging."

"Like, nothing!"

"At all. I would've noticed."

"Me, too."

"And, aren't you on birth control?"

"I thought I was. Apparently, it's somewhere floating in my fucking womb, too!"

"What nigga done pushed your stuff all the way up

there, Baisleigh? Let me find out you're rolling with the big dogs."

"If size is the factor, there's only one man capable of that and it's Laike."

"So, what do you mean you're pregnant with Nicholas' baby?"

"Laike pushing my birth control out of place means that it was still very much so working, active, and in me the night that we were intimate and that was four months ago. I'd at least be sixteen weeks by now – at minimum. Two weeks after that is when Nicholas and I made our relationship official, and we did things that we obviously shouldn't have been doing. Now, here I am."

"Are you going to tell him?"

"No. Well, not yet, anyway. I'm just trying to figure this all out."

"He deserves to know," Ditto expressed.

"I know. I mean... I don't know. I don't want anything to do with Nicholas, Ditto. I'm trying to start a life with Laike and give him babies... not my ex. If it's left up to me, he'll never have to know about this baby. But, I know I can't have it my way. When Laike finds out, that will be the end of us and my child will need a father. I'm kind of just stuck. This is not the way I imagined my life going. If you'd told me six months ago that any of this would be happening, I'd call you a lie to your face. But, look at me, now. Pregnant and about to be a single mother with no man and no ring. Why does

God keep punishing me like this? Every time I try to get my love life together, it falls apart even more."

"Don't say that. It's not fair. Things were getting better, Bais. Just bad timing."

"And, bad paternity, too! I wish this wasn't Nicholas' baby. One of the women that reached out to me is pregnant with his child right now and the other one just had his baby. The child is not even a year old, yet. I'm not trying to be part of their circus. That's why I called off the engagement. He's going to have three children around the same age. I'm not subjecting my child to that, Ditto. I don't have to, either. He's not doing enough for the one he has or the one he has on the way. I'll do this alone before I do this with him."

"But, you're not alone. You're never alone. You know that as well as I do."

"This is so fucked-up, Ditto. Like, I don't understand."

"Life is far too complicated for us to ever truly grasp any concept it shoots our way. Our only option is to deal with it as it comes, all of it. I'm truly sorry that you're dealing with this – any of it – but I would like for you to think about the greatness that follows. You've always wanted to be a mother and here's your chance. Yes, the circumstances are shitty, but we can't change that."

"As far as Laike, I'm so happy he is getting his shit together, but if he decides not to stick by you during this time, then fuck him. Honestly. Please excuse my language. I hate talking like that, but seriously. I love you guys together and it warms my heart to see him trying to make amends but this happened before he decided to get himself together and as a result of him not getting it together sooner. No one is to blame here but him."

"If he doesn't see the error in his ways, then he can crawl back underneath whatever hole he crawled from under. Him leaving will hurt, again, but it'll be worth it. At the end of the day, you have to choose this child over all else."

"I will," I assured her. "From this moment forward. It's so weird, but I already feel the connection. It was almost instant. I'm willing to go to the ends of the earth protecting this child."

"Good, because so am I."

"It's a boy," I cried out. "I'm having a son."

And, he's not an Eisenberg. The thought haunted me.

TEN

laike

ANOTHER UNANSWERED CALL to Baisleigh had me tight in the chest. For the last week, I could hardly get a hold of her. Though I spoke with her several times throughout the day, her dryness made our conversations awkward and filled them with pockets of silence. When she wasn't silent on the other end, she was finding a way to rush me off the line.

The two nights that she'd stayed over to my place

in the last seven days were hardly enough time with her and left me fending for more. Because I knew that her period had come, I was trying my hardest to understand. It was the most difficult five days of her life and everything leading up to those days felt like pure hell for her.

She was on day four, and I was praying things got better as we closed out the chapter for the month and moved on. I made sure to jot down the date so that I could remember when to give her more grace and fill her with even more love.

Whatever I could do to ease her discomfort and remind her of her greatness, I would. Today, flowers were on the menu. When she walked into her home, I wanted her to be reminded of how beautiful and how loved she was.

The sound of my front door opening caught my attention. I grabbed the iPad from the charging dock so that I could get a look at the camera. There were only a few people who could gain access to my home without me unlocking or opening the door for them.

Lyric, I finalized after seeing the Bentley truck in my driveway. When she rounded the corner, heading straight for the kitchen, I shook my head. She was overly pregnant, irritated, and still stuffing her face.

"What are you doing in here?" she inquired, frustratedly as she pulled the fridge open and walked inside.

"Well, I do live here and what's the matter with you?"

"Besides the obvious... you know, pregnant and hungry as hell... Nothing. Just ready for this baby to come. My back has been killing me for two days. Let's not mention these fake ass contractions. Like, why put me through this hell?"

"That's what happens when you're spreading your legs or whatever."

"Oh, shut up!"

She reappeared with a bowl of freshly cut fruit that were a result of the weekly grocery delivery. I watched as she devoured them while taking a seat on one of the stools that were underneath the island.

"Don't you want to cook for me?"

"Not really. I've got shit to do. What if I order you something?"

"From *Baisleigh's House*?"

Her eyes widened as she perked up.

"If that's what you want."

"No. Not really. Food sounds good, but I can't keep anything down right now. I just wanted to see if you still loved me."

"Always," I assured her. "Don't insult me like that."

"Speaking of Baisleigh, where is she?"

"Dodging me, it seems."

"I doubt that one. The woman is smitten, okay? What makes you think she's dodging you, anyway?"

"She's pretty much been MIA on me for the last

week. We were kicking it and everything was going good. Then, bam. I can't even get her to answer my calls or stay on the phone with me longer than a few minutes. She's been super short and dry lately."

"Completely unlike Baisleigh."

"Exactly! Before you walked in, I tried to call her. She didn't pick up."

"Oh, man."

"I'm just wondering what the fuck is going on. Like, what's up? Is it me? Is it something I'm doing or not doing?"

"Have you considered the fact that she might just be overwhelmed and needs a little quiet time? In the last few months, she's gone from single to dating exclusively to screwing her ex to getting into a relationship to being engaged to calling off an engagement to being back with her ex... all while working and keeping her business afloat. It's a lot. You should take that into consideration. I'd be pulling my hair out right now if I were her."

"I have thought about that shit. That's why I'm wondering if shit between us was too soon."

"I don't think that one bit. I just think you two need some time together and away from all the distractions."

"Yeah, but she's been working her ass off."

"That's even more of a reason to get her out of that damn restaurant. Take her somewhere with little cell-phone reception and make her really focus on finding peace even if it's temporary. Show her a good time. Reconnect and get her to open up to you. Help her communicate."

"Something like a little cabin in the wilderness?"

"That's perfect. A cabin. One of the ones with a full layout, though. Not the basic shelter ones. My girl will be even more stressed. Put her up nicely. One of those small, glamping settings will suit her well."

I was already on the iPad searching for a spot that we could kick it for the weekend.

"You going out with them, tonight?

"Yeah. Meeting them niggas in about two hours."

"I'm so jealous. I can't wait to have this little girl so that I can finally go outside. I miss outside." She pouted.

"What's outside for you, Lyric?"

"Niggas and drinks and music."

"Ken going to cut your fucking head if you play with him."

"Keanu knows not to play with me. I keep that thang on me. Okay. And, I have no problem showing him how well it works. And, I like seeing but never touching, okay. I have exactly who I want but it doesn't hurt to look."

"Yeah, aight."

"So, tell me you don't even look another woman's way since you made things official with Baisleigh?"

"We're not talking about me, though.'

"Exactly!"

"Come on. Get your fruit bowl and get your ass out of here. I've got shit to do and it's late. I don't want you going in the house alone this late. Where that nigga at, anyway?"

"Dooley. He'll be back in time to get ready."

"Aight. Then, I'm about to follow you home."

"Laike, the boogeyman is not going to get me." She sniggered.

"I know, because I'll be right there waiting on his ass."

laike + baisleigh

"I'M WITH MY NIGGAS. But I miss you. Girl, don't get it twisted. Can't wait 'til I see you, hug you, and kiss you."

Rod Wave amongst others was the soundtrack to my shower. As I wrapped the towel around my waist, I sang along to *Letter from Houston*.

"I've been thinking 'bout you. Yeeahhh."

I stepped into my bedroom where my clothes were laid out neatly on the bed. Beside them was a bottle of lotion that I'd been using more than my own. It was Baisleigh's honey and oats body moisturizer. Before grabbing it, I halted and took a second to really consider all that she'd been through in the last few months. It hadn't been easy for her and for a while, I'd contributed to her stress.

Come on, B. Talk to me, I urged as if she could read my thoughts.

I turned on my heels and headed back into the bathroom where my phone was. She was so heavy on my heart, and I just wanted her to know that I was thinking about her. Whatever was going on in that pretty head of hers, we'd get through.

Face recognition unlocked my cell. I chortled, realizing it was still on her contact. She was giving me the blues. I tapped the message button and opened our text thread.

> Take the weekend off (no exceptions). I'm kidnapping you so that we can spend some time loving on each other. I miss you very much. I'm not sure what's on your mind or what's on your heart, but I'm here. I see you. I feel you. Call me when you're feeling up to it. Don't take too long, or I'll be forced to come and see about you. I love you, B.

I sent the message and laid my phone on the counter. With a lighter heart, I could finally get dressed and head out. I was running a little behind, but we hadn't set a definite time to meet at our usual spot. If Luca and Ken arrived before me, they had no issues keeping themselves busy until I showed my face.

It didn't take very long to throw on the Balmain jeans, shirt, and shoes that I'd chosen. It was a light night, nothing too over the top was coming out of my closet. I topped it off with a quilted jacket to shield me from the November winds of Channing. They weren't a joke and would have you sneezing and coughing if you played with them.

I stepped out of the house with a blunt to my lips and a cup in my hand. When I slid into my whip, I sat my cup in the holder and stashed a full tin of blunts in the dash. I wasn't sure what type of night I was in for with the guys, but I was hoping for a good one. If it ended at Baisleigh's crib, it would be the perfect end cap. I wasn't banking on it, though. I wanted to give her whatever space she required. I knew that she'd come to me when she was ready. If it wasn't before our weekend trip, then we'd hash shit out then. Either way, she wasn't going to keep last much longer and neither was I.

When I arrived at *Oat + Olive* for their Tuesday set, I wasn't surprised to see the valet line down the street. Refusing to wait, I whipped through traffic and pulled into the parking lot beside the waiting cars. The attendants immediately recognized my whip and came running to assist me. I stepped out and dug into my pocket to retrieve a few bills.

I handed four twenties to the first attendant that reached me and told him, "The fob is in the cup holder. Don't wreck my shit."

The line to get inside was even longer than the line to park. There was no way I was going to wait in either. I made it up the slight incline and to the door. Just as I was about to motion for Dooney, the bouncer we'd all grown to love, I felt a hand on my arm. I turned, quickly recognizing the voice that followed.

"Hey stranger," Ashlyn said, smiling from one ear to the other. "You want to take me inside with you?"

"Na. Not really," I admitted, removing my arm from her grasp and putting space between us.

"The line is long and my feet are hurting, already. I was thinking I could go inside with you, have a few drinks, and end our night at my place."

"You got you some toothpaste yet, or you still holding onto empty tubes?"

"Laike, are you serious right now?"

"Dead serious. Whatever we had going on is dead, Ashlyn. I'm spoken for and even if I wasn't, it wouldn't be shit between us. But, you know this already."

"Is it the girl I saw you with?" She sucked her teeth and placed a hand on her hip.

"It doesn't matter who the fuck it is. It ain't you. Cut your losses. It's a whole spot full of niggas. Choose one. They'd gladly wash your back with them dirty ass washcloths."

I wasn't sure what she said or if she even said anything else because I'd tuned her out, completely.

"Dooney. What's up, my boy?"

As we slapped hands, I slid him the hundred-dollar bill that I'd retrieved along with the valet money when I got out of my car.

"Shit. Shit. Them niggas in there waiting on you."

"Right on," I said, stepping forward and past the metal detector.

If my strap didn't make it in, neither would I. Wherever it wasn't invited, I couldn't attend. It was that simple. My safety and security were above all else. Dooney understood that which was why he said nothing as I walked through. It was understood that my piece was present.

At our usual table, I found Luca and Ken, both with drinks in their hands. In front of the empty seat was a third cup that I could see was filled with brown liquor. The sight of it quickened my pace. I made it to the table in little to no time.

Yeah. It's about to be one of those nights. I nodded before greeting both Ken and Luca.

"What y'all old, washed ass niggas got going on? And, where the wings at? My stomach is touching my back!"

"Your woman owns an entire restaurant. You should never be hungry," Ken pointed out.

"She ain't fucking with him like that this week, remember?" Luca tapped his arm.

"Oh yeah. My bad."

"Fuck both y'all. After this weekend, we'll be back

straight. Just wait. And, I'm not telling you niggas nothing anymore. 'Cause why the fuck would your fat head ass bring that up?"

"Man, have a seat and drink your drink. I know you're stressed and shit. We're here to have a good time. Get out ya chest."

"Whatever," I responded to Luca, taking my seat at the same time. Before my ass hit the seat, I'd tossed back the drink and was ready for another one. "Next round on me."

laike + baisleigh

IT FELT like it was taking forever to get home. The thought of popping up on Baisleigh crossed my mind, but I didn't have the energy to travel the distance. My house felt closer, even if it wasn't. The liquor I'd consumed was settling in, and my intoxication level had gone from *semi* to *highly* on the short drive. When I pulled into my driveway, I closed my eyes for a brief moment and thanked God that I'd made it safely.

I stumbled out of the car but managed to straighten up by the time I reached my door. I was scanned in quickly and given access to my home. When I walked in, my first stop was the half-bath. My bladder was screaming for relief, and I couldn't wait to give it exactly what it needed.

When I made it into the bathroom, I quickly unzipped and unbuttoned my pants before pulling them down my ass. My dick sprang from my briefs. I leaned over and placed a hand on the wall as my world began spinning. My urine hitting the toilet was loud yet satisfying. The balloon that felt like it had been inflated inside of my stomach was finally gone.

"Shit," I breathed out as I shook the head of my dick.

I managed to pull up my briefs but didn't bother with my jeans. They would be coming off as soon as I made it upstairs, anyway. The warm water and soap worked simultaneously to clean my hands. I grabbed a paper towel when finished and headed out of the bathroom.

The kitchen was my next stop. I grabbed a bottle of water and put it to rest within seconds of opening it. I turned it up and didn't lower it until it was empty. I tossed the plastic into the recycling bin and headed out. Too intoxicated to even consider the stairs, I took the elevator, instead.

I entered my bedroom shortly after. The journey down the long hall felt never-ending, but I managed and I made it. The moment I stepped inside, I was hit with a scent of warm vanilla and amber. My heart pounded against my chest at the realization that I wasn't alone. And, for the first time, I hated that my room was so fucking big. It took nearly a lifetime to reach the bed and confirm my suspicions.

Baisleigh laid underneath my covers, comfortably, with a satin scarf protecting her hair. That could only mean one thing. She'd been to Fatima. Otherwise, she didn't bother with the inconvenience. I loved running my fingers through her shit while stroking that pussy from behind so she wore her hair wild and free for the most part.

Excitement drove me to the bed where I stripped out of all my clothing. When I finally climbed in behind B, I was in nothing but my briefs. For once, my dick didn't harden at the sight of her. I was just simply happy to be in her presence. I'd been sick without her, although it was only for a few days.

"I've missed you," I whispered in her ear even knowing she was asleep.

When she maneuvered, turned, and rested her head underneath my chin, I was taken by surprise. She smelled divine and just like that shit she had all over my shower.

"I've missed you more." She yawned. "You smell like liquor."

"You had me tossing them back, trying to get you off my mind."

"Now, why would you ever want to do that?"

"I never said I did. If I was going to survive another night without you, then I didn't have another choice."

"Well, you don't," she assured me.

"I know."

All was well in my world. I wrapped her tightly in

my arms and kissed her forehead. The weekend couldn't come quickly enough. I was ready to take her away from the madness of her world and become engrossed in our own.

"Goodnight."

"Goodnight," I whispered, ready for sleep to have its way with me.

ELEVEN

baisleigh

IT WAS beautiful and just what I needed to reconnect with myself. For the last week, I'd been distant – even with myself. Laike inviting me to spend time with him at the cabin for the entire weekend was the break I didn't even see coming. Luckily, there was a manager on the night shift now, so I wasn't too worried about Baisleigh's House. I was just hoping they didn't destroy the place in three days.

Sideways, I turned and pushed my joggers down slightly. *Nothing.* Not even a pudge was visible. At fifteen weeks, I was at least expecting a bulge. There was nothing. My reflection in the mirror saddened me and excited me, simultaneously.

A mom. In a few months, though I didn't know what my life would resemble otherwise, I'd be a mother. A little baby boy would be peeking his head out of my vagina before finally pushing him out into the world. The thought was both magnifying and heartbreaking. His birth would mean the death of Laike and me, but it was a sacrifice I was more than willing to make.

Laike had chosen himself before. It was time I chose myself, no matter what the outcome was. Over the last week, I'd been mentally and emotionally preparing myself for our ending. No matter how I tried to think about it, I always ended up with sharp pains through the chest, sweaty palms, and shallow breaths.

"B," Laike called out, startling me.

I hurried and lowered my shirt before he stepped into the bathroom. I was so wrapped up in my head that I hadn't even heard him coming in. When he appeared in front of me with curious eyes, I began to wonder if he'd been watching me or somehow suspected I was keeping something from him. My mind was all over the place, which was why I'd tried putting distance between us, but Laike wasn't having it.

The more I pushed away, he pulled me back. Hadn't the circumstances been as they were, then I would've loved the effort he was putting in. But, now, I simply wanted to cut both our losses so that we could get on with our lives. It was obvious that this lifetime wasn't the one we were meant to be in together. Maybe it was the last one or the next one – anything but this one because it simply wasn't working out for us. As painful as it was, it was reality.

"Yeah?"

"The fire is ready. You coming out?"

"Yes. I'll be right there," I assured him.

The helplessness in his eyes was like a dagger to my heart. I wanted so desperately to put his worries to rest, but I couldn't. Anything that fell from my mouth pertaining to the depths of the situation I was in would do more harm than good. So, for now, I'd keep choosing to remain quiet and enjoy the little time we had left together.

"Is it me? Am I fucking up, again?" Laike asked after staring at me for so long without saying a word.

"No. No. No. It's not you, baby. It's me. I promise it's me."

"Then, talk to me, B. You made it clear that you wanted to communicate and here I am... communicating. Talk to me and tell me what's wrong. I can't fix it if you don't tell me what's broken."

"I'm just trying to wrap my head around some things, baby. That's it."

"First it was your period which I completely get, but that has passed and you're still leaving a nigga out here to rot. This isn't you, B. I feel so empty, and I'm right next to you. It's like you're here, but you're not. If this is too much, too soon, then let me know. I'll back up, but I'm not letting you go. I don't care what it is that's happening right now. We'll get through it. I just need a sign or something. I have nothing."

I'm going to be the one to break your heart this time, I wanted to tell him, but the words never came out.

"I'm just having a moment. Please bear with me, Laike. You've done nothing wrong, okay? This will pass."

But, it won't. I cringed.

"Whatever you say, B. You coming out here with me?"

"Yes. Of course. Just give me a second."

"I'll be out by the fire waiting. I'm taking the blankets with me so don't worry about it."

"Thanks."

Defeat covered his handsome features as he turned and walked in the opposite direction. My shoulders sagged as I watched from behind, wanting to call out to him and admit that his intuition wasn't the liar, I was. I hadn't exactly lied, but I was so close to it.

"Laike," I called out to him.

He turned, curiosity replacing defeat. "Yeah?"

"I love you, deeply and wholeheartedly. You are my world, and I just want you to know that. My love for you is unconditional and without restrictions. I'd go to the ends of the earth if it means I'd find you there. I love you. I really, really love you."

"I know, B," he said as he turned, again, and finally exited the cabin.

Too much. What happened to too much? The realization that he hadn't responded with the famous phrase made my body heat all over and my skin itch all over. *Why didn't he say too much?* I panicked, feeling like my heart would explode at any second.

The thought of Laike not loving me back hurt like hell. I'd always thought it wasn't possible, but now I was second-guessing it. With all that I had going on, I doubted that he'd maintain the love he's always had for me. *Always love me, yes, but remain in love with me... no.* That was way too much for my heart to consider.

Feeling him drift too far, I rushed out of tiny bathroom, into the small space that we'd be sleeping in, and out of the door. When I made it outside, there he was, sitting near the fire with a small table in front of him. On the table was raw fish that he'd seasoned and allowed to marinate over the last few hours. My stomach growled at the sight, knowing that it would be divine. Laike had a way with food that I appreciated.

"You good?" he inquired, picking up one of the whole-body catfish and laying it on the grill that he'd started when he did the fire. It was the tiniest thing, but it could easily fit two fish. That's all we'd need in addition to the salad that I'd made and brought along with me.

Because I couldn't leave work until after traffic died down, Laike headed to the cabin without me so that he could get everything set up and ready for my arrival. He wanted to stay and wait for me, but I didn't want to risk ruining the weekend by sharing my secret with him. If we spent that time together on the road, I knew that I would. The hour-drive alone gave me time to myself to think although it was almost all I'd been doing for the past week.

"Yes. Just hungry, now," I admitted with a forced smile.

Nothing felt genuine about the moment except the man in it. I hated that for him, and I hated that for me. But there was no changing the course my life was on, now, and there was no traveling back in time to change the odds of my situation. It was here and once I got a grasp on things myself, I'd put on my big girl panties and share the news with him.

"The doctor says my mom is getting better. It doesn't look like it and neither does it feel like it, but that's what they're saying. Her tumors are shrinking but chemo is so fucking hard on her. The other day, I wanted to just snatch all the cords away, pick her up, and walk her right out of that place. She was ill the entire day, complaining of stomach and chest pains. Even her lips are dry to the point that no amount of moisture will help."

"Her fingertips are so dark. They're at least four shades darker than her skin tone. She hides underneath scarves and hats. My father has covered all the mirrors in the house. She hates to even see her own reflection. I'm trying my hardest to be here and be strong, but shit, B. It's like cancer is eating me up, too. I've done this with her before but this time feels different. It's more aggressive. She's much older. It's like... I just don't want her to leave this earth. I'm not ready for her to go."

"She won't. You said the doctors are saying she's getting better, babe."

"I know, but you just never know with this stuff. What if she doesn't get better? Or what if the chemo stops working? What if her body can no longer handle the torture of it? Ya know? That shit just been on my mind. I haven't been sleeping too well the last few nights."

Me, either.

"You're not there, which means I have far too much time on my hands. All I do is sit and think, sit and think."

"I'm sorry I've been home. I had no idea you were having trouble sleeping. I would've come over. Why didn't you call?"

"Because I didn't want to burden you with my shit."

"Your shit is my shit, Laike. It wouldn't be a burden. Ever."

"Yeah?"

"Of course."

"Then why are you fighting your silent battles alone? Why isn't your shit my shit?"

"It is, babe. It's just some things even I can't explain."

"You could try."

"I would if there was something to explain."

With a nod, Laike signaled that he understood. I knew that he couldn't possibly comprehend though, because not even I did.

"I just wish I could pay a fee and this all be over with. All of my problems are easily handled with a few dollars, but some just don't work that way. This cancer shit surely doesn't."

"You're right, but there's a bright side here. She's getting better. It's only been a few months. How much longer does she have?"

"They were talking six months to a year of chemo. It's looking like she'll be going the full year. It's already taken her breast and her pride," he scoffed, painfully, "I trying to figure out what the fuck else it wants from her? From us?"

I didn't exactly have the words for Laike. So instead of continuing to say things that didn't quite make a difference, I stood to my feet and walked over to him. I pushed his arms apart and lowered onto his lap. His arms felt so inviting. He wrapped them around me as he continued to watch the fish that he'd placed on the grill. After a few seconds, he leaned down and kissed my forehead.

"Are we okay?" he asked, gazing into my eyes.

"Yes," I lied, hoping he didn't recognize the dishonesty.

I'd never lied to Laike, and I'd never planned to, but I was unable to look him in the face and tell him that I was to have another man's child in a few months. I wasn't ready for the loss that I'd just recently gained.

laike + baisleigh

MY BELLY WAS full and my eyes were heavy. Laying in Laike's arms, I watched him scroll his phone, checking sports analytics and returning text messages in his family's group. The security and serenity I felt in his arms were inexplicable. For the moment, all my troubles disappeared. I laid still on his chest as he inhaled, taking in the smoke from the blunt in his hand.

"You remember them stories you used to read a nigga back in the day?" he asked.

"I do."

"You still read that shit?"

"Sometimes. I hardly have time to now, but I sneak at least a novel in every month."

"What you reading right now?"

"*Catch me if you Can* by Alexandra Warren."

"Is it any good?"

"It is, actually. It's a story that happens a little like ours," I explained to him.

"You got it with you?"

"No. I don't. I didn't think about bringing it."

"Aw shit. I wanted you to read it out loud. I used to love that shit."

"Me, too. Even your interest in my addiction to Black Romance books was intriguing."

"Niggas don't know what they're missing. Them little stories got some kick to them."

"They make you feel good, too, about love and the possibilities."

"Yeah. All of that shit."

"I love them so much. I just love Black love."

"I love our love," he exhaled as he said, "and I can't wait to see where it takes us. You and me, for the rest of our lives. That shit excites me more than you know."

"Woah." I giggled, not expecting him to lift from the bed so quickly and pin me down.

He put out the remainder of his weed and shared with me that smile that I'd fallen for so many years ago. When he lowered his lips, I accepted him into my mouth. The gum that I chewed slipped from my tongue onto his. When he pulled back, chewing it, I couldn't help the curve that formed on my face.

Laike sat straight up on his knees and peeled off the shirt that he was wearing. Then, he removed the soft, pajama pants that I'd purchased specifically for our weekend away. He didn't have underwear underneath. When his dick hit his thigh, I swallowed the moisture my mouth created as a result of it.

Once he was completely bare, six-pack staring back at me, Laike began removing my clothes. The shorts that I had on that matched his were the first to come off. Then, the cami followed. His head lowered almost immediately after my breasts were exposed, taking the right one into his mouth.

"Fuck," I groaned, squirming beneath him.

My body was set ablaze. It felt like pins were piercing my body from head to toe. My sensitivity was upped a few notches and so was my arousal.

The amount of pleasure I received from nipple stimulation was almost embarrassing. Shameful, to say the least. However, my man loved sucking my titties as much as I loved having them sucked, so it was a win-win situation for us both.

He switched from the right one to the left, exposing its wetness to the air. The cold breeze kept it hard as Laike's thumb swiped across it over and over. He wasn't being fair because this felt far too good.

"I want you to ride this dick for me," anxiously, he commanded.

As the words left his mouth, he was lifting me from the bed like a limp doll. He sat down, pressed his back against the wall, and positioned me right above his stiff pole. My pussy salivated at the thought of his request.

When he lowered me onto his dick, my creaminess made his entry a bit smoother.

"Sssss," I winced, closing my eyes as he stretched me to fit his girth. Once I hit rock bottom, I rested my hands on his shoulders and balanced my body with my knees piercing the air. Slowly, I slid up and down his hard dick, completely mesmerized by the moment.

"Maybe we should consider some type of birth control. I can't keep pulling out of this shit. It's too fucking good."

"Then don't," I suggested.

There wasn't any more harm to be done. I was already expecting. His semen couldn't produce another child in my womb while one was already growing inside of it. At least, I didn't think it could. Women's bodies, I was learning, were unpredictable and almost anything was possible.

Nothing more was said between us. The sound of my wetness became the soundtrack to our lovemaking. With as much passion and just as much pain, I rode us both into oblivion. Deep down, I felt like it would be the very last time that I'd spend such a precious moment with Laike. He didn't deserve the pain that I was about to bestow upon him. For the rest of my life, I'd be forced to face the fact that I caused it.

As a result, I poured my whole heart into every move that I made. His hands gripped my sides, assisting me in my climb to the top. However, it was his climax that I was chasing. Tonight, it was all about him.

Because for the rest of my life, it would be all about the child that I'd unknowingly created with a man that I wanted no dealings with.

"Baby... fuck," Laike moaned. "Fuck. Cum for me."

"Tonight is yours," I revealed, tightening my pussy muscles around him, trying my best to extract his cum from the head of his dick.

"Fuck. I'm about to cum all in this shit, baby."

Underneath me, he stiffened as the hold on my waist tightened. His soldiers went marching as beads of sweat trickled down my back.

"Shit," he howled as he finally released my waist and wrapped his arms around my entire body. "Shit, baby."

laike + braisleigh

REST MISSED every opportunity to locate me. As Laike slept peacefully beside me, I remained still, staring into the darkness. My thoughts were running wild. Though nature was all around us, the station still played through the Bluetooth speaker that blasted sounds of rushing water and chirping birds through the small cabin.

Because I could no longer sit in silence, allowing my thoughts to consume me, I slipped out of bed. I grabbed my cell phone from the table in the corner of the cabin and tiptoed through the small walkway. When I reached the bathroom, I twisted the knobs on the sink. The water began to run, drowning out the sounds inside.

I rested my bottom on the toilet and my head in my hands. For the first time since I'd visited my doctor's office a week ago, I allowed myself to feel the emotions that had been building. When they hit me, they nearly took me out.

My chest caved and rose as the tears fell from my eyes. The tiny whimpers turned into deep, low sobs that affected my breathing. I felt as if the walls were closing in on me while my world was simultaneously falling apart. Through the blurriness, I managed to unlock my phone and find the contact that I'd been avoiding for a week straight.

I prayed for an answer, noting that it was after nine. She was an early bird and went down with the sun, almost. Her children and business both wore her down, even with the assistance of her loving husband. When I heard ruffling on the other side, there was a calm that settled over me that only she had the capabilities of producing. She was just that damn good.

"Hello," Ever answered the other end.

"I'm going to lose him," I wept.

"Baisleigh, what's the matter, babe?"

"I'm sorry for calling so late, but I just need someone to talk to."

"What's wrong?"

"I'm pregnant," I whispered.

"Oh, babe. What's with the tears, then? This sounds like good news."

"It would be if Laike was the father, but he's not. I found out last week that I'm pretty far along in my pregnancy. About fifteen and a half weeks, now. Laike was nowhere to be found fifteen and a half weeks ago, Ever. He'd left me high and dry. Fifteen weeks ago, Nicholas asked me to be his girlfriend, and I vividly remember us going round for round. I'm not sure that he pulled out each time, but I'm certain he didn't at least once."

"Baisleigh." She sighed, remorsefully.

"I'm afraid to lose him again. I'm going to lose him, Ever. But, I don't want to."

"And, you won't. At least, I don't think that you will. Laike may be a lot of things to a lot of people, but none of those things when it comes to you. He's not that cold-hearted to just leave you because of something that happened in his absence."

"You weren't there the first time. He left me for less."

"No, he left you for so much more. He left so he wouldn't hurt you."

"I wish I had the power to do the same. It feels like way back then, only this time it's me that's going to break his heart. I'm going to hurt him, Ever."

"I won't deny that, Baisleigh. You will hurt him... bad. But I don't think it will be the end of you guys."

"How? I don't see it any other way."

"You won't know until you tell him. Keeping it a secret, that's what will crush you guys. Telling him and allowing him to deal with his feelings so that you guys can see where you go from there, that's the best option here. I just can't see him walking away again. Not after finally getting you back."

"I don't know, Ever. This isn't something small or that can be concealed. It's an entire child."

"Baisleigh, over the last few weeks you've watched Laike do something that he simply doesn't do and hasn't done in over a decade, right? You've seen him fight for your love. You've seen him fight for you. You've seen him out of his shell and ready to risk everything to save the love you both suppressed all those years. You've seen him plead and you've seen him beg for a chance to be in your world again. Right?"

"Yes."

"Then, why are you above that?"

"I don't understand."

"He messed up and even though far too many years passed before he got it together, he did. And, when he did, he put something aside that Eisenbergs just don't. He put his pride aside, finally, and has been fighting nonstop for your love.. For you... for the both of you. Why haven't you considered the option if this goes left? Is your love not potent enough to fight for? Is he not worth fighting for? Pleading for? Risking it all for? You're on my line right now, tears streaming down your beautiful face because you're afraid to lose a man you feel you're meant for. Please help me understand why you're giving up and not gearing up for war."

I remained silent, taking in her wisdom.

"He can only walk away if you let him."

Her words resonated with me, hard. I had nothing to say. I just wanted to listen to her all night long as she filled me with her peace and her love and her protection.

"He showed his behind to get you back, Baisleigh. Don't be afraid to take a page from his book. If that's your man, then act like it. Don't compromise yourself or your sanity doing so but beat him at his own game when it's all said and done. Then, give him a baby, too, because he's going to want one. They're spoiled like that."

"I'd give him one without a second thought. I wish this one was his."

"But it will be. Trust me. You can't tell Luca those oldest two don't belong to him. In his mind, they came out of his nut sack and I'm okay with that. I have no doubt that the same will be for Laike."

"I don't want anything to do with Nicholas. I literally need him. My son will need a father."

"Ahhhh," she sighed, "we're having a boy."

"Yes, I just wish he was an Eisenberg," I groaned.

"He is, by default. By the time you're pushing him out, Laike will have gotten over himself and will be at your side. Trust me on this one, Baisleigh. You have nothing to fear."

"I'm sorry I called you so late."

"It's fine. Luca ran out to get Laura something to settle her stomach. She's not feeling so well. I'm waiting on him to get back."

"I have to get over there to see her this week. I must."

"She'd love that."

"I'm going to let you go. I need to get back to bed before he realizes I'm gone."

"Cheer up, babes. You've got this. It will be hard and your emotions will take a few blows but it'll be worth it in the end. You'll have your man and you'll have your beautiful baby boy."

"I hope so."

"You will. My gut says so."

"You don't even have a gut, Ever."

"Well, you know what I mean. And, congratulations. If you need me, you know how to find me."

"I know. Love ya, honey."

"Love you, too. Goodnight."

"Goodnight," I said as I ended the call.

I stood, afraid to look at myself in the mirror. When I did, I found the puffiest set of eyes, swollen lips, and redness all over my face. I sighed deeply before running my hands over it to clear the tears. Afraid that Laike would wake up at any minute, I turned off the water, flipped the light switch, and stepped out into the hall. I was pleased to find him still sleeping in the bed.

My body fit into his like the perfect piece to the puzzle. When I finally closed my eyes, Ever's words looped in my head.

You're on my line right now, tears streaming down your beautiful face because you're afraid to lose a man you feel you're meant for. Please help me understand why you're giving up and not gearing up for war.

She was right, absolutely and positively. As I allowed sleep to consume me, I began preparing myself for the battle that was to come. No matter how long and how dreadful, I had to come out victorious and with my man at my side.

TWELVE

laike

I COULDN'T REMEMBER the last time I'd slept so well. When I woke up with Baisleigh at my side and numb fingers, I knew that the cabin had served its purpose. The peace and tranquility paired with that powerful ass pussy between my woman's legs left me unconscious.

Fuck. I picked up my phone just to discover it was dead. With it hooked up to the speaker all night, it finally gave out. With only the bit of light that came from the light on the Bluetooth speaker and the rising of the sun, I searched for a charger to get some juice on my phone before my run.

I tried my hardest to refrain from waking Baisleigh, but it was beginning to look like I'd have to. Ten minutes later, and I still hadn't found the charger I thought I'd packed with my belongings. Just as I was about to tap her leg, I remembered seeing her stuff a charger in her purse as I was helping her out of her truck.

I rushed over to the table in the corner where her purse sat. With the little light that I had to work with, I dug through her belongings to find a charger for my phone. I was ready to hit the trail for my daily run. The change of scenery had me anxious.

I located the charger, but not before nearly emptying her purse completely. Just before I began to stuff it with the unnecessary content I'd taken out, one, in particular, caught my attention. The sepia images printed on shiny paper that seemed to go on for miles rested between my fingers, piquing my curiosity. I'd collected enough nieces and nephews to know exactly what I was looking at, but it didn't clarify anything for me. I was still confused as to why it was Baisleigh's name that I saw across the top.

The wind left my body as I lowered it to the ground. My legs felt like slime, unable to manage the weight of my frame or my heart. When I was finally resting on the floor, emotions that I didn't know existed within me were unearthed.

I wasn't a fucking genius, but neither was I a fucking fool. I'd only been in Baisleigh's life for a few weeks. That wasn't nearly enough time to garner such results. It wasn't even enough time to miss a period.

But, she just had a period, I thought to myself. Nothing was making sense to me.

Or was it something else? Another thought entered my mind soon after. It would explain things much better for me.

Is that why she was acting so distant? Had to be. I'd been on my best behavior, yet she'd been pulling away from me constantly.

Did she abort this nigga's baby? I shook my head, completely disregarding that thought. That wasn't like Baisleigh. She'd never do such a thing. She was one to live with her choices and make the best of them.

She's having this nigga's baby? I asked, already knowing the answer. *She's having another nigga's baby*.

The thought was repulsive. I could feel everything I'd eaten over the last twenty-four hours resurface. I stood up, rushed to the bathroom, and hunched over the toilet.

"Urrrrgggggggggghhhhh!"

Everything inside of me spilled from my mouth and into the toilet.

A fucking baby.

"Urrrrrgh."

More came to the surface before coming out.

"Fuck."

And, then there were more. I felt as if I was releasing my insides. At any second, I expected to see my heart in the toilet. I was almost certain it had been excavated from my chest.

This can't be fucking life, man. This can't be life.

My pores opened and sweat poured from them. The cabin felt about twenty degrees hotter than it was when I woke up. My world felt as if it was spinning, forcing me to the floor with my back against the wall.

This couldn't be.

The needles to my eyes, finally released the tears they were after. Like a fucking baby, I sobbed for old and new. The only girl I'd ever wanted and saw myself with for a lifetime was having a baby and it wasn't mine. That was enough to make any nigga drop a tear. I wasn't just any nigga and this wasn't just any girl, so I shed a few.

I wept for the time we'd lost together. I wept for the time we'd spend together. And I wept for the future we were planning for that would never happen. I wept for the losses we'd taken over the year. I wept for the memories we'd made. I wept for me, and I wept for B. Because no matter how hard we tried, life just didn't want to let us be.

laike + baisleigh

I WASN'T sure how long I'd been sitting in the same spot, but it must've been hours. I could still taste the vomit on my tongue as I heard her voice. That sweet, angelic voice of hers called out to me.

"Laike?"

The pain that rested in my chest cavities just wouldn't allow me to look at her. *Fuck.* My eyes stung. This wasn't the way I'd planned to spend our weekend. This certainly wasn't how I'd planned to spend my morning. Yet, here I was, stuck on the bathroom floor with a set of ultrasound pictures next to me.

While this should've been one of the happiest moments of my life, it was the exact opposite because it wasn't my child that was on the ultrasound. It wasn't my child that Baisleigh was carrying. The child, as innocent as it was, didn't have shit to do with me, and that hurt like a motherfucker. Another nigga's seed was swimming in her and that was too hard of a pill for me to swallow.

"Laike," she called out to me, again.

"Another nigga's baby, B?" I asked, words packed with as much agony as I felt.

"I... I'm. I'm sorry," she expressed.

Without even looking in her direction, I could feel

the tears that swelled in her eyes and fell down her pretty face.

"This shit we have... as good as it might be and as much as we might want it... I doubt it will ever survive the unfairness of life. That's a whole fucking baby in your stomach."

"I know. And, I've been wanting to tell you. It's just that as soon as we got our shit together, I'm hit with this. I've been sick thinking about how this will affect us."

"How long have you known?"

"A week."

"Day one, B. Day one. That's when the fuck you were supposed to tell me."

"I was still processing it myself."

"And leaving me in the dark, wondering what the fuck I'm doing wrong. Pushing me away, making me think I'm the one that's insane. Baisleigh that shit was foul."

"I needed time to figure this out."

"When we're in a relationship, you don't get to figure out shit like this on your own. Weren't you the one telling me we need to communicate? Hmmm? You knew that you had information that would crumble me to the core and you chose to keep that from me, anyway? How is that communicating, Baisleigh? How is that fair?"

"I was afraid of losing you. I still am."

"As you should be, Baisleigh. 'Cause, where are we

supposed to go from here? Huh? You think I want to watch you co-parent with another nigga for the rest of my life? Hmmm? Does he know? Did you tell him?"

"He doesn't know, Laike."

"This shit..." I pointed at the ultrasounds, "this shit hurts like a motherfucker."

I found the strength to finally stand on my feet. When I did, I pushed past her and made my way back to the front of the small cabin.

"Laike, talk to me."

"I don't know what you want me to say, B. You could've been talking to a nigga, but you chose not to."

"You did the same!" she yelled, attempting to reason.

I turned around, swiftly, and closed the space between us.

"I did what, B? Left before I broke your heart? You're right. I did. But, if you're trying to justify that with a baby, then try again."

"Hadn't you, then none of this would've happened."

"Blame everything on Laike. That's your plan? Though it sucks, I'm willing to take the blame for this shit if it makes you feel better. Whatever for Baisleigh, right? That's my motto, huh?"

I began packing my things, desperate to get the hell out of dodge. I was over it all. This shit was beyond me. Some things there just weren't any coming back from. A baby, in my opinion, was one of them. She'd already fucked up my head when she agreed to marry that nigga.

Then, when she told me that she was happy with his bitch ass, she broke my shit into pieces. Knowing she was carrying his seed was just too much for me to handle. Baisleigh was a big girl. She'd figure the shit out. I wasn't worried about that.

"If it's whatever for Baisleigh, then why are you packing your things? Hmm? Why are you already planning to end this? Why are you thinking about a future that doesn't include me? Why are ready to walk away and toss everything that we're trying to build?"

"Because I'm not giving you another chance to break my shit. You've already done it twice," I stopped to tell her.

"Third time's a charm, right? Isn't that what you said?"

I chuckled, remembering the words I'd spoken at Lyric's baby shower. They weren't true.

"Say something!" she bellowed.

"Ain't shit to say." I shrugged, continuing to pack my things.

"Yes. There is, Laike. There's so much to say. Tell me what's on your mind!"

"You don't want to know what's on my mind, B," I warned.

"But, I do." She pushed back.

"You getting rid of the fucking baby. That's what's on my mind," I admitted.

"I know what that feels like. I can't do that again," she revealed, stunning me into silence as I finally turned around to face her.

"I made a promise to myself that I'd never do it again and I won't. It doesn't matter... the situation doesn't matter. This baby deserves a fighting chance."

"Again?" I asked.

"The morning that we went for a run and you told me that you no longer wanted to be tied down in such a serious relationship at such a young age, we both had something to tell each other. I assumed your news was as good as mine, so I allowed you to share yours first. I wasn't expecting you to break my heart. After you finished telling me that our journey had come to an end, I was gutted."

"Suddenly, the news I had to share wasn't so exciting anymore. And the last thing I wanted was for you to think I was trying to trap you into staying. If you weren't ready to be in a committed relationship, I knew there was no way you were ready to be a father. That's a lifetime commitment. So, instead of sharing the news of my pregnancy with you, I focused on gathering the pieces of my brokenness."

"That very day, I scheduled an appointment with the abortion clinic. Two weeks later, I laid down a young mother and got up a grown woman. When I fell apart, it wasn't only because I'd lost you. It was because I'd lost my child in the process."

"Lost? You didn't lose shit, B. You aborted it."

"I did what I felt needed to be done, Laike. 'Til this day, it's the one decision that I regret in life."

"So not only did you kill my child without my knowledge, but you're telling me that you're willing to keep this nigga's child? Tell me what the fuck I ever did to deserve this type of pain, B? Hmmm?"

"It's not that simple, Laike," she tried to explain.

"Baisleigh, fuck you!" I spat, the words killing me as they exited my lips.

As much as I hated talking to her that way, the pain that settled in my chest wouldn't allow me to be as gentle and as caring with her as I'd always been. I was angry, furious even. The news she'd just delivered was news that I wasn't at all prepared to receive. Leaving anything that I hadn't already packed, I pushed through the cabin, out of the door, and got into my ride. I burned nearly all the rubber from the rims getting the fuck out of dodge.

laike + baisleigh

I DIDN'T TAKE my foot off the pedals until I reached my comfort zone. With the heaviest heart I'd ever carried, I stumbled onto the porch and dug in my pocket to retrieve my key ring. I hated that every home didn't have a system and the fact that some required keys, but tonight wasn't one to complain about anything other than the brokenness I was suffering through.

The sun had risen completely, serving as light through the coziness of the dark dwelling. One foot in front of the other, I continued until I reached the master suite. The sight of the tired, resting body underneath the covers made my heart beat, again. I quickly removed my joggers and jacket, then climbed in bed with my briefs and tee still attached to my body.

"Laike?" my mother asked, eyes still closed.

I wrapped my arms around her warm body and planted my head on her chest without a word. The tears that I'd been suppressing wet her shirt before reaching her skin. Though words failed me, I was hoping she knew my heart well enough to understand what I was facing.

When I felt her hand rubbing against my back, all felt well, but only for a brief moment. Right after, the pain resurfaced. Though I'd gotten a good night's rest, the morning had exhausted me, and I felt far more tired than normally at this hour. On my mother's chest, I closed my eyes and tapped into the serenity her presence offered.

The sound of her heartbeat lulled me. When her hand slowly drifted from my back, falling onto the bed, I knew that she'd fallen asleep, again. I followed suit, allowing rest to rescue me from the hell I was in.

laike + brisleigh

"WHENEVER YOU'RE READY," my mother said to me as she sat across from me at the kitchen table.

On the plate before me, my father had prepared a full breakfast. Though I wasn't interested in eating, my stomach let me know that eating was my best option. With turkey bacon, turkey sausage, scrambled eggs with cheese, breakfast potatoes, toast, and a bowl of grits sitting in front of me, it was hard not to dig in.

"She's pregnant," I said between bites.

Neither my father nor my mother said anything. Forks and spoons colliding with plates were the only sounds heard. After a deep, exasperated sigh, reality finally settled in my soul. I dropped my utensils, hardly wanting to chew the food that was already in my mouth.

"Fuck!" My fist pounded the custom-built, wooden table.

No one said anything. Both kept enjoying their meal as I crumbled. The heaviness weighed me down, pushing words out of my mouth that I'd never utter in their presence if pain wasn't involved. I closed my eyes, squeezing them tightly as I tried my hardest to imagine my world without her, again. As much as I didn't want to, I had to.

"This shit wasn't supposed to happen like this," I explained.

Finally, my father spoke. "How was it supposed to happen?"

"We link back up, fall in love, and start our lives together. I'm supposed to marry her, and she's supposed to carry my child. This isn't how it's supposed to happen."

"Remind me, again, son. Who left?"

"Not right now, Pops."

"Yeah, right fucking now, son. I understand your frustration and your pain, but there's nobody's ass you should be kicking more than your own. You damn near let the girl marry some other cat. You thought a kid wasn't coming next?"

"I thought she was more careful. I thought she was on birth control."

"Well, you thought wrong, Laike. Let's just be honest here, son. You know I love you to death, but I've got to call you out when you're on bullshit and that's exactly what you're on. You talking about you want to marry this woman. You don't even know what the hell marriage looks like. It's more than kisses and hugs. It's the determination to make it no matter what. Had I left your mother for such an extended period of time, whatever she had going on when I returned, I'd be willing to deal with."

"And vice versa," my mother agreed.

"Because, it was my decision that allowed another

nigga to sneak in and bury his bone. You acted a damn fool for weeks when you found out she was marrying someone else. Then, you begged for another chance in her life. All for what? You to chicken out once she gives it to you? Because of a baby?

"A baby that wasn't conceived during your relationship? A baby that could've happened at any time during the what? Twelve or thirteen years you played in every pussy under the Channing City sun? Hmmm? Put your fucking tears away and man up, nigga. Karma is a bitch, and she's a bad one. But, you're an Eisenberg and ain't a motherfucker on earth badder."

He picked up his fork, again, and resumed his meal. I turned to my mother for support, but there wasn't any given. She simply shook her head before she began.

"I wish I could say something to ease your pain right now, but I can't. You asked for another chance and you have one. It's not ideal, but it's the chance you asked for. When you think about it, son, like really think about it... Baisleigh has done nothing wrong.

"I've watched her love you from a distance for so many years. I've seen it in her eyes when she looks at you. I've heard it in her words when she speaks to you. I've seen it in her actions when she's servicing you. She loves you, deeply, but she was forced into a corner. You wouldn't love her back, not fast enough at least.

"That gave another man time to creep in and do damage that can't be undone. Does that mean she loves you any less? No. It just means that you have to love her a little more, even through the pain. Because she'll already be beating herself up the rest of her life for conceiving a child with someone other than you."

My head shook from one side to the other as I listened.

"What are you thinking? What are you feeling?"

"Betrayed," I admitted. "I'd never... never impregnate another woman. Ever."

"I know Baisleigh, Laike. I'm almost sure that this wasn't intentional. You even said it yourself, you thought she was on birth control. Last week you mentioned a period."

"She had one, or at least that's what she told me."

"It's pretty much impossible to have a full period while pregnant. Her body is probably still adapting to the changes. This was not her intention, Laike."

"But it's happening and the baby isn't mine. Do you know how that makes me feel?"

"Like a motherfucking man. That's how it would make me feel, knowing I have a kid on the way. Oh, it's the greatest feeling in the world."

"Pops, it's not my boy!"

"And, a son? Oh, yeah, I'd be popping a bottle of the finest champagne. I remember finding out your mother was pregnant with Luca. I finally felt like I had a purpose in life. I celebrated for seven days straight. I know damn well she was tired of me, but I didn't give a damn. My legacy was going to live on. I was building on the Eisenberg tree."

"Fu– Forget this. I'm out," I hissed, standing to my feet and preparing to leave.

"If you don't sit your yellow ass down and shut up, I'll make sure that you're never able to stand again. Whining like a baby because life is doing its due diligence with your ass, finally. You broke that poor girl's heart all those years ago, and she never fully recovered. Now that it's your heart that's hanging in the balance you want someone to feel sorry for you. I don't."

He never looked up from his plate as he threatened me and then came down on me harder than anyone ever had.

"I'm not asking anyone to feel sorry for me," I assured him.

"Then, why are you here with us instead of working on that future you spoke so highly of with her? Hmm?"

"Because she's carrying another nigga's baby. Have you not been listening to anything I've said?"

"I've been listening, but you haven't said anything worth holding onto. Other than the beauty of welcoming a son."

"It's not my son, Pops," frustrated, I reminded him.

"Oh, but it is. And, we're going to begin preparing as such."

"We're not preparing for nothing," I told him.

"He's not too far off from Lucas. It'll be like watching you and Luca as boys."

"Mom, can I be excused?" I asked.

My pain was quickly depleted by the anger that was festering in my body. My father's inability to see the issue with the situation at hand was even more frustrating than the situation itself. I didn't want to spend another second in his presence.

"Your father means well, Laike. When has he ever meant any harm?"

"Never, but today ain't the day, Mom. It's not the day."

"Go ahead," my father chimed in. "and when you're ready to put on your big girl panties, come holler at me."

Without another word, I stood and bolted out of the door. When I finally settled in my car, I rested my head on the steering wheel. As much as I hated my father's words, I knew he meant well by them, and that's what killed me the most. The type of man he was, I wasn't sure I could ever be. He chose to see the good in every situation and handled the bad accordingly.

As for me, I didn't have the same discipline, maturity, or patience. I wasn't half the man he was, but I imagined it was with time that he'd grown to be the man he is. My time hadn't come yet. Shit, I wasn't sure if it ever would. Because in no lifetime did I want

Baisleigh pushing out the next nigga's seed. I didn't give a fuck how old, wise, or mature I was.

My engine howled as I reversed out of the driveway in pursuit of my home. Everything was a blur on the drive. I didn't even realize I'd made it home until I was inside my garage with my head in my hands, again.

"Fuuuuuuuuuccccccck!" I screamed. "FUCK!"

I exited the car and made my way inside the house through the garage entrance. Without stopping to even drop my keys on the counter, I headed straight for the shower. I needed the water to coax the anxiousness I felt and help me calm my raging heart.

Boom. Boom.

Boom. Boom.

It sounded in my chest, far too loud and far too fast. I arrived at the shower door before sliding it back. The sight of Baisleigh's products that lined the shelves made me sick to the stomach, again. I rushed to the toilet and stood over it, but nothing came out. Once I knew that it was certainly a false alarm, I returned to the shower. This time, I didn't wait for sickness to overwhelm me. I stepped inside, fully dressed, and removed every product that Baisleigh had purchased from the shelves.

I didn't want to see anything that reminded me of her. It made me ill, physically, mentally, and emotionally. I wasn't equipped to fight all those battles at once. So, I found the nearest trash bin and began tossing them inside. One by one, they hit the back of the bin before falling inside and on top of whatever else was inside. I got to the last jar of the body scrub before pausing. It was her favorite. It smelled like a sugar cookie and left me with a sweet tooth that only she could satisfy.

After a long, deep breath, I dropped it into the trash along with the others and stepped away. Now, at the counter, I stared at my reflection in the mirror. Visions of Baisleigh and I over the last few weeks came rushing to the forefront of my mind.

"URGH," I howled, hardly recognizing the strife in my voice or the strength that sent my arm flying in the air.

However, the sound of breaking glass wasn't one that could easily be mistaken for anything else. Neither was the feeling of the warm blood as it trickled down my knuckles and dripped onto the counter. The mirror above my sinks shattered, creating what felt like a million reflections.

I brought my hand closer so that I could see the damage that had been done. With my adrenaline hiked, I didn't feel an ounce of pain beyond what Baisleigh had caused. She'd done a number on me.

THIRTEEN

braisleigh

TWO WEEKS LATER...

IT FELT like an eternity had passed us by, though it had only been two weeks. Laike left the cabin much earlier than I'd anticipated, forcing me to spend even more time alone with my thoughts. I waited for him, two days in a row, but he never showed. As much as I hated the way he'd left and things between us had ended, the time that I was gifted alone was a blessing.

My thoughts settled after the first six hours of nature sounds and constant tears. Once my emotions were under control, my problem-solving skills kicked in, and I began searching for a solution to the issues at hand. By nightfall, I'd come to the realization that I didn't want to fix what was broken between Laike and me. Not yet, at least.

The time that it would take to birth my child into the world, I needed that to focus on the changes that were pending. Trying to fix a relationship just didn't seem to fit on my schedule. I had less than six months to prepare for my world to change forever. There was no time for chasing a man around Channing, begging him to love me when the love I had for myself was enough already.

Did I want to lose Laike? Gosh, no. Not even a little. It hurt to even consider, but I was okay with it, now, because I didn't see any other outcome for the situation. The only fight I had in me at the moment would be geared toward a healthy pregnancy and birth. I refused to let the stress of my love life murder my child in cold blood.

Even with me forcing myself to believe that everything would be well in my world without him, I couldn't quite convince my heart. It yearned for Laike Eisenberg and Laike Eisenberg only. It craved his presence day in and day out. It was as if I desired him most because he was not around.

I missed him. I missed the waking up to him in the

morning. I missed laying down for bed with him at night. I missed our showers together. I missed our meals together. I missed our time together. I missed his heart. I missed his home.

I grabbed a few paper towels from the dispenser in my personal restroom and pushed a stream of hot air from my nose. The weight of my heart was almost too much to bear, but I had no other choice. Laike had made his decision once again. This all felt like deja vu, but this time, I refused to be left broken and ashamed. I'd hold my head high and keep pushing forward. There was more to live for now. My son needed me and somehow, I needed him, too.

I grabbed the apron from the back of the door as I exited the restroom. While making my way back to the front, I tied it around my waist. It was still early morning, but it felt like I'd had a full day already. When I made it to the floor, I noticed the seats had quickly filled with guests that were waiting to be served.

Get it together, Baisleigh, I coached myself. *You've got this.*

"Well, if it ain't Baisleigh motherfucking Carmichael!" Kleu belted in the middle of the restaurant.

I hadn't seen her come in, and I certainly wasn't expecting to see her. Channing wasn't a place she frequented, but when she did, it was always love. Sister of Ditto and easily the finest thing the family had ever seen, Kleu Carmichael was a dream. Her dark skin was completely opposite of Ditto's and evidence that Carmichael genes were strong. With different fathers and the same mother, Ditto took after her dad's people. She even shared their last name.

"KLEU?" I squealed, rushing through my place of business to meet her halfway.

When we finally made contact, our bodies collided and my head immediately fell onto her chest. She was the closest thing to a sister I'd had for many years. Then came Ditto. It wasn't until Kleu turned eighteen and left the city that Ditto and I became a duo. Prior to, there were three of us.

"What brings you in town?" I pulled back as I asked.

"That sad ass face and that sad ass voice of yours. Ditto told me you're having nigga problems, so I thought I'd slide through to cheer you up. 'Cause, if it's one thing we don't do is cry over niggas – not when there's always a better one with bigger pockets waiting for the chance to trick it all."

"I don't want just anybody, Kleu. I want him, specifically."

"Well, I hate to break the news, baby, but it doesn't look like he wants you. But, that's okay, 'cause like I said..."

"He does. He's just sorting things out, Baisleigh. Please don't mind her," Ditto appeared.

"Baby, what type of parking where you trying to

find? I thought I was going to have to send the search team," Kleu said as she turned to face Ditto.

"I was waiting for a spot closer to the door. Thank you very much. Anyway, back to you. How long has he been missing?"

"Two weeks," I admitted, cringing at the thought.

"Oh, baby. We're definitely not chasing that one. He's for the streets, now."

"Please don't listen to her," Ditto interjected, pulling Kleu in the opposite direction.

"Oh, but she should."

"You two have a seat, and I'll be right over to your table." I chuckled, knowing that Kleu was serious.

Finessing men was her specialty. It was her day shift. Exotic dancing was her night shift. She was a force to be reckoned with. Men hated to see her coming... so did their pockets. I didn't blame them one bit. Kleu was irresistible, in every way, which was why I was itching to get back to her. I missed her so much. However, duty called.

"Hi. Welcome to Baisleigh's House. Have you had a chance to look over the menu, love? If so, what are we having?"

I pulled out my pen and pad from the apron but there was no reason. My memory was sharp while on the floor. I could wait on five tables and not get a single order wrong. Once I exited the building, that's when things got foggy for me.

"Baisleigh, is it?" the guest asked.

The small table that she occupied alone was to the far left of the floor. It was reserved for parties of three or less. She'd chosen the perfect spot. It happened to be my area whenever I was on the floor. It was rare that I ventured to the other side, but if necessary, I would.

"Sure is. What can I get for you to drink?"

"You don't remember me, huh?" she asked, followed by tittering that somehow managed to make my flesh crawl.

I finally looked up from my pad to see if I recognized the guest. Nothing came to mind.

"Gas station a few weeks ago."

"I'm sorry. I don't recall. Have you decided on what you'll be eating? Drinking?"

My only goal was to take the order so that I could get the rest of the orders around us and then get back to Kleu and Ditto. They were waiting for me.

"Seeing you kind of made me lose my appetite. I didn't know you worked here. Laike sure knows how to pick 'em. Every one of you that I run into is another downgrade."

"If you haven't noticed, you're sitting in Baisleigh's House, love. Where'd you go to school, again?"

"I didn't say."

"Right. Right. And, I guess Laike has taught you nothing because if you were actually relevant in his world, then you'd be able to identify a boss when you see one, babe. Now, what will we be having? Either you're ordering or getting out of my restaurant."

348

"I'll have an orange juice to start. I need to get my energy up after the night he and I had at his big, big mansion. And do you happen to have warm tea? My throat is a little tender from him getting all excited while down it."

"Orange juice and tea coming right up," I said with a smile.

Hadn't she included the line referring to Laike's home, then her words would've cut me to the core, but I was calling her bluff. Even if what she was saying had happened, it hadn't happened as she'd recalled them. Laike bringing a woman to his home was simply out of the question and that had little to do with me.

He wasn't a careless man, and he protected his privacy by all means necessary. Random women just didn't have a place in his home and for good reason. Laike wouldn't allow it. Lyric wouldn't allow it. Luca wouldn't allow it. And Liam damn sure wouldn't allow it.

I could feel the scrunching of my features as I poured a glass of orange juice from the freshly squeezed jug of juice that we kept refrigerated. I grabbed a tea bag and plopped it into one of my favorite mugs. It was clear and allowed you to see its contents. When I poured the steaming hot water into it, I watched it change to a gorgeous blue before picking it up to examine it. With both the orange juice and tea in hand, I headed for the table that I'd just left.

"Hey, Liz. Do me a favor and get the two tables

over in my section. I haven't taken their order. Just get them started, and I'll handle the rest."

"Sure."

"What's the matter?" I heard from behind.

"And who is that over there? I didn't miss the way your face balled up while talking to her."

"She says she's someone that is dealing with Laike. According to her, I'm a downgrade. Also, according to her, he made her throat sore from sticking his dick down it throughout the night," I explained with a heavy sigh.

"So, why is she still here... sitting in your restaurant?"

"Why are you two not at your table and behind my counter?"

"No, you answer me, first."

"Because, Kleu, you know she likes to keep it professional and she's not with the drama."

"Oh, well, I am."

Before I could stop her, Kleu bolted for the table that I was headed for. I could only shake my head as I watched her approach the guest.

Please, Kleu. Please don't cause a scene," I begged.

"Oh, you know she is," Ditto confirmed.

"Oh God." I cringed when she tapped on the guest's shoulder.

"Ashlyn!" I mumbled, finally remembering her name. She was the woman we'd bumped into the night

Laike had surprised me with my new truck. *How didn't I remember her?* I asked myself.

"Huh?" Ditto posed, puzzled.

"Her name is Ashlyn."

Not too many words were exchanged. In fact, I wasn't sure that Kleu said anything at all, yet I watched, remorsefully, as she wrapped the long, braided ponytail around her arm and hand. By the hair, she dragged my guest out of her seat and toward the door.

"That has to hurt," Ditto winced as if it was her hair being uprooted from the scalp.

"I'm sure it does," I agreed.

Though Ditto and I were in tune with each other and the situation at hand, my employees were too preoccupied with our guests and our guests were too busy stuffing their mouths to notice the commotion until Ashlyn began yelling.

"Let my fucking hair go!" she screamed, trying her hardest to detach Kleu's arm from her body.

Her small frame didn't stand a chance. Kleu was a Carmichael through and through with legs long as the week and a lengthy reach. Just as quickly as she'd come with intentions to disturb my peace, she was gone. I handed Ditto the tea that she was supposed to consume, and I sipped the orange juice myself. Kleu returned to our sides as if nothing had happened.

"Now, I came to spend some of these niggas money

on you. Take that apron off, honey. We're going shopping."

"I'm literally at work," I reminded her.

"As of this moment, you're not," she responded as she reached behind me and untied my apron. "We came to kidnap you."

"Ditto," I turned to her, "you didn't tell me this was part of the plan."

"I didn't even know we had a plan." She shrugged, just as confused as I was.

laike + baisleigh

NIGHTFALL CONTINUED its pursuit of the sky's beauty as I made my third trip from the car to my house. The constant trips were indicators of how my life as a single woman and mom would be. It wasn't a very good feeling at all, but it wasn't anything to cry about. I'd already made it up in my mind that I'd be hiring a full-time nanny so that I didn't have to do the work alone. There would always be Ditto, but she had a life of her own.

"Damn it, Kleu," I fussed, realizing just how much we'd gotten from the stores.

Everything she laid her eyes on that seemed like it was meant for a boy, she grabbed. The things that were too big for any of us to even consider carrying, she ordered to be delivered to my home. Though I was thankful for the generosity, it left me with so much work to do alone.

My phone buzzed in my pocket. Unsure of who was calling, I sat a few bags on the concrete behind my truck where I was standing. I'd cleared the front seat and back seats. The trunk was last because it seemed to have the most.

"I'll call you back when I get inside and settled, Mom," I whispered, after seeing who was trying to contact me.

I missed her and my father so much, but they had raised their children and were having the time of their lives traveling the world. They were living in London for now, with plans of moving in two years. It was beautiful where they had settled, and I couldn't wait to visit. The pregnancy would more than likely push the visit back, but I'd be there as soon as I felt better about everything that I had going on in my world.

"Promise," I said as if she could hear me. After silencing the phone, I slid it back into my pocket and resumed the task at hand.

"Pay attention to your surroundings," the voice that owned every key to my heart said, forcing me to snap my neck in its direction.

In the dark, there stood Laike with his hands clasped together in front of him. Either he'd gotten finer in the last two weeks while away, or I was just horny and seeing his features in a new dimension.

My heart rejoiced at the sight of him. I wanted, so desperately, to run into his arms, but I held my ground. For once in the last two weeks, all was right in my world. Afraid to blink for the fear of him disappearing, I stretched my eyelids as my orbs bloomed. I couldn't bear to miss even a second of him.

This man is my whole soul, I admitted. The achiness of my chest and the spinning of my thoughts weren't even proof enough. It was the magnetic pull that his presence possessed, commanding all of me every single time. And I wanted to give it, too. All that I had to give, Laike could have. I wouldn't hold back. I couldn't hold back.

"You scared me."

"I'm sure," he responded, unmoving.

"What are you doing here?"

"Not running."

His answer left me baffled. I didn't understand what he was saying.

"I don't understand."

"This is me not running... This is me not wasting another decade plus getting back to you... This is me accepting responsibility for the role I played in our current situation... This is me showing you that no matter what the outcome of the situation is, I'm here."

His words left my cheeks streaked with tears. I remained silent, unsure of how to respond or what to respond. I simply nodded my head to assure Laike that I'd heard every word he'd said and understood them as well. When he stepped closer and closer, and then into my personal space, I caved. He pulled me into him, resting my head on his chest.

"I love you so much," I managed through the sea of tears.

"Too fucking much," he responded as he lifted my head and looked me square in the eyes.

"Don't ever stop, B. Even when I'm being stubborn and bullheaded. Keep loving me. Keep needing me. Keep wanting me. Keep choosing me. Keep forcing me to see the fault in my ways and then drag my ass back home by the ear if you have to, aight?"

"Speaking of draggin," I chuckled, wiping my face, "Kleu dragged that girl Ashlyn out of Baisleigh's House this morning."

"Oh yeah?"

"Yes."

"Good. She doesn't seem to know when to quit. Maybe that'll help her understand the time is now."

"I'm sure."

"It's Kleu who bought all this shit, huh?"

"Yeah."

"Figured. I see I'm about to have some real fucking competition. I can't let her outshine me when it comes to my little nigga!" he exclaimed.

Hearing him claim my son forced me to stop dead in my tracks. There was so much I needed to tell him and I would, but there was one thing in particular that couldn't wait.

"Laike, I just want you to know that I've decided against Nicholas being in my child's life. He's chaotic, and I don't do chaos well, at all. He has a new baby and one on the way. I don't care to be a part of that. I haven't told him about the pregnancy, and I never plan to. I wholeheartedly believe that it's the best decision for my son."

"*Our son*, baby girl. Fuck that nigga. I've been waiting to stamp my legacy on the Eisenberg tree, anyway."

"Your legacy?" I laughed out loud.

"Yeah. This little nigga right here," he responded, falling to his knees in front of me and raising my shirt.

The visual was astounding, filling me with so many unregistered emotions. I was so tired of crying over the last two weeks, but I couldn't help the fresh tears that hit my face. I quickly swept them away, but more appeared.

The moment Laike's lips touched my belly, all was right in my world. My hands rested on his head, stroking his curls as he planted kisses all over me. The last one landed on my lips after he'd gotten up and cupped my face between his palms.

"I need help getting all of this stuff into my house."

"We're going home, baby girl, and all this shit is coming with us."

"Some are already inside."

"Get in the truck. I'll go grab them. I'm leaving my car here."

"Your car?" I asked, taking a look at the Mercedes that I didn't recognize one bit.

"Shit. A nigga bout to welcome a baby and shit. I had to get me an official dad car and shit. What you think?"

"I think it's uh... I think it's gorgeous."

The black paint, dark tint, and black wheels were perfect. I loved the sleekness of the body and its girth. It was a bigger model, though I wasn't exactly sure which one.

"Bet."

"That's why I didn't hear you pulling up."

"If you were paying attention to your surroundings, then it wouldn't have mattered what I pulled up in."

"My mother was calling," I told him.

"You could've waited to check it when you got inside."

"Here we go, Mr. Secret Service Agent."

"Just trying to make sure my baby momma safe," he joked.

"Laike, I'm no one's baby mother. That title doesn't even suit me. Your woman, yes. Baby mother, nah. Please don't ever fix your lips to call me that."

"I'm just fucking with you, B. Let me go grab this shit. Get in."

"It's too much to fit in the backseat alone. We will need the front seat, too."

"I'll make it work. Get in and start it up."

Laike walked around to the other side of the car

with me trailing behind him. He opened the door and waited until I was in. Instead, he rushed around to the driver's side and started the engine himself.

While he ran back and forth from the truck to the house, I tried returning my mother's call. The phone rang and rang until her voicemail eventually picked up. I ended the call and waited impatiently for Laike to return.

The amount of gratitude I felt within was unreal. Since he'd entered my life again, he continued to stun me. His evolution was heartening and exactly what I'd waited all these years to experience. I thought I'd had an amazing version of him when we were young, but this version of Laike proved to be the better version. The best version.

"Ready?"

He slid into the truck and bumped up the heat.

"That cold front is about to come through and cause hell. I hope you're ready for a snowy fall and winter."

"Snowy sounds good as long as hot tea, cuddles, and unlimited mushy movies are involved."

"It's your world, B. We're doing whatever you want to do."

"Including dress up in matching pajamas for Christmas?"

"Including that corny ass shit."

"And cooking for Thanksgiving?"

"That shit in two days, B. What you talking about cooking? I know the stores are going to be packed."

"Laike, did you forget that you don't do your grocery shopping? You have a service to fill that big fridge. Besides, I wouldn't be surprised if you already have most of the stuff we need."

"Me, either. Let's make a list when we get home and figure out what we'll need. Luca is hosting this year, and I have the menu he and Ever finalized. We'll just prepare shit you want that isn't on it."

Home. It truly felt like that's where I was headed, and that's where I wanted to be. That's where I wanted to spend the rest of my days. That's where I wanted to raise our son. That's where I wanted to make our second child.

"Okay."

Laike slid his hand over onto my side and squeezed my thigh. Needing to feel his skin against mine, I placed my hand on top of his hand. My heart hummed in my chest, causing a smile to raise my cheeks.

FOURTEEN

laike

"LOOK at this little nigga's head. I'd swear he was an Eisenberg if I didn't know any better!" I exclaimed, showing my mother the sonogram images.

"He is," she corrected.

"You know what I mean. Biologically."

"Technology is so advanced these days. Look at his face."

My mother was in awe each time she held one of

my son's sonograms in her hand. According to her, she didn't think she'd ever see such a moment. It didn't matter that Luca had an entire circus and Lyric had birthed a beautiful baby girl. She was appalled by my addition. Those two, she knew would be parents long before they had children. Me, on the other hand, she wasn't banking on it.

"This reminds me of Keanu and Lucas," she continued/ "Have you seen their 3D ultrasounds? Laiken's isn't too far-fetched. The tiny little features. Oh God, we're having another baby."

"We are and very soon."

"How much longer do I have to wait?"

"A few weeks or whenever this nigga decides to quit playing and come on out."

"It'll be soon. I'm so proud of you, son. I know this wasn't the easiest but you stepping up to the plate makes me so happy."

"See, that's the thing, Ma. It's been the easiest thing I've ever done. Loving Baisleigh has never been hard. It's almost as natural as breathing. Our son is just an added bonus."

Finally, I could see the improvements in my mother's health. Her smile was brighter and her spirit was lighter. In two months, she'd be ringing that bell and we'd be putting cancer behind us. Her tumors had shrunk and vanished, but we were still finishing out the treatments as the doctor suggested.

"I'm so happy you two got it right."

"Baisleigh always had it right. It was my stupidity, but we're locked in now. I wish I could've made her my wife before she became a mother, but I can wait. I know, B. She wants the big wedding and fancy reception. She's more like Lyric than even she knows."

"Yes. Yes, she is. But, I don't think it has much to do with her. She'd probably be okay with a tiny wedding in the backyard. Her parents... that's who she wants to give fond memories. I don't blame her. They already won't have any real pregnancy pictures. The girl look like she ate at a buffet with that little pudge of hers."

"According to her mother, her aunt was the same way during one of her pregnancies, and B's grandmother didn't know she was pregnant with her mother until she was almost seven months. It wasn't until then that she started feeling movement and her stomach started to protrude. Maybe it's a genetic thing."

"Has to be. At least she doesn't have to worry about stretch marks."

"Not this time, at least. Next time, she might be swollen around here," I replied.

"Oh, so there will be a next time?"

"Yeah. I'm with that, but not until I've given her the wedding of her dreams and we get accustomed to the little person we're waiting for right now."

"Good. Give her body the rest it needs."

"Old man," I called out to my father as he approached us.

"What's up, Laike," he greeted. "You ready, Honey?"

"You know I can take her home, right? You don't come get her on nobody's day but mine. I'm not even in the Hellcat on days I have to come see her. I'm in the Benz."

"Laike, it's not about the car. It's about the fool behind the wheel."

"Do you need help?" I asked my mother, ignoring my father. He swore I couldn't drive a bit, but I found that hilarious when I'd never wrecked a car and always returned home in one piece.

"No, son. I've got it. I'll talk to you later, okay?"

"Yeah. Of course."

"I love you, Laike."

"Always," I responded as I watched her stand from her seat.

She looked a lot healthier than she did six months ago. Even three months ago, she wasn't nearly as healthy as she was now. The differences were dramatic. With lower doses of chemo and a pill that sufficed for most doctor's visits, her body was beginning its recovery process. It was beautiful to watch.

My phone began vibrating in my hand, pulling me from my thoughts. I didn't have to look at the screen to know who was calling. Baisleigh was the only one blowing my line down all throughout the day.

"I'm on my way, baby."

"Okay. Come on. I miss you and my back hurts."

"Well, good thing it's your last day standing for so many hours. It's time to kick your feet up and wait on our son's arrival."

"I can feel the bed already. Oh my God, I can't wait to get home. But, first, I need to eat."

"Of course, you do." I chuckled. "I'm on the way."

laike + baisleigh

I LAUGHED as I watched Baisleigh exit Baisleigh's House in a cut-off top and gray leggings. Her belly wasn't getting any bigger because the baby was in her ass. That thang was twice the size it was when she found out she was pregnant. I wasn't complaining a bit. I was hoping that motherfucker stayed. It was better than any pillow on the market, even the ones I'd spent hundreds of dollars on.

I reached over and opened the door for her. When she sat down in the car and passed me a container full of food, I couldn't help but shake my head. That only meant her appetite was far too vicious to wait for my arrival.

"Don't laugh," she whined. "I couldn't wait so I had Liz make up something to hold us over until we have dinner."

"I'm not laughing." I chuckled.

"Yes, you are. You probably think I'm such a fatty, huh?"

"I don't think nothing, baby. The only thing fat on you is that ass, and I happen to like that. You see how hard you got my dick right now?"

I reached over and grabbed her hand. When I placed it on top of my dick, she squeezed it.

"Good, because I'm so horny I want to cry right now."

"Don't cry 'bout no dick, baby, not when I've got plenty of that shit for you. Take all that you can stand. Cry on the dick, B. Not 'bout the dick. This mother-fucker yours... any time, any place."

"Well, I'm still crying," she sobbed, finally releasing whatever was pent up in her.

As much as I wanted to laugh, I knew that it would only make shit worse. We went through the same thing, daily. It was as if she had to release a daily dose of salty tears to feel better about the simplest shit. Pregnancy hormones were kicking her ass, and I couldn't do shit about it most times. Even my solutions warranted tears. She'd cry because she was happy and because she was sad. There wasn't a preference – just tears.

"It's okay, baby. Let me get you home so you can cry right on this dick."

"Okaaay," Baisleigh wept, tickling my soul.

I peeled out of the parking lot, ready to break every traffic law to get my baby home. Halfway through the trip, I remembered we'd decided to stay at her crib for the week while we finished packing up her things. She'd moved into my space months ago but had yet to consolidate our things. This caused a lot of back and forth for her, which we were ready to eliminate with the baby coming in a few weeks.

I made the necessary changes to my direction and ended up at Baisleigh's place a few minutes later. By the time I made it around to her side of the car to help her out, she had finally gotten herself together and dried her tears.

"Feeling better?"

"A little."

"Well, I got something that will make you feel a whole lot better once we get inside."

"Okay."

Her sniffles were the cutest thing ever. I grabbed her hand and led her toward the house after closing the door behind her. Like a sad puppy, she followed without hesitation. When we stepped onto the porch, Baisleigh leaned into my side, placing her head on my arm. My baby was juggling so many big feelings and having so much trouble balancing them perfectly. While there was not anything wrong, those feelings still existed.

"Come er'," I demanded, pulling Baisleigh back toward the door after we'd made it inside.

I grabbed both of her of her hands and placed them on the door. Baisleigh quickly understood the assignment and spread her legs. Desperate to reach her center, I tugged at both sides of her leggings, ripping them right at the seam.

"Laike," she moaned.

The large hole exposed her perfectly round ass and cellulite that had grown along with it over the last few months. Her thong was buried so deep between her cheeks that it was almost impossible to retrieve but I managed and then ripped it to shreds, too.

"Baaaby."

I lowered my pants and freed my dick from my boxers. With my mouth to her ear, I shared a few choice words with her.

"Shut the fuck up, bend that fat ass over, and take this dick you've been crying for."

As the words left my mouth, I slid into Baisleigh, not stopping until I felt my ball pressed against her skin. She arched her back, giving me unrestricted access to her sloppy wet pussy. It should've been illegal for her shit to be so good. Even if it was, I'd still be slipping and sliding. I wasn't above the law. A nigga like me had made a living off breaking them.

"Laaaaaaaaaikkkkke," she cried as she creamed.

Her stickiness coated my dick, covering the skin up to the base. Baby girl was oozing from her center so beautifully. The sight of her creaminess and the feel of her walls locking me in made my toes curl. I closed my eyes, trying to mentally check myself. I was so close to nutting though I'd only slid in less than three minutes prior.

"This shit ridiculous," I groaned, pulling out of Baisleigh before she ended my ass.

I replaced my dick with my fingers, dug into her pussy, and found her G-spot. I curved my index and middle finger toward me and massaged her internally until she began to scream.

"Please. Please. Oh God. Ummmmm."

"Let that shit go," I coached.

"I'm cummmmmming."

The waterworks began. Her ejaculation squirted out and all over my hands and forearm. Just as it slowed to a creep, I removed my fingers and re-entered her contracting pussy. It pulled my nut from the head of my dick where it sat, waiting to enter her oasis.

"Uhhhhhhh. Shit."

Heavy, labored breathing followed our climaxes, forcing both of us against the door. Her face rested against the coolness and mine rested against her back. It wasn't until I heard her soft sniffles that I lifted and turned her around to face me.

"What's wrong?" I asked, concerned with the tears that was on her face.

"Nothing," she assured me, attempting to wipe them away.

"B, you've got to tell me what's wrong, baby."

"It's just that... That felt so good," she cried even harder, falling into my chest.

This time, it wasn't as easy to conceal my laughter. I pulled her into my chest for her to rest her head as the deep cackle erupted. Humiliated, she cried even harder. Baby girl was going through it, and I couldn't wait until she dropped my son so that we could get past this stage.

"Come on, babe. Let me get you to the shower. I think you just need a nap. We can save the work for later. Shit, I can hire somebody to come do this shit if you want me to. It's about time for you to take your rest."

"Okay," she blubbered with a face full of tears.

Her clothes were destroyed, which would only give her another reason to cry even harder. I eliminated the risk by scooping her up and carrying her up the stairs and to her bedroom. We continued through the large space until we reached her bathroom, where I finally placed her on her feet and began stripping her clothes from her body.

"Hey."

I slid up onto the counter and pulled Baisleigh between my legs. Her tears still hadn't stopped, which prompted me to believe there was a lot more to them than what she was letting on. My intuition had never steered me wrong, and I doubted it would start. At least not when it came to Baisleigh.

"What's the matter, B? Talk to me. What's wrong, mommas?"

I pressed my hand against her belly. Though it hadn't grown much during her pregnancy, it had hardened. The presence of a child was now obvious. She simply looked around three or four months though she was at the end of her pregnancy.

"I just have so much anxiety. I don't understand what's going on," she finally admitted as a gush of air left her mouth and nose.

"That sounds so much better," I told her. "You have every right to be nervous, to be anxious, and even afraid."

"I'm scared to death."

"Giving birth is no walk in the park, B. Shit, I don't even have to push the big head ass baby out, and I'm scared shitless." I sniggered, bringing a smile to her face.

"Yeah?"

"Yes. I can hardly sleep at night, just sitting there waiting on the moment your water breaks or you complain of contractions. I know we have a few weeks, but shit... It feels like everything is happening so fast already. I just don't want to miss a second or not be there when it finally happens."

"Thank you," she said, lowly, dropping her head. "I know this must be so awkward for you sometimes. And, I know I never tell you, but I just want you to know that I'm so thankful for you."

"Awkward?" I scoffed. "I'm not that nigga, B. And, I'm glad you've never thanked me because then a nigga would be offended. Whatever is on your head, I'm off that and you should be too. We have a son *together*. End of story, aight?"

"Alright."

"I'm going to run you a nice, hot bath with bubbles and shit. Then, I'm going to run to the car. I bought you something I think you'll enjoy while in the tub. When you're ready, I'm going to come in here and wash your body down. Then, we're heading to the bedroom so that I can lotion you up. After that, we're both going to take a long ass nap. Obviously, we could both use one. You down?"

"Yes. That sounds like the perfect plan. Can we watch a movie on the way to sleep?"

"Nah. 'Cause, it'll be watching us before it's said and done. We can cut on that nature shit you love to play, though."

"Even better," she cheered, "I love you."

"Too much," I responded, "And know that you're not alone in this thing. It's no easy walk in the park, but you're not walking alone. You're scared... I'm scared, but we're going to thug this shit out. You're going to bring in a healthy baby boy that we both get to enjoy for the rest of our lives."

"I want a push gift," she revealed.

"Then, a push gift you're going to get. I was thinking of putting a ring on that fucking finger, but I can settle for something else."

"A ring sounds good, but I want it once this is all over. I don't want the birth of the baby to overshadow our engagement. I want the events to stand alone."

"I feel ya on that. Let's get this young nigga out and in my hands and then we can work on the ring."

"Yes," she agreed.

"Aight. Scoot back. Let me start your water."

Baisleigh had all types of shit to help calm her during a relaxing bath. I chose a few different salts, bubble bath, and some scrubs I knew she'd want to use before getting out. They were new. The other ones already in the shower were nearly gone.

I adjusted the water temperature to hell, just like she'd want it and poured a decent amount of bubble bath inside. As the tub filled, I sprinkled salts all around it. By the time I was finished, I was ready to jump in myself. The mixture of fragrances was a treat.

"Go ahead. I'm going to be right back, aight?"

"Okay."

Baisleigh lifted one foot after the other into the tub. I watched for any signs of distress as she lowered her body into the water. Of course, she loved it. That shit was scolding hot. I cringed at the thought of my balls touching it.

I made my way out the door and to the car to retrieve the bag from my trunk. It only took a few seconds for me to return to the porch. When I made it back into the house, I headed straight for the stairs. My adrenaline was pumping as excitement drove me straight into the bathroom where Baisleigh was resting.

"Check this out," I said to her, causing her to look in my direction.

"Shut up!" she squealed. "Shut up!"

"Nah. I ordered this shit 'cause I figured you'd like it. I was too happy to get this one. It's from the one book you read me the month before last. She got some new shit out. I think it might be the one after the one we read."

"It is. Alexandra Warren. And, what's this? Before I let Go? Kennedy Ryan? K.C. Mills? Shanice x Lola? B. Love? BriAnn Danae? Baby, where'd you find all of these books? Oh my God. I don't even know where to start!"

"It's a new bookstore that just opened right here in Edgewood. All they sell are Black Romance books. I was thinking we could go check it out. In July, they have a few authors coming through to do live readings. I was thinking we could roll through."

"Yes. Of course. Laiken will be a few months by then."

"Three. I think we'll both be ready for the break."

"I'm sure," she agreed.

"Oh my God. I don't know which one I want to read first."

"I was thinking I could read one to you. I just want you to relax. We can start with the sequel to the one we've already read."

"You... read to me?"

"Yeah. I just thought of that shit just now. What you think a nigga can't read?"

"No. I'm aware that you can read, silly. I'm just...

nothing. Yes. You read to me. I'll shut up and listen now."

"Thank you. I thought you'd never say it."

"Don't make me pull you into this hot water."

"Please don't do that shit. I'll fuck around and have third-degree burns all over my ass."

"Read the book, Laike. I'm closing my eyes and shutting up now."

"'Bout time."

laike + baisleigh

THE LONG, hot bath that Baisleigh had taken had proved to be effective. She was finally settled and her tears had dried. As we lay in bed, waiting for sleep to overcome us, I rubbed her belly in circles.

"I was thinking that maybe next time we'll have a shower. This time, I just didn't feel up to it. I mean, I didn't find out until I was so far along in my pregnancy. Then, there was the thing with you and me. After all of that was over, I just wanted to focus on getting my business in order for my lengthy departure. Everything just flew by. The months have felt like days or is it just me?"

"Na. It was just Christmas and we were matching pajamas and sipping hot chocolate. Now, it's April, and we're about to drop our first litter."

"First litter?" Baisleigh hissed. "You can't be serious right now, Laike. It's one baby and it's not an animal. What do you mean our first litter?"

"Load? Does that sound better?"

"No. It doesn't actually. Baby sounds just fine. Son, that works, too. Child, there's another one."

"Shit boring," I teased.

The sound of her phone chiming in the background halted her train of thought. I wasn't complaining about it, either. I reached over her and grabbed her cell so that she wasn't straining too hard. She'd pulled a muscle earlier in her pregnancy and was down for two days. We didn't want that happening, again, especially not so close to the end.

"Hello," she answered.

There were a few seconds of silence before she spoke again.

"Hey, Mom... No, I'm fine. Just waiting for this baby to decide it's time... Where's Dad?"

Baisleigh turned over, onto her side so that she wasn't yapping away in my ear. Though I wasn't bothered a bit, I appreciated her for the move she'd just made. She'd gotten in the perfect position.

I lowered my briefs and my dick sprang from its confinements. Its heaviness had always amazed me. I tapped it on Baisleigh's ass as a fair warning as to what type of time I was on. She didn't budge.

"No. My last appointment was a few days ago. Laike and I are just trying to sort things out with my belongings. It feels like a never-ending task at this point. We're staying here for the night and trying our hardest to finish up tomorrow... No, today was my last day at work. I'm officially on maternity leave for the next three months."

I wet the tips of my fingers and then brushed the saliva onto the tip of my dick. Slightly, I lifted Baisleigh's leg, careful not to disrupt her too much. With little resistance, I was able to slide into her.

"Moooooom. Uh. I have to," she stuttered.

"Don't hang up that phone. Be a big girl," I whispered.

Long, deadly strokes were the remedy to her soul. Her focus was dismantled as she tried hard not to sound off on the phone. Her pussy creamed for me, making it easier and easier to slide in and out of her.

"Umm... I don't... I don't knoooow."

Her words were exaggerated as she continued the conversation with her mom, barely responding to whatever was being said. The internal and external struggle she faced was gratifying.

"One second, Mom," she said clearly.

I watched from behind as she placed the phone on mute. When she pushed back into me, forcing me to flip over onto my back, I was ill-prepared. When she mounted herself on top of me, sliding down my dick like a stripper on a long pole, I wanted to scream.

"B," I moaned. "What the fuck you doing?"

Skillfully, she worked her pussy muscles as she

rode my dick like the champion she was. Her wetness coated my shaft and slid down further with each stroke, eventually forming a pool on my balls and thighs.

"B, what the fuuuuuuck?"

Her body was hypnotic, summoning my hands. I ran my fingers along her waist, up her back, and her shoulders. When I finally reached her neck, I wrapped my right hand around the back and shoved her forward. She broke her fall with her hands, planting them firmly on the bed.

Perfect, I rejoiced inside. She was right where I wanted her. I raised up from the bed, still lodged inside of her, and stood firmly on my knees. With Baisleigh now on all fours, I began assaulting the same pussy that had me moaning a few seconds earlier. Now, it was her time to whimper and moan.

Wham! I slammed my hand on her ass. The other, I used to grab her long, flowy hair. She'd been wearing it piled at the top of her head in a ponytail that made her even finer. The natural baby hair and shit framed her face perfectly, bringing out those big eyes and those chunky lips.

"I'm cumming. I'm cumming!" Baisleigh screamed. "I'm—"

"That's right. Cum on this dick," I groaned in her ear.

I could feel my nut rising. As she reached euphoria, my strokes intensified. Her strands remained locked in my fist as I fucked her senseless. The sound of our connection was glorious in the quiet space, bringing me right to my peak.

The stars between my lids aligned as beads of light shined through. *Outer body.* It was the only way to explain the tranquility I felt. My limbs stiffened as I spat my seeds into Baisleigh's canal. It felt like buckets of cum that just kept coming. If she wasn't already pregnant, then she would've been after that.

I fell backward after releasing her from my grasp. She crawled around in the bed until she was back in her spot. I chuckled when I saw her lie down and close her eyes.

"Your phone," I reminded her.

"Shoot!"

Her eyes popped open, and she reached for her cell. Sluggishly, she pressed the screen to unmute the call.

"Sorry, Mom. That was someone on the other end. You mind if I call you back when I wake up from my nap?"

There was a brief pause.

"I love you, too. Tell Dad to call me when he sits his behind down somewhere."

A long sigh escaped her body as she ended the call and laid the phone beside us. I pulled her closer and deeper into me before wrapping my arms around her body. I closed my eyes, ready for the stillness that followed our lovemaking sessions to consume me. Baisleigh was easily my peace.

FIFTEEN

"BABY. BABY, WAKE UP! BABY!"

Though she seemed far away, I knew that Baisleigh was right beside me. I felt her shaking my body, trying to wake me from the coma she'd put me in. the urgency in her voice paired with the inability to breathe jarred me right from my sleep.

"Laike. Please. Please wake up!" she howled. "Wake up!"

I lifted straight up in bed.

"What's... what the fuck?"

What I thought was the fuzziness of my vision from the sleep I'd been awakened from turned out to be something totally different. My lungs were immediately filled with the smoke that filled the room. The lack of clean, breathable air quickly explained my lack of oxygen.

"Fuck!"

I quickly dug through my memory to recall leaving on a stove or anything that would catch fire. There was nothing. We'd come straight inside, handled Baisleigh's emotions, made it upstairs for a bath, finished each other off, and fallen asleep. Nothing we'd done would've warranted our current situation.

"Baby!" Baisleigh tapped my shoulder over and over, pointing with her other hand.

I followed her lead. What I found at the end of the path that she'd directed me to made every drop of blood in my body halt, briefly. The dryness in my mouth tripled, forcing me to swallow down what little moisture was in my mouth.

"What the fuck?"

"If it's not me and you, Laikie, then it won't be you and anyone else," Ashlyn cackled.

She stood at the edge of Baisleigh's bed dressed in black from head to toe. Even with the fogginess of the room, the image on the black hoodie caught my attention. My face was printed across the front with a large heart around it.

This bitch is ill!

Growing sick to my stomach, I lunged forward and in her direction. Just as quickly as I made the move, I realized it was a miscalculated mistake. She wasn't the goal and using my energy for her would prove to be deadly. I had a son and a woman to save. I retracted, slamming my body against the bottom of the bed instead.

"My water. My water. I think my water... Laike," Baisleigh whimpered, drawing my attention.

"Oh, wow. Three birds with one stone," Ashlyn chanted, throwing her hands in the air. "At least we will all be in heaven, together."

It was a difficult task, but I managed to tune her out as I scooped Baisleigh up from the bed. Fluids gushed from her as I carried her to the door. It was as if they'd never end, continuing to leak from her body as I neared the bedroom door.

"Ah. Shit!"

The knob was scorching hot, burning my palm and fingers on contact. I clenched my teeth to relieve myself of the pain. I couldn't focus on it at the moment.

"Oh God," Baisleigh grunted. "The baby is coming, Laike. He's coming," she cried out. "Oh God."

Desperation sat in as I realized it was impossible to open the bedroom door. Whatever was behind it was obviously worse than what was inside of the room, so I knew that it wasn't the direction we should be headed in.

"Hold on, B. I'm going to get us out of here."

Smoke slid through the cracks of the door, confirming my suspicions. The entire house was in flames. I searched for a possible solution, thinking quickly on my toes.

"Window," Baisleigh made out through slow, chest-caving coughs.

Yes. Yes. The window. Relief washed over me as I made my way across the room.

"Shirt. Shirt. Please," Baisleigh pleaded.

There wasn't enough time to grab a shirt to cover her naked body. Thinking quickly on my feet, I snatched the flat sheet from the bed with one pull, knocking the comforter to the floor. The loud thud that followed reminded me that I'd left my Glock under-neath the pillow. Before placing the end of the sheet in Baisleigh's hand, I swooped down and grabbed my piece.

"You have to get on my back, baby."

"I can't," she admitted.

"You have to. It's the only way we'll make it out of here. I'm going to do all the work. I just need you to hold on tight. Aight?"

"Okay."

"I love you, aight? We've got this."

"How cute?" Ashlyn's voice rang through the room, pissing me the fuck off.

"You know it's a very slim chance that your baby will survive that fall. It's literally like tossing it out of the wind—"

Click. Clack. Fow. Straight through the center of her head, the bullet that flew from my gun landed. Precision was my specialty. My father had taught me that. It's the reason why, even in the haziness, I still hit my target.

Shut the fuck up! My thoughts rang out.

Quickly, Ashlyn's body hit the ground with a loud, crashing sound. She'd ended up on the glass fixtures that Baisleigh had packed from her bedroom that would've been going with us to my crib. It was bittersweet, being the cause of a female's demise, but it wasn't time to dwell.

There hadn't been a time in my life when a female was at the other end of my barrel, but she deserved every bullet that came from the clip. If I had time, I would've emptied the entire thing in her ass. Her intention was to kill my entire family, so she had to go.

"Baby." Baisleigh gasped as she closed her eyes tightly and turned her face toward my chest.

"I'm sorry. That bitch had to go. We'll meet in hell someday."

For once, I was thankful for the easily opened windows and the ladder that I always felt was a security threat. Baisleigh lived in a Victorian-style home with a bedroom balcony that was extremely accessible. A ladder, covered in greenery, led to the long, wrap-around balcony. I hated the sight of it, especially with Baisleigh being a single woman living alone.

Today was a little different. It was our only escape route from the burning home. For that, I was finally thankful.

When I opened the window, cold air came rushing through. I could finally breathe healthy, untarnished oxygen into my lungs. My overheated body appreciated every bit of the breeze.

"On my back, B. I'm going to climb down. I just need you to hold on."

I maneuvered her frame until she was on my back. She hooked her arms around my neck, her legs around my waist, and held onto me tightly. Her tiny belly was the greatest gift from God at the time. It allowed me to begin our descent down the ladder with her clinging to me.

As I managed to lock my hands on the side and carefully lower us both, our combined weight proved to be a bit much for the wooden ladder. *Fuck.*

"Baby, it's wobbling."

"Just hold still, B. We're getting down this motherfucker even if I have to jump and break all my limbs to make sure y'all straight."

I picked up the pace, stretching my legs far enough to skip a full step for every step that I did land. This cut our time in half but came with extreme risk. In my opinion, however, the closer we got to the ground, the better our chances were of arriving safely.

"Oh God."

Baisleigh, in obvious pain, loosened her grip around my neck and clenched her stomach. The unexpected movement shifted the weight, throwing off our balance and nearly sending us plummeting to the ground.

"Woah!"

"Shit!" I yelled, feeling us both slip from the ladder.

My reflex was quick and effective. There was no way either of us was landing unless it was on our feet. I placed a hand on her back to secure her or else she wouldn't survive my next move.

"We're jumping! Hang on!" I screamed out as I leaped from the ladder and onto the grass.

"Laike!"

"I know, baby. I know."

"He's coming," Baisleigh belted, "He's coming."

"Fuck. Aight. Come on. Let me get you out of here."

Looking back at the house as I scooped Baisleigh up in my arms, again, my heart sank into my soles. The home she'd worked so hard for had been destroyed. The raging fire forced me to pick up the pace and jump into my car. Thankfully, I never removed the fob unless absolutely necessary. After I got Baisleigh settled into the passenger seat, I ran around to the front and got the car started.

Baisleigh was always on my ass about leaving the

fobs in my vehicles but I was known to lose keys. For that reason, I'd installed the smart security system at my home and at the homes of the people I loved. If they still used a key, it was because they preferred it. I, on the other hand, hated them.

"Ahhhhhhhhhhh!"

"Hold on, baby."

I wanted no time burning out of her driveway. The smell of rubber and burning wood penetrated the air. With a final look at the house before peeling off down the street, I made a promise to reimburse Baisleigh for the loss of her home. It was my fault. All of this was my fault. Everything that had gone wrong in her world in the last year was my fault or at least it felt like it.

Something had always seemed off about Ashlyn. It was the main reason I'd cut ties with her in the first place. Her hygiene was the final straw. Over the last few months, I'd bumped into her, but I never thought much about it. As I sped down the road, I began connecting the dots. Our run-ins were never coincidental. They were intentional, on her end, at least.

"Oh my Godddddddd."

Sweat beads formed on my forehead as I watched Baisleigh's scrambled features. The pain was intensifying and there wasn't anything I could do to help her. I pushed the petal, hoping to give her relief sooner than later.

"He's coming. He's coming."

"Right now?"

"Right now!" she assured me with dramatic nods. "Oh God. He's coming."

I wasn't sure how the hell I'd ended up at the end of Luca's driveway, but it was obviously the place I was headed all along. The hospital was in the opposite direction. I quickly punched in the numbers for the gate to open.

As I waited for the gate to part, I lay on the break. Patience wasn't on my side. When it looked like I had enough room to squeeze through, it's exactly what I did.

WHAM! The impact of my side mirrors slapping against the gates sounded. I didn't give a damn about the casualties. I'd have them repaired once my son was here and Baisleigh was resting.

"I need to push. Baby, I need to push."

"Hold on, B. Hold on. I got you."

I wasn't sure what the hell I was saying. I felt queasy as if I'd faint at any given minute. The thought of a baby exiting the hole that I enjoyed often was just too much to consider. *Because, how?* I asked myself as I stopped in the driveway, so close to the house that one would've thought I was aiming for the front door.

The moment I put the car in park, I bolted from the driver's seat, leaving the door open as I ran up to Luca's door. Before I could begin pounding, the door swung open with Luca standing behind it.

Click. Clack. I heard him ready his gun. The seriousness of his expression let me know that he was ready for whatever, but there was no need for armor. I'd already laid my enemy to rest.

"What's up?"

"Baisleigh's having the baby. Get Ever!"

I wasted no time turning around and heading back for the car. It was then that I realized I was still in my boxers. As quickly as the thought surfaced, it disappeared.

"He's coming ouuuuutttt!" Baisleigh screamed as I opened the passenger door.

Her hands were positioned in front of her and what I saw inside of her palms nearly sent me crashing onto the concrete.

"Is that his fucking head?" I screamed, unsure of what to do or where to turn to.

"Oh God!" Baisleigh pushed a final time.

The baby's full body lunged forward and slipped right through her hands. Acting fast, I leaned in, catching him right in my hands. His slipperiness was challenging, but I steadied him by placing him against my chest.

"Fuck, little nigga. You trying to hit the floor?" still in utter shock, I asked.

Hot, fresh tears stung my eyes and fell onto my cheeks as I stared down at the blonde-haired, brown-eyed baby boy. There was no doubt in my mind that I was staring down at the newest Eisenberg. And, not an honorary member, but one that shared the same DNA as me.

"He's mine," I choked out.

"Oh God," Baisleigh continued to repeat, unaware of the blessing I'd just received. "Oh God."

She was too exhausted to even give a fuck what was going on.

"He's here?" Ever yelled, finally reaching us. "Oh, baby, he's here," she said to Luca, hands covering her mouth.

Luca walked up on me, examining the newest addition to the family.

"A fucking Eisenberg," he confirmed. "A fucking Eisenberg."

"Let's get you in the house, Baisleigh. Do you think you can walk?" Ever asked B, springing into action.

"Yes. I can walk. Can I just... Can I see my son first?"

Exhaustion was apparent. She could hardly keep her eyes open as she requested our son. My heart was so full of joy that I hardly even wanted to hand him over. I did, reluctantly, because I needed her to understand how divine timing was. We weren't expecting Laiken for another few weeks according to the timeline that her doctor had given us. However, the information we'd been going by was inaccurate. The timeline was off. My timing, however, was perfect.

"Baby!" B called out to me the moment our son was in her hands. "Baby. Look."

She rubbed his full head of sandy blonde hair. "Baby! Is he? Is he..."

"Was going to be mine regardless, but you fucking right. He's mine."

"Give or take a week," she quoted her doctor as tears streamed down her face.

"Or, two," I added.

"Or two," she repeated."

laike + baisleigh

"HOW ARE YOU FEELING, HOMIE?" Luca asked while sipping the Hennessy he'd poured himself.

"Like a bitch," I admitted. "I just feel all these emotions and I feel like the only way to truly release them is to–" I paused, not even believing what I was about to say.

"Cry," he finished for me.

"Yeah. That. I spend her entire pregnancy thinking I was about to become the father of another nigga's seed and was still head over heels for the young nigga. But, to see his face and his features, man that shit nearly made my heart explode. I'm still just sitting here in awe. Like, what if I would've ran this time, too? Ya know. This situation would've been too much for anybody to handle, but I stood ten toes down."

"And, look at the reward."

"Look at it, man. A beautiful ass baby boy that looks just like that nigga, Lucas."

"Fucking twins. That shit is bananas. You would think Ever push that nigga out."

"Just like Keanu." I chuckled. "Her little fat ass just got her dad's nose. Everything else is us."

"Them Eisenberg genes strong," Luca added.

"Strong as hell. You think they're finished?"

Ever had called over her team of natural birth workers. They were hard at work making sure that Baisleigh and the baby were good. If we could avoid the hospital at this point, we wanted to. She'd already done the hard work. Visiting would almost be unnecessary.

"Nah. They'll come down when they are. Right now, I need you to tell me how you ended up at my crib in your boxers and Baisleigh wrapped up in a sheet."

"Fuck."

"What?"

"I dropped a body, tonight."

"And you're just saying something, nigga?"

"It's not like that."

"Then, what's it like?"

Luca was already on the phone making calls.

"Ashlyn, a chick I was dealing with a while back... that's who is to blame for all this shit. We were at Baisleigh's crib. She wakes me up with urgency. I'm guessing it was because she was beginning to feel contractions and shit. When I finally get up, it's hot ass shit and I can hardly breathe. I'm coughing and shit.

Baisleigh points to the end of the bed. I follow her finger to find this ditzy ass bitch at the end of that motherfucker. She laughing and talking about us all dying together and shit. I quickly realize she done set the fucking house on fire. You know that ladder I've complained about since B moved into her crib?"

"Yeah, the one you threatened to remove on your own if she didn't?"

"Yes. That one. Well, that one saved our fucking lives because that's how we got out of there. But, before we did, I made sure to blow that bitch brains out. I wasn't leaving until I did. I didn't give a fuck how close we were to burning alive."

"Damn right,"

"I need to make sure they never find out what really happened. Burned in a fire is how I want to keep that story."

"I'm on it. In the meantime, I'm going through there to see what's up. I'm sure the fire department is still there. Randy on the squad. He'll give me details."

"Bet. In the meantime, I need a phone and some fucking clothes. I'm walking around in boxers and a tee like this my pad. Give me something to throw on. I can shower down here and maybe they'll be finished when I get out. I'm ready to hold my son."

"Be patient, homie. I'm about to grab something for you since you're being ungrateful. I thought the tee and boxers were a good look on you."

"You could've brought some joggers down, too. A

tee? We're not at our old crib. Lyric and Mom aren't the only women in the house anymore."

"Told you. Just ungrateful. Ever ain't thinking about your little dick ass and neither are those women upstairs."

"Yeah, aight. You saw how the older one was eyeing me."

"Nigga, you're full of yourself."

"I bet I could knock the cobwebs off if I wasn't already committed."

"How you even know she has cobwebs?"

"Can you go get my shit?"

"Yeah. I'll be back."

Luca exited the mancave with his glass in hand. I turned mine up and groaned from the slight burn of my chest. When I stood from the leather couch, I stretched my limbs until they popped before journeying to the bathroom. It was right on side of the full bar.

I shut the door behind me and locked it to be sure that no one could disrupt what was brewing in my chest. My heart was full and broken at the same time. It was as if I was straddling an unfamiliar fence and hoping to come out on the better side.

Human. I was human. The fact that I'd nearly walked away from Baisleigh and left her alone to be a single mother while she was, in fact, carrying my seed left me feeling undeserving and unworthy of the moment. Unworthy of them. Unworthy of him.

Laiken. He was mine. All mine. That was the silver

lining in all of this. His presence was encompassing. And the love I had for him, immediately couldn't be compared to anything else. I loved him more than life itself. I loved him more than I even loved myself, and the revelation of it all knocked me to the ground with tears spilling from my eyes.

Like a baby, I wept on the floor of my brother's bathroom. Because, though I didn't realize it, I'd been waiting all my life for this moment. No amount of money or success had ever driven me to my pinnacle. I'd never truly felt fulfilled, no matter how many millions my family acquired or how much success we experienced. It was them, Laiken and Baisleigh, that filled the lifelong void that I was unaware of.

Finally, I felt like I'd gotten it right. Finally, I wasn't fucking up. Finally, I was being the best man I could be. Finally, I felt like the reflection of my father that he would be proud of. Finally, I felt complete.

"Too much," I bawled, "too fucking much."

Because it was true. I loved my son, and I loved his mother *too much*.

EPILOGUE

baisleigh

SIX DAYS LATER...

"HEY. Hey. Hey. Is it really that bad, baby boy?"

Laiken was screaming at the top of his lungs as if I was killing him. I was only trying to get him into his onesie after a sponge bath. He hated water touching his skin, easily reminding me of my brother when we were younger. My parents had to stand by the door to watch him shower. Otherwise, he'd sit in the bathroom and allow the water to run and never touch his skin.

"Okay. Okay. Just a second."

The sound of Laike stirring in his sleep pained my heart. He hadn't gotten more than an hour or two of sleep each night since the baby had been born. He was so afraid of missing any of the precious moments that he forced himself to stay awake even when he couldn't be of service.

"Shhh. Shhhhh. It's okay, man. It's okay. I promise. Mommy is going to give you some good ole milk in just a second."

I scooped him up, although he was halfway dressed, and placed his skin against mine. The second we connected, his screams turned to low whimpers.

"It's okay, man. I'm right here. Mommy just wants to get your clothes on you. That's all. That's it."

I pushed his arms through the onesie before lifting him to zip it all the way up. Before he realized I'd removed him from my chest, I cradled him in my arm and pulled down the latch of my nursing bra. I found humor in his puckered lips and the unsuccessful search for the milk. With his eyes closed, he moved his head from one side to the other.

"Here we go. Here we go."

I braced myself for his latch. It was powerful and hurt the first few seconds. But, once he got going, it felt much better.

"Ummm," I groaned as I bit into my bottom lip.

Laiken's little jaws began rising and caving, assuring me that he was getting the milk he was about to have a fit about.

"There we go," cooing, I rubbed his sandy hair and those chubby cheeks.

He was Laike all over again. I'd seen enough baby pictures to know. The irony of it all was both unbelievable and heartening. The odds of Laike being the father of my child were very slim, so slim that I never considered them. However, the imperfect timeline of my pregnancy due to the period-like bleeding that I was still having up until the end of my fifth month, the size of my child, and the proximity of my sexual encounters was to blame. I'd prayed for a good outcome in this situation and God had presented me with the unthinkable. Nevertheless, I was appreciative.

Staring at my high yellow, deep-blonde boy was comical. I'd expected the cutest chocolate offspring as a result of Nicholas' dark skin and mine. I'd checked his ears a few times to see if he'd be changing any time soon, but they were yellow, too. A twinge of jealousy caused me to roll my eyes into my head. I'd done all the work, yet Laike was reaping the benefits. I was looking forward to my chocolate king.

So precious. Laiken was a doll. Aside from his tantrums during bath time, he was the calmest, coolest baby I'd ever met. He hardly made a sound and preferred sleeping over everything else – even eating.

Ding Dong. The doorbell sounded. I sighed, deeply, knowing that there was no hope for my man, now. He sprang up, immediately.

"Huh? What happened? Where's Laiken?" He looked around from side to side.

"He's right here, baby. Someone is at the door."

"Oh. Shit. That's what I heard?"

"Yes."

"You invited someone over?" was his next question.

"No. I thought maybe you did."

"Na. Not until you tell me it's cool. My priority is making sure you two aren't overwhelmed. If you want, I can have whoever it is to come back another day."

"It's fine, baby. Whoever it is, maybe they can help me out for a few hours so that you can finally get some rest. Your eyes are so tired."

"I'll be aight."

Laike stood from the bed and then circled around it, ending at my side. My robe was wide open with one of the flaps of my nursing bra open, giving Laiken access to his favorite boob – the right one.

"You good?" he asked as he kissed my lips.

"Yes, baby. I'm the best I'll ever be. I just need you to get some rest for me."

"I will."

"When?"

"Tonight. I promise. I'm going to. Let me go grab the door. I'll be right back, aight?"

"Umm hmmm."

He leaned down and kissed Laiken's forehead before stepping off.

"Aye. That nigga got a fucking forehead on him. I hate to beef with him in school and the nigga headbutt me. Sheesh. Instant concussion."

"Laike, really? Goodbye."

"I'm saying, you don't think so? His head doesn't seem a little big to you?"

"No."

"Well, your head bigger than a motherfucker, so I wouldn't expect you to think so. That's where he got that shit from."

"Well, at least he got something from me. He's all Eisenberg if you ask me."

"He is. He is."

"Bye, Laike."

He disappeared behind the bedroom door. I listened for a clue of who had come into the house, but it was impossible. I'd forgotten just how large our home was. The bedroom seemed miles away from the front door.

Minutes passed before I heard anything close to human interaction. Kleu's voice was the first I recognized. Ditto's was next. I could feel the upward turn of my features as I perked up. I hadn't seen either of them since Laiken's birth and was dying to see my girls. They were both trying to give me the seven days I'd requested in my birth plan before people began bombarding the baby and me. However, nothing about the birth or baby had gone as planned, so there wasn't any use in utilizing the rest of the plan, now.

"Babe?" I called out as they neared. "Do I hear my favorite cousins?"

"The loud one and the little one... yeah. It's them," he confirmed. "The tall one must've been on the way to work and decided to stop by. Ain't no way she's been walking around with these shoes on all day."

As everyone entered the room, I was overcome with gratification and stunned speechless. Not only was Ditto and Kleu standing before me but so were my parents. Beside them stood my brother, whom I hadn't seen in four years. The beautiful sight left me in loud, chest-collapsing tears.

"Mom... Dad... Brandon? What are you guys doing here?"

"You thought we'd spend another minute on the phone listening to our new grandboy cooing without coming to see him in person?"

"I ain't even got the privilege to hear that," my brother interrupted. "I'm here for it all."

"We have to stay in here with your titty out or whatever? 'Cause, this is a little too serious and motherly for me. It's making me itch," Kleu complained.

"Where are you headed?" Her silliness helped me manage my emotions. I wiped the tears from my face and tried my hardest to stop crying.

"I have to be headed somewhere?"

"It would make your outfit make more sense," I admitted with a shrug.

"Focus on not sounding like a beast when crying. I'm sure you're scaring the baby. And for your information, I'm going on a date when I leave here."

"In that?"

"Nothing is wrong with my outfit. He's paying fifteen hundred to see me in these at dinner. I might look silly but that deposit didn't when it hit."

"I'm not mad at you, honey. Get your money."

"Oh, that's just how I am. I'm going to do that anyway," she assured me.

"We know," Ditto concluded.

"We're going to go downstairs and get cleaned up. I know this is your personal space and the last thing we want to do is invade. I'm going to get some dinner started and when you're ready, you can come down. I'm ready to hold my little baby, but I know he's eating right now."

"Yes, and he doesn't play about that titty milk," Laike chimed in.

He'd faded into the background. I'd forgotten he was in the room. I loved the way he was able to blend and transform in any situation or setting. He was highly adaptable when he wanted to be and that was intriguing. Lately, he'd been less of an asshole and more of the gentleman that he kept hidden. I admired both, but the Laike I was seeing was my favorite.

Everyone filed out of the room except Laike. He

stood at a distance looking as handsome as he did twenty years ago. Knowing that we'd finally gotten it together and would spend the rest of forever with one another made my inner child smile. I'd loved him since the young, ripe age of eleven.

"I guess I should get dressed to go downstairs and join everyone, huh?"

"I guess you should. That's why I laid something out for you."

I hadn't noticed the floor-length cotton dress until he mentioned it to me. It was gray in color and one of the lounge pieces I'd chosen for moments like this one. Laiken was sound asleep on my breast, making it easy to pull him away. When I did, his little lips puckered as he whimpered, silently, before resting his little features.

"Can you grab him and lay him in the bassinet, the one with the wheels?"

"Yeah. I'll get him downstairs and into the nursery so that it's not too loud for him."

"Okay, make sure the cameras are on."

Laiken's nursery was two stories. From one floor to the next, his belongings filled the enormous room. The idea came from Laike, who refused to separate his things or waste money buying two of everything for the same house. He'd mapped out the design and got to work on it immediately. There was even a set of stairs that allowed us to move from one floor to the other if we needed anything that wasn't within our reach.

We spent a lot of time downstairs, which was what determined he needed a nursery on two levels. The rest was history. Laike had the time of his life seeing his vision evolve. Having a man that loved creating things was so amazing. Once he put his mind to something, he didn't stop until it saw the light of day.

"Aight."

Slowly and carefully, Laike laid Laiken's tiny body into the bassinet. As he pushed him away, I busied myself with trying to get at least somewhat decent for my family. Six days postpartum, and I didn't look like I'd ever been pregnant. I imagined I had my family's genes to thank. Apparently, we carried small for the most part.

Though it was appreciated for the postpartum period and the sake of my postpartum body, I was a bit bitter about never experiencing the large, round belly I saw women carrying around. I wanted to complain, wobble, and sit the food that I was eating on top of it. That wasn't possible with my tiny bump.

There. I pulled the dress over my head and down my body. The ponytail I'd worn for the last four days was hanging on by a thread. I headed for the bathroom to grab a brush. While in there, I slid into my fluffy UGG slides that I wore as house slippers.

After brushing my ponytail and reapplying the hair tie, I slathered my lips with lip butter. Though I didn't look my best, I felt damn good. Exhaustion was written all over my face, but my adrenaline wouldn't allow me to rest. Not right now, anyway.

I rushed through the hallway and to the elevator. The stairs weren't even an option at this point in my postpartum journey. The less energy I put into things, the more energy I saved for Laiken. He required all of it.

The thought of joining my loved ones downstairs was exhilarating. It brought a smile to my face. It had been far too long since I'd seen my brother. I couldn't wait to spend whatever time he had with him. And, the thought of enjoying one of my mother's dishes. *Ummmm.* My stomach growled. It had been over two years since I'd tasted anything she made.

I stepped out of the elevator and was pleasantly surprised to find the first level exceptionally dim. Baffled, I rounded the corner to find a trail of rose petals that I followed without even thinking about it. It felt like I was walking forever, but it was only about a hundred feet into the family room.

"Nooo," I shrieked, turning around and running in the opposite direction.

"Baisleigh," Laike's voice stopped me in my tracks. I didn't move another muscle. I couldn't. His voice was so commanding, paralyzing me.

"I'm not running, and neither can you," he said to me.

He wasn't. He hadn't. Even when our relationship was faced with adversity, he remained.

"Why are you doing this? I thought we agreed that–" I started, unable to continue, too overcome with emotions. "Laike."

"I know what we agreed, but I also understand that some things can't wait. Making you my wife is one of those things. You didn't want to strip your parents of the opportunity to see you walk down the aisle, so I figured what better time than now? However long it takes for you to put together the wedding of your dreams, I'm willing to wait, but I can't imagine another second not being able to call you my wife. I believe, wholeheartedly, that I was put on this earth to be your husband, and I'm ready to fulfill my role. If you'd have me."

Turning around and finally taking in the beautiful scene before me, I sobbed. "Of course. All I've ever wanted was to be your wife."

"I know, baby, that's why I'm ready to make that happen."

"The babies, Laike?" I questioned, looking over at Essence, Emorey, Elle, and Lucas.

Will. You. Marry. Me, the signs they were holding read.

"Please, just don't get on one knee," I chuckled through the tears, "because I'll just end up down there with you."

"Baisleigh Carmichael," he said, closing the gap between us, "Will you do me the honor of being my forever?"

"Did you even have to ask?" Coughing back the tears, I nodded. "Yes."

"Tonight?"

"Whenever. Wherever. However. Yes, I'll be your forever."

Cheering erupted from behind us as he pulled me into his arms. They were the safest place on earth. They were the only place I wanted to end every night and start every morning.

"I love you," he whispered to me.

"Too much," I responded.

THIS IS NOT THE END... *keep reading*.

THE END OF AN ERA

To my dearest reader,

Before you flip this page and have your life changed forever, I'd like to thank you for loving on, supporting, standing behind my crazy idea to write an extremely long series that featured three siblings and a family with an unbreakable bond. My goal with the Eisenbergs was to showcase a healthy family dynamic, healthy Black love, and healthy hearts. While the world wants us to believe people like Luca, Ever, Lyric, Keanu, Laike, Baisleigh, Liam, and Laura don't exist in our community, they do.

In the beginning, Luca was supposed

to be a full-length 50,000-word novel that would be released, simultaneously, with another one, giving you guys the task of choosing which you'd read first. Well, obviously, that didn't happen. He had bigger plans, much bigger plans. He and Ever's story was so beautiful that I felt like I could tell it forever and ever. Even now, there's so much more story to be told, but my time with the couple has ended. Lyric followed up and now we have Laike.

It's going to be so hard saying goodbye to the Eisenbergs, but they've been so much joy to write. Luca was the most freeing. Lyric was the most difficult. Laike was the easiest. In the end, I love them all for their own little reasons, but mostly because they're Eisenbergs.

Ending the year with this family is perfect for me. I feel complete. Don't worry. Next year will bring more series, extremely long novels, and more siblings. I'm in love with the idea already. Go ahead and turn the page to get a glimpse

of what's next. It'll blow your mind.
Don't say I didn't warn you.

g

INTRODUCTION

The beginning...

"To the bravest, baddest baldie in the history of cancer. Beat that thang not once but twice," I chanted as we held our glasses near one another.

"Cancer a bad motherfucker, but ain't a mother-fucker badder than an Eisenberg," my father added.

"To health and wealth," Luca chimed in.

"May our pockets continue to get fatter as we get finer," Lyric finished with.

Glasses clinked before they were lifted up to our lips and sipped from. I watched as Baisleigh sipped the mocktail that Ever had made them both. With a new Eisenberg budding in her belly and Baisleigh breast-feeding our son, they were both automatically excluded from the real festivities.

After over a year of treatment, my mother was officially cancer free. We'd gotten the news two weeks earlier, and she'd finally rang the bell two days ago. We waited for Sunday dinner to celebrate. Everyone had plans of gathering already, so we saved the toasts for our moment together.

The smile on her face as she sipped the red wine from her glass warmed me inside. When she'd announced her cancer had returned all those months ago, I feared for her life. Her health hung in the balance once, and we'd barely made it out on the other side of the deadly disease. This time, my faith was low but my hopes were high.

It was her cancer that had led me to Baisleigh's home. It was her cancer that led to my son's conception. It was her cancer that woke me up and forced me to see the fault of my ways. As much as I hated it, I appreciated what it had done for me and my family.

Baisleigh slowly turned, noticing my gaze. She matched it. Her lips curved upward into a smile that still made my heart skip a beat. The large diamond on her finger glistened, slamming against the glass in her hand as she brought it down from her lips and to the table.

My wife. At our home, in a very private ceremony that only included family, we'd wedded. However, that was only the beginning. The Eisenberg women were planning a white wedding that would take place in a year. I couldn't wait to meet her at the altar.

I love you, she mouthed.

Too much, I responded.

The sound of Laiken's wailing raised both of our brows. We headed out of the dining room, simultaneously, meeting in the hall that led to the nursery. My parents had changed almost every room in their home to reflect the new additions of our family. There was now a nursery, two girls' rooms, and one boy's room. Almost every trace of their older flock was erased from the bedrooms.

"I got it," she said to me just before we entered the nursery.

"You sure?"

"Yes."

"He's hungry. Unless you have some breast milk, then go back in there and celebrate with our family."

"I don't know. Maybe if I squeeze hard enough it might," I joked, squeezing my nipple through my shirt.

"Bye, Laike. Go back in there. We're fine. I got this."

"Call me if you need me."

"I will. Promise."

She kissed my lips and then my forehead. Her jealousy was apparent. Though she had the milk, she knew that Laiken favored me. As much as she could, she tried to get him alone to convince him that he should fuck with her more. He wasn't buying it though. He was a daddy's boy, through and through.

A little saddened that Laiken had to spend a little time with his mother alone, I made my way back to the dining room. When I arrived, almost everyone had cleared out. Baffled, I searched for any signs of where they'd gone.

"They're outside," Lyric said, bouncing a whiny Keanu on her lap.

I quickly marched over and snatched her from Lyric's arms.

"Heeeeey. Heeeey. What's the matter uncle's baby girl?"

"She wants her dad," Lyric hissed.

"Not you, too," I tittered.

"Me, too, what?"

"Jealous because you've got a daddy's baby. B on that same bull."

"I'm not jealous, not at all," she lied through her teeth.

"Then, why is your face flushed red and you have sad eyes?"

"Shut up, Laike, and give me my baby."

"She don't even want your ass," I teased, handing her Keanu.

She'd managed to settle down a bit.

"Gone back there and pout with Baisleigh. She's looking just as sad as you right now. Y'all need to follow Ever's lead. She don't give a damn about them kids getting on Luca's nerves.'"

"Probably because she has a million of them," Lyric noted.

"Hey, now. Not a million... just five and a half.

Four accounted for and one on the way."

"Close enough," Lyric responded, "I'm going to the nursery. She's hungry, and I'm sure you guys don't feel like seeing my titties today."

"Sure don't."

"If you'd go outside and get out of our faces, then you wouldn't have to see them anyway," she fussed, obviously fed up with my bullshit.

"Aight. I'm gone. When I come back, you better have fixed that attitude or me and Ken stealing the babies and not bringing them back until the morning. Let Baisleigh know I'm dead serious so that lip better not be poked out when I return."

"Mom, can you get this man out of your house? Please."

Before she could even begin chastising me, I sprinted out of the kitchen and out of the door. I found the fellas posted up against Luca's new truck at the end of the driveway. The fine buds they were both in possession of could be smelled a mile away.

"You niggas snuck out here without me?"

"You in there playing daddy of the decade and shit. We needed something to go with our little cocktail," Ken spoke first.

"Nigga was probably in there trying to breastfeed the fucking baby," Luca put his two cents in.

"The way Lucas be up your ass, I thought you had titties, too. And, you, my nigga, we're not even going to talk about how you've spoiled that fucking brat in there."

I pointed toward the house for emphasis. Ken didn't have any room to speak about my situation. He was in one far deeper than mine. Keanu was a problem already, spoiled just like her mother.

"Stop talking about my baby before I down your ass out here," he warned.

"I've never been scared. But, you already know that. I used to beat your ass back across the street."

"You're remembering it wrong. Both of y'all soft, suburban boys used to jump me after I kicked one of y'all's asses. And, you, my nigga, tried to shoot me for kicking your ass when we were barely even fourteen. About to fuck up everybody's life," he reminded me.

I shrugged, remembering the incident vividly. He'd gotten far too many good ones in on me. I had to get my licks back, one way or the other.

"You had it coming. You talked too much shit."

"I backed it up, too."

"He did. He did," Luca agreed with Ken.

"Whatever. This nigga a hoe."

"Whenever you're ready to show me I'm one, I'm ready, too," he rebutted.

"Aye," Luca called out, catching both of our attention.

A tall, brown-skinned nigga climbed out of a clean ass old school on 22" wheels. From the tiny glimpse, I managed to get before he shut the door, I could see that the inside was just as sickening as the outside. He walked to the other side of the yard where a path to the front door was carved with concrete, completely ignoring our presence.

"Does this nigga not see us or what?" I posed, looking from my left to my right.

"I know the motherfucker not blind because he can obviously see the house he's headed up to," Ken added, puffing from the blunt in his hand.

"My nigga, take another step and you'll have a minimum of three bullets in your body. Neither of us will miss. I'm hitting your kneecap."

"Are we killing 'em or?" I asked.

"Na." Disappointingly, Luca answered.

"Then, I'm hitting the stomach. A shit bag will teach 'em a lesson."

"I want to see the nigga dance. I'm hitting that big toe. Knock a nigga balance off," Ken claimed, puffing on the blunt in his hand.

"Not that any of that will be necessary," he finally spoke, cutting through the grass and backtracking his steps.

"Oh, it's very necessary." I let the nigga know.

"You look like smart men. I'm sure you know they didn't stop making guns when they made yours."

"State your business, nigga, or you won't make it to yours," I assured him.

"I didn't come for any trouble."

"Then what you come for?" Luca belted.

"'Cause, that's what we're all trying to figure out," with a shrug, Ken stated.

"I– uh. I'm looking for Liam Eisenberg."

The hairs on the back of my neck stood as I stepped forward. Luca was right beside me, using his hand to block my path, but we both knew that if it came to it that wouldn't stop shit. Ken wasn't far behind, stepping up and beside Luca.

"For what?"

"My mother died three months ago. I just gathered the courage to go through her shit at the house. I came across a letter in her nightstand drawer that explains a mystery that's haunted me my entire life."

"And, what's that?"

"The identity of my father. According to her letter, Liam Eisenberg is the father of my brother and I."

Without hesitation, I bolted for my parent's door. I busted through, in search of my father. When I didn't see him in the common areas, I was forced to call out to him.

"Pops!" I yelled, breathlessly.

"Laike, is everything okay?" my mother asked as she approached me.

It wasn't okay. Nothing was, because if what I'd just heard was true, then life as I knew it was about to change. My world... *our worlds*, were about to bit hit with a blow so devastating that we'd all have to hold on tight if we wanted to survive it.

"Nah," I answered quickly. "POPS."

"Yeah?" His voice rang out from a distance. My eyes followed his baritone, spotting him almost instantly.

He appeared with a paper towel in his hands. He'd emerged from the bathroom with enough worry lines across his face to create a journal entry.

"What is it, Laike?"

"This nigga out here claiming he ya son!"

The **Domino** Effect

Coming in 2023

Now available for pre-order on Amazon

MORE FROM GREY HUFFINGTON

SYX + THE CITY
SYX + THE CITY 2
SYX THIRTY SEVYN
SXYTH GIVING
SYX WHOLE WEEKS

WILDE + RECKLESS
WILDE + RELENTLESS
WILDE + RESTLESS

MR. INTENTIONAL
UNEARTH ME

THE SWEETEST REVENGE
THE SWEETEST REDEMPTION

HALF + HALF

THE EMANCIPATION OF EMOREE

SLEIGH
SLEIGH SQUARED

THE GIFTED
MEMO
GIVE HER LOVE. GIVE HER FLOWERS.

UNBREAK ME
UNCOVER ME

AS WE LEARN
AS WE LOVE

JUST WANNA MEAN THE MOST TO YOU
SENSITIVITY
10,000 HOURS
DARKE HEARTS
MUSE.

SOFTLY
PEACE + QUIET
PRESS REWIND
JAGGED EDGES
MY PERSON
**THE REALM OF
RIOT THIMBLE**

WHOSE LOVE STORY IS IT ANYWAY?

WEB EXCLUSIVES:
ghuffington.com

HOME*
BLUES*
31ST*
WHAT ARE WE DOING?*
NOW THAT WE'RE HERE.*

THEN LET'S FUCK ABOUT IT*
GIVING THANKS

LUCA
LYRIC
EVER
LAIKE

PAPERBACKS
HARDCOVERS
SHORT STORIES
AUDIOBOOKS
MERCH
AND MORE...

Made in the USA
Middletown, DE
18 May 2025

75697982R00245